Split Feather

Book 4 of Feathered Dreams
By: Brittany Putzer

Split Feather

Editing by: Kat Pagan

Formatting by: Frankie Page

Cover design by: Rae Lumpkins

ISBN: 979-8-218-06870-7

Published in the United States

Dedication

To those I've lost over the years: may you rest in peace. And to the mourners: I hope you uncover your happiness again.

#LiveLaughRead

Contents

WAKING UP 1

LIGHT IN THE DARKNESS 11

LIMITED TIME 16

STAND STRONG 21

JUST DANCE 29

SHOCK 43

FORGOTTEN GIFT 49

SWEET PEACHES 55

FUNKY MONKEY 71

CHICK ON BOARD 77

DIFFERENT BEANS 84

VACATION 88

LEVERAGE 92

MR. SUNSHINE 97

BLOODY TRUTHS 106

NEW PAL 120

INTENTIONS 128

SACRIFICES 136

LONG LIVE THE KING 143

DISARMING 153

LOYALTIES 173

OUT OF THE ASHES 192

CIRCLE BEARD 197

TRUE LOVE   207

VOTE FOR PEACE   217

THE BLACK ROSE BEGINNINGS   223

SALLY AGE 35   224

JEREMY AGE 12   230

MARY AGE 12   236

SALLY AGE 35   242

JEREMY AGE 12   248

MARY AGE 14   253

SALLY AGE 37   257

JEREMY AGE 14   263

MARY AGE 16   267

SALLY AGE 39   272

JEREMY AGE 18   276

MARY AGE 18   282

SALLY AGE 44   288

JEREMY AGE 21   295

MARY AGE 21   300

SALLY AGE 46   308

JEREMY AGE 23   312

THANK YOU   314

ADDITIONAL TITLES BY THE AUTHOR   316

ABOUT THE AUTHOR   318

Waking Up

My feverish world is a blur of nightmares but I fight to keep conscious long enough to focus on a shadow.

"I'm right here, Ann." Karen squeezes my hand.

"Are you really here or am I dreaming?"

Her mocha-colored eyes swirl with unshed tears. "You aren't dreaming, honey. The infection in your neck was spreading, but the doctor took care of it. And when you were stable, they moved you to your room to recover."

"What about the Black Rose rebels, Max, and the rest of the Palace?"

"Shh, it's all going to be okay. Rest now. You are safe."

No matter how hard I attempt to keep my eyes open, my dreams take control.

I'm imprisoned with King Mark's twisted guard. Derek smirks at me, promising to punish me for attempting to escape with Prince Christian. Then the scene blurs, and I'm in Prince Christian's arms until I'm snatched by his devious wife, Mary, who is also a member of the Black Rose Rebellion. With a flick of her regal wrist, she sends me to her morbid brother, Max — the same man who murdered my father. He tugs my hair and smashes his lips to mine.

"No!" I scream.

A gunshot rings out and crimson oozes from Mary's angelic mask. I can't celebrate this victory because Joey, the palace guard who is protecting me, clutches a piece of wood sticking out of his abdomen.

I cover my ears while dropping to my knees. "Stop! No more!"

The dream spins until I'm naked in Prince Ryan's strong arms as we wait to be rescued from the safe room, while an

1

infection courses through my body.

Suddenly, the door slams open, and Max glares before laughing maniacally as he rips me to pieces.

I jolt in a puddle of sweat, his haunting glee ringing through the room. I rub my eyes, still unsure if this is a dream or not, while wondering what other monsters are lurking in the shadows. I let one foot touch the floor. Then the other. The cold weaves up my ankle and confirms my state of consciousness. From the corner of my room, a white ball barrels towards me. I retreat to the bed with a squeal.

"Ann? What happened?"

I stare at Prince Ryan and then down at my intruder. Once my mind stops playing tricks on me, I relax, realizing the blur is the Palace hen. "Snowball?"

Ryan tucks me under the covers. "I'm sorry if she frightened you. Karen thought you would like to see a feathered face when you woke up."

"Wait. When did Karen return from the hospital? Where are the twins?"

"Rest. We can talk soon. I will place your security hen back on the bed to ward off trespassers. Unless, of course, they have breadcrumbs. Because we both know that's her weakness."

My fingertips graze the scabs on his face. "You took a punch for me." I snuggle into the blankets, knowing I'm safe with him and Snowball near.

When I stir again, I groan at the rock now crushing my chest. My eyes shoot open, and I stare into Snowball's beady eyes.

"You need to stop eating so many carbs. You weigh *more* than an overweight cat." I run my fingertips through her plumage. "But I'll take you over a feline any day."

Snowball tilts her head at the mention of goodies and flops to the floor. The sudden thump takes me back to the raid when the jail door exploded off its hinges. Darkness closes in around me and I rush to my open balcony. I suck in gulps of the warm night air as I clutch the railing, my knuckles turning white. Once I catch my breath, and the hammering in my ears ceases, I take in my surroundings. The moonlight shimmers off the pedicured grounds, and for a moment, it feels like the world is exactly as it was *before* the attack.

Snowball rubs her head on my ankle as she struts over. I reach to pet her, but she takes off, chasing after a moth. They dance on the terrace, but the insect doesn't stand a chance and is quickly pecked to oblivion.

"Eww," I push out.

She takes a moment to narrow her eyes, reminding me that I lectured her about carbs, and insects are certainly not breadcrumbs. Then she stalks after another one. I aim to smooth things over, so she doesn't peck my eyes out while I sleep.

"You know, King Christian should give you a medal. Afterall, you did trip that rebel. You were very brave."

When she continues to ignore me, I wander back into my room and pause at the full-length mirror. My fingertips trail over my pale cheeks and bandaged neck. Why can't I catch a break? My head shoots to my adjoining room as I hear movement. I tiptoe over, before cracking the door and sneaking inside. I scan the room

3

and notice it looks the same. Except, instead of Christian's blonde hair poking out of the covers, it's Ryan's dark locks now sprawled across the pillowcase.

Ryan turns in his sleep before he sits upright. "Ann?"

I swallow down the lump in my throat. "After everything that has happened, I'm still trying to figure out if I'm dreaming or not."

He slips out of the bed, collecting me in his arms and carrying me back to my room. "Ann, please, you need—"

"Rest, I know," I grumble into his neck as he lays me down. "But how much longer do you think you can drug me and keep me in here? What is so terrible out *there* that you feel like you have to protect me? Especially considering all the events *we* just endured."

"I'm not hiding anything from you. The medicine is to help you sleep better. And no one is forcing them down your throat." He tries to pull away but my arms drape around his neck. "Ann, you can let go of me now."

"Never," I whisper into his ear.

He pulls back far enough to look into my eyes before he runs his fingertips over my face. "I missed you."

"I missed you too."

His words sooth my insecurities as images of the safe room flash in front of my eyes. Our heated night and countless physical encounters under the sheets. I press my lips to his, and passion fuels my desire to be close to him again. To feel *something* again. Anything.

He steps back.

"Ryan?"

He rubs his face. "You need to rest. We can talk later, okay." He kisses my forehead quickly and backs out before I can pull him down.

I pout at his slumped shoulders as he departs. Then I turn my watery gaze to the ceiling. What did I do wrong? I slowly fall back to sleep, wishing I could obtain the answers plaguing my every thought.

But…

Also knowing the responses could very well be what I *don't* want to hear. Like, maybe, I'm not *enough* to keep Ryan.

I rise before the sun, ready to hunt for the answers I seek. While I'm slipping on my boots, I side-glance Karen sneaking in.

"Ann, it is so good to see you moving. I missed you so much." She suffocates me in a hug.

"How long have I been out?"

"It's been a week since they pulled you and Ryan out of the safe room."

"A week?" I rub my face before I scan the room. "Where are the babies?"

"Olivia and Carter are safe in their nursery downstairs, with a great nanny Elizabeth recommended. The woman is old as sin but spunky and super sweet."

I beam as my eyes mist. I missed so much. "Olivia and Carter? Those are beautiful names. Where is Vinny? Is he all right?"

"He is pretty shaken up and bruised, but he will be fine. He is now on a constant rotation, keeping the King

5

guarded."

I swallow the lump of guilt. "Christian… is he okay?"

Karen runs a finger over my bandage. "Why don't I call the doctor to check your wound?"

"Why is everyone diverting my questions? I'm not five years old."

"Ann, all I know is that the King was shot in the attack. We are only trying to ease you into everything. But you're right. You deserve all the answers. I can accompany you to check on him." She rubs my arm. "And if you want, I can introduce you to the twins. Their room is on the way to the hospital wing."

I swallow at the mention of the hospital and what I might find when I see the condition Christian is in after getting shot. "I didn't mean to jump down your throat. It's just… I'm so out of the loop. You know what? I would love to see the babies. It's about time they met their aunt."

She locks arms with me and prattles on about how her labor and delivery went. I try to listen, but once we step out of my room, I'm shocked at the state of the Palace. Even though it's been a week, there are still bullet holes and blood splotches littering the once dazzling walls.

Karen's warm hand on my arm pulls me to the present. "Ann, are you sure you are feeling up to this?"

"It's better than cowering under the covers." I lift my chin. "Let's go."

As we make our way to the ground floor, the nutty aroma wafting from the kitchen beckons to me. My heart tightens. After that horrific attack, will I discover Jock and the rest of the kitchen crew alive and performing what they love to do? I can't stop my feet as they demand to know. With a shaky palm, I push the double doors.

"Dale, you better have a good excuse for walking in

6

here an hour late! And blaming your mother is not going to work. You are a grown…" Jocks stops short as he turns to us, and a smile replaces his scowl. "Lady Ann! It's so lovely to see you!"

He embraces me and I hold tight, trying to contain my tears of joy. As my name echoes around us, the kitchen team stops their prepping and offers their gratitude for saving them.

"It is so good to see everyone. You all look great." I cough on the last word, unsure what else to say. I clear my throat and nod to the coffee machine. "Do you mind if I make a cup?"

Jock shoos everyone back to their stations. "Of course, anything for you."

I cringe as he limps with effort to grab a mug. I put a hand on his arm. "You know what? I've been stuck in bed for days! Let me stretch my legs a bit and get it." The steaming liquid fills my cup. I take a whiff and cry with relief. "Just the way I remember it."

Jock returns to his stirring before he grabs a bowl and ladles a heaping. "You must be famished. Here, try this broth and then I will make your favorite pizza."

"Chicken noodle soup? Wow, Jock, I don't think I've ever seen you make something this… classic."

He slides a bowl to Karen and ushers us to a pair of unoccupied bar stools. He chuckles as he adds more shredded carrots. "Classic, huh? Yes, I have learned to… how do you say… enjoy the *simpler* things in life. Plus, a little birdy told me it was one of your favorites."

I let the warmth of the broth flutter to my toes. "This is delicious. Thank you."

"Thank *you*, Lady Ann. Now, please, take your time eating, ladies." Jock walks with effort around the corner, my eyes glued on his injured leg. Visions of Max pulling the trigger and Jock crumbling at my feet cause me to squeeze my spoon handle until my knuckles ache.

"What happened to all the rebels who attacked us?" I ask Karen.

"From what the other maids and I have learned, the guards killed most of them during the raid, others were tortured for information, and some are rumored to have escaped but we are combing the countryside for them."

"And what about Max?"

"He's buried six feet underground, where he belongs."

I let out a breath, glad for that bit of news. Max was an absolute lunatic. How I got stuck with his crazy affections, I will never know. "How many people did we lose?"

"Only one that I'm aware of. And twenty-five others are still recovering in the hospital."

"And Elizabeth?" I inquire about Christian and Ryan's mom.

"She led the office staff into a safe room and is unharmed."

I squeeze my eyes shut. I forgot about the office workers. The same individuals I worked with every day. I'm so happy they made it to safety.

But those twenty-five others...

I can't imagine all the anxious families. I rest on my elbows in despair. Could I have done a better job at protecting them?

Karen squeezes my shoulder. "Tell me what's going on in that head of yours. I'm a great listener."

"I don't even know where to begin."

"How about you tell me what happened to *you* during

the raid. I've heard *heroic* tales of Saint Ann of the Palace."
She elbows me. "And I must admit I'm very privileged to
call her *my* best friend."

I suck in a breath before I retell the horrible tale, up
until the point Ryan and I... Should I explain that we
had sex? Or is Ryan keeping it a secret until he speaks to
Christian?

"What I'm about to say can't leave your lips."

"You mean there's more? And it's worse than what
you've already told me?" She tips back and shakes her
head before she leans towards me again. "What is it? I'm
here for you. And I promise I won't say a word."

"Ryan and I, well... You know how we were barricaded
in that safe room? While we were in there, he told me he
wanted to marry me. That he was going to stand up to
Christian and demand he let us choose each other."

Her mouth drops as she looks around. Then she
whispers, "He *said* that to you? But what about Christian's
feelings? I mean, he is his *brother*. Oh, that man! Surely he
could have said this ages ago."

"We thought we were going to die in there. It was
terrifying. And then my infection started." My fingertips
graze my neck. "Well, Ryan and I *did* it." I meet her gaze,
not wanting to say the word out loud. It felt too real if I
spoke it to the air between us. And it was already eating
away at me.

"Did what? Like it, *it*!"

"Yes."

The silence is deafening. Emotions pass behind her
eyes, and I can tell she is choosing her words carefully.
She pushes her meal aside and collects my hands. "Oh,
Ann. Didn't your mom ever warn you that men will tell
you anything to get you in bed with them? It's a classic

man thing to do. Even if he is a literal Prince."

Tears brim my eyes as I stare at my soup. "Karen, you know my mom died when I was young and way before I hit puberty. And Dad, rest his soul, never even had the *talk* with me. He used chicken metaphors. I learned everything in school and from books. Do you really think Ryan lied just to sleep with me?"

"It doesn't matter what I think. What he said to you was inappropriate. I mean, you are still engaged to King Christian. Ryan took advantage of the situation. You had a fever and an infection coursing through your body. You were both trapped in a high-stress atmosphere."

"I was involved in the decision too."

Karen scoffs, "I know plenty of men who do this, girl. They prey on innocent women already in a relationship."

"Wait just a minute. You are being incredibly sexist."

"I am just pointing out the obvious, okay? After everyone voted for you to be queen, Ryan never gave his brother a chance to win your heart. The cottage Ryan designed, the wedding dress he planned, and then he ran to you after being ordered to stand down..." She lets her words flutter between us before she clears her throat. "The kids should be waking up from their nap soon and I need to feed them."

Karen brings our bowls to the sink and strides out. She isn't wrong. Ryan did have a hand in the cottage and the dress but those were gifts to Christian and me. I thought she liked the idea of Ryan and me together? Why is she being so hard on him? Surely, his actions weren't as manipulative as she is making them out to be?

Light in the Darkness

Karen quietly pushes open the nursery door. Then we both peek inside and watch as the nanny rocks the newborns, one in each arm, while she sings softly. When she notices our presence, she pauses to greet us. "Miss Karen, Lady Ann. Good morning."

The older woman extends a pink bundle to Karen, who coos at the sleeping child. "Thank you, Rose. You can grab breakfast if you want. I can take it from here."

"Not a problem. I should stretch these old limbs anyway. Maybe I'll head to the kitchen and make a cup of Earl Grey, then stroll the gardens."

Rose attempts to pass me the blue bundle, but I take a step back. "Oh, I—no, I am not sure if I'm ready for that."

Karen giggles as she sits in a rocking chair, preparing to breastfeed Olivia. "Ann, that is your nephew. Don't be afraid." She shares a smirk with Rose as she taunts me. "I mean, *seriously*, she can fight rebels, deal with unruly cocks, but *this* is too much for her?"

I narrow my eyes before I hold my palms out. Rose places him in my arms and my heart swells. Carter opens his eyes and watches me. It feels like he is reading my soul. I trail my fingertip over his cheek. "Hello, little Carter. I'm your Auntie Ann." I bite my lip as he settles. I grin up at Karen while Rose slips out of the room. "He fell asleep."

The comforting quiet soothes my previous concerns. Karen pats the rocking chair next to her, and I rock little Carter while she feeds Olivia. "I'm sorry. I just got protective of you back there in the kitchen. I know you are inexperienced, and when I heard what happened, it rattled me. I love you, girl. And I hope you know I'll always be here for you, no matter what."

11

"I love you too and I appreciate your honesty. Don't be afraid to share your opinions with me. I value them more than you know."

We both glance at the door as it creaks, and Ryan pops his head in. "I saw Rose leaving and thought you may need a hand." He shuts the door and saunters over. He stumbles when he notices me. For a second, he frowns and looks towards the door, like he might bolt. But then he clears his throat and plasters on a fake smile. "Didn't Karen warn you? I'm Carter's favorite."

Why is Ryan acting weird?

"Well, get ready to be bumped to *second* favorite." Carter wiggles as I hold him tighter.

"See that? He can hear me." Ryan kneels and offers a pinkie to Carter. "You tell her that you want Uncle Ryan."

Karen shakes her head as she rises from the rocker. She hands him Olivia with a scowl. "There will be *no* favorites, you two."

Ryan collects Olivia while Karen grabs Carter. Then she adjusts Carter to get him to latch on.

"Karen! We have talked about this! Put those milkers away *before* you grab or pass the kids," he demands as his face turns red. Olivia cries from the loud noise and he bounces her. "That's right, Olivia, you tell her!"

I burst out laughing. "Milkers?"

"Breasts! Okay? Are you happy now?"

Karen and I giggle at his discomfort like a pair of school children. Karen stares at him while she covers herself with a blanket. "Why don't you change Olivia and then take Ann to see King Christian?"

He wiggles a finger at Olivia. "You know what? This is really a *lady's* job. So, as Prince of this Palace, I dub you, Lady Ann, diapering lady." He passes the baby to me.

12

"Seriously?"

"Absolutely."

I stride over to the changing table, ready to figure this out. I narrow my eyes at the diaper as I undo the flaps. There's nothing to this. Ryan is a big baby for pawning this chore off. I open the fabric and gag at the stench while frantically closing it to contain the toxic gas. I glare down at the stinky enemy and snatch a wipe. I need to tackle this challenge before Ryan notices my hesitation. I suck in fresh air and return to the mission.

Then Vinny enters. "Rose just gave me a status report, and I thought I would pop in real fast and give everyone some love."

I shove the wipe into Vinny's combat-ready palm. "Thank goodness! Daddy is back to lend a hand! Here you go, old man!"

Vinny's smile widens as he notices me. Then he returns to Olivia and tackles the task like a pro. "I'm not old yet." He hugs me one-handedly. "I hope you realize how many lives you saved during the attack. People are calling you a hero."

"Then they don't know me very well."

Vinny kisses Olivia as Karen stands to change Carter. Once she is done, she sits in the rocking chair next to Vinny. They both reach over and peck each other on the lips.

Ryan clears his throat. "We should be going, Ann."

"I should probably get back too." Vinny sets the baby in the crib and smiles at Karen. "I'll see you tonight."

"You got it." She winks as he guides us out.

We stride towards the hospital wing. I look around, surprised that the front of the Palace appears untouched from the recent attack. Vinny catches my gaze. "They

13

slipped in through the servants' quarters. They were mostly unseen because some of them had Palace guard uniforms on." His jaw clenches. "Then, once they were safely within the walls, they attacked and helped other rebels enter, ensuring the coast was clear."

"I'm sorry, Vinny. That must have felt like salt in the wound, to have them enter with your uniform."

He only nods, but his eyes tell it all. Dark and brooding.

Ryan pauses mid-step and turns to Vinny. "Could you give us a moment, please?"

"Of course." And he continues without us.

Ryan runs a hand through his hair. "What happened in the safe room will not be discussed until I say so."

I step away from him. He's acting like Karen said he would. "What? Why?"

"I don't want to add any more stress to the situation. Just until things settle down."

Like so many times today, I swallow past the lump in my throat and nod. What more can I do? I can't very well argue with him, especially here. We turn the corner towards the hospital wing. I stop short. It's packed. The crowd looks up with sad smiles and nods of acknowledgement as we pass. Some ignore us and continue to pray or cry.

One woman rushes over. "Lady Ann, you saved my brother in the kitchen. Thank you so much."

"Of course, Miss…?"

"My name's Emily."

I glance into her dark eyes, now brimming with tears. "Emily, it is nice to meet you. Was your brother injured?"

A tear slides down her face. "No, my brother is fine

14

and back to work already. I'm here waiting to collect my husband's remains. Joey, he was a guard in the prison."

My knees go weak, and I falter as Joey's face swirls in front of mine. My vision blurs and I'm taken back to that horrendous day.

I'm sitting with Max. He leans forward to tell me it was all a trick, and that the rebels are attacking. Joey orders me to hide behind the desk. Before I can take cover, the door is blown off its hinges and shots are fired.

When I come to, Vinny is cradling me on the floor. "Ann?"

I can still smell the gunpowder and blood. I clutch his uniform, trying to ground myself. Vinny settles me on my feet.

"My heart goes out to you and your loved ones. I'm sorry. Please forgive me." I rub my temples. "I'm still recovering from the raid myself." Once my legs stop shaking, I straighten my back and place a hand on the woman's shoulder. "Emily, before you go, leave your phone number for me. I would love to talk again soon."

Emily nods, and Ryan quickly ushers me forward with a hand on the small of my back. "Hey, it isn't your fault. You don't owe her anything."

"Her husband gave his *life* to save mine! How is that not my fault! I owe her *everything*."

"It was his *job*. They all sign up willingly and know the risks."

I cringe at his tone and the darkness that's presently slithering in his eyes. Where is the man I fell in love with? The man whose compassion met mine head-on? I swallow and look away, afraid of the answer.

15

Limited Time

We past the crowd and make our way to the last room in the hospital wing. Two guards stand outside watching our approach. Ryan lifts his chin at them and they open the door. There, in the middle of the sterile room, is King Christian, my fiancé.

My heart clenches with regret as I watch his chest rise and fall. I choke on a sob and run to his side. I gaze at all the machines surrounding his pale body. His eyes are closed, but I know behind those heavy lids are the icy-blue orbs I've grown fond of. I run a shaky hand over his dirty-blonde strands as silent tears strike the blanket with soft thuds.

"Christian, you need a haircut," I whisper. "It's unseemly for a King to have bangs. Although… we could braid the ends and add some bows."

For a second, I fear he's already gone, but then his lids flutter. At first, his pupils appear unfocused but then he blinks. "Ann?"

I kneel so our eyes meet. "Yes, it's me. I'm right here."

"I had hoped I would see you again."

"I would never let them take me without a fight." I kiss his knuckles.

"You are a stubborn woman, through and through."

"Well, I learned from the best." I elbow him.

His smirk dissolves into a frown. "Ann, I apologize… I…"

"No apologies necessary. We can talk more when you are feeling better. Rest. That's an order."

"I have made so many mistakes."

I grab his chin. "Stop it! You are a great King and have

accomplished many wonderful things. And you will continue your reign as such!"

"My reign is coming to an end." He closes his eyes. "This is one command I am afraid I cannot follow through with... for you."

"What are you talking about? You are strong and more tenacious than I am. You'll be fine."

Christian throws back his sheet and I cringe at his bandaged leg. "The doctor is struggling to get the bone and wound to heal, and it's not looking good."

"So we'll transfer you to another hospital and get another opinion."

"It has nothing to do with the physician, and everything to do with my body's inability to mend itself."

I sit on the edge of the bed and cover him back up. "Your body will battle *this*, just like it fights everything *and* everyone."

Christian closes his eyes, and my heart aches to see him like this—giving up. I open my mouth to protest further, to beg him to stop acting like a baby, but I feel a warm hand grasp my elbow. I look at Ryan and he guides me to a chair.

Sitting next to me is Elizabeth, his mother, and she offers me a bottle of water as she dabs her cheeks. I thank her before I wipe my eyes and then return my attention to Ryan as he speaks with Christian. They whisper softly to one another, words I'm not meant to hear. I weep into my hands as Elizabeth wraps her arms around me.

After a while, we are escorted out of the room and into the hallway so the doctor can give us an update. He explains that the injury to Christian's leg was not fatal, but it shattered his bone and left a massive wound where the bullet broke through the skin. It was exactly as Christian had said: his body is rejecting the medications and the infection is spreading. When he concludes, he apologizes, wishing there was more he could do. He informs us that at this point their plan of action is to continue the treatment and keep Christian as comfortable as possible. Once he is done breaking our hearts, he nods solemnly and stalks off.

"We should take him to the lake house." I frown at Christian's door.

"What? This is no time for a vacation," Ryan grumbles.

"But he shouldn't wither away in a hospital bed. He should enjoy the time he has left."

"Didn't you hear what the doctor said? There is still hope! We can't just take him out of the hospital and give up!"

"I never said we should *give up*. We can send the medical equipment and staff to the…"

"No! End of discussion! *You* may be ready to let him go, but I'm not!" Ryan blares.

My breath catches. "How can you say that?"

"Enough, you two. Ann, we will consider moving Christian to a more comfortable environment when we are *sure* nothing else can be done. And, Ryan, I know you have a lot on your shoulders, especially with Christian's prognosis. But you *will* control your temper or, so help me, I will take the crown before you ever ascend the throne." Elizabeth sniffles. "What we *must* focus on is keeping the country stable. We should do a press conference and delicately update the public."

I need to keep busy or I'll lose my mind. "I can do it."

"Are you sure?" Elizabeth asks.

"Yes."

"Okay. Next order of business… Where is Vinny?"

Vinny makes his way over. "Yes, Queen Elizabeth?"

"How are we doing with the rebels? Have we found them all?"

"It's not an easy task, but we are doing our best."

"Well, you need to do *better* than that." Her jaw ticks. "Now, go."

He nods and walks off.

"Mom, Vinny has been working night and day to locate their hideout."

Elizabeth raises her chin. "It was *his* job to protect the King! And he failed!" Her lip quivers as she storms off.

Ryan goes after her, but I grab his wrist. "Everyone is hurting right now. I think it's best to just let her cool off."

"This is all my fault. If I had just stayed by his side instead of chasing after *you*, I could have protected him."

"Ryan, do not say that. Everything happened exactly the way it was supposed to. Remember what we said in the safe room? *No regrets*."

Ryan doesn't answer. He clenches his fists and brushes past me.

"You can go back in," a nurse calls.

I enter the room, grab Christian's cold hand, and bring it to my lips. This time he doesn't stir, and his eyes remain closed. I glide a fingertip down his cheek as I remember all the wonderful times we've had together. We struggled to get along, but we developed a strong partnership. Even though our relationship and engagement were not of our own choosing, we still made it work. We love each other as all great friends do. I kiss him before resting my forehead on his.

I wish things were different. Ryan is so cold and distant. Christian is wounded and giving up. It makes me wonder if they would have been better off without me meddling in their lives.

"I'm sorry, Christian." I pull off the chicken engagement ring he gave me and twirl it between my fingers. I place it on his large pinkie. "When your brother and I were in the safe room, you said to let Ryan take care of me. Well, I can't do that. But I'm sure you saw that coming." I let out a laugh. "Ryan wants nothing to do with me," I sob. "And I don't blame him. Especially when pain and suffering surround me wherever I go."

Stand Strong

I drop into the office and ask Tim, Christian's assistant, to set up a press conference. Then I scurry to my room. I glance around the huge space with a sigh. Snowball waddles over and looks up into my eyes expectantly. I offer her some freeze-dried mealworms and stroke her feathers. Why can't I live a carefree life like she does?

I take a long, hot bath to try to take the sting out of the day's events. My best friend's words float around my head as I swirl the bubbles. Is Ryan really looking to work things out with me, or did he get what he wanted all along?

After I finish my bath, Karen is back in my room and helps me into an elegant baby-blue sundress edged in pink lace. Then we pick out silver flats, wispy blue feather earrings, and I clasp on the black feather necklace my dad gave me. We discuss her family as she primps and we both avoid talking about my current situation. As a finishing touch, she styles my hair and applies light makeup.

When she steps back, I stare into the mirror at her masterpiece. "Wish me luck?"

She nods as she opens the door for me. "You don't need it. I know you'll do great."

I clutch the banister as I descend the stairs. The guard nods to me before he opens the door leading to the gardens. I shield my eyes and glare up at the sun as sweat forms on my forehead. When I turn the corner, I see Elizabeth is already helping set up the space for the reporters. Knowing she has everything under control, I stride to the flowers and run my fingertip over their petals. My lip quivers as I remember the last time Christian and I strolled through the flower beds. I pluck a forget-me-not and tuck the blossom behind my ear,

21

making a mental note to give it to Christian.

"Ann, you look lovely." Elizabeth smiles as I move towards her.

"Thank you."

I approach the podium that's been placed under the cool shade of a large oak tree. I scrunch my nose at the waiting reporters as several of them take a few quick photos. Elizabeth stands next to me and gently places a hand on my back, signaling me to begin.

"Thank you all for joining us today. As most of you may have heard by now, the Palace was attacked a few days ago. The group that attacked us calls themselves the Black Rose. They raided the Palace, wounded twenty-five individuals, and killed one guard. The medical staff is working around the clock to treat those affected and promises to do all they can." My eyes water. "What we are asking of everyone is: if you know anything about this terrorist group, please call your local authorities." Tears fall onto my stack of prepared notes.

"What about King Christian?" a reporter shouts.

"The King was shot in the attack and is fighting hard to return to the throne. For the time being, Prince Ryan is taking on his Palace duties."

"What are the chances of the King making a *complete* recovery?"

I glance at Elizabeth, who shakes her head. Of course they want to keep it quiet. I swallow my unease and answer, "The King is strong and we hope he'll return to the throne as soon as possible."

Before they can throw more queries at me, I nod my farewell and retreat to the solitude of the pond to catch my breath. As the burden of the situation weighs heavily on my heart, I chuck my heels across the manicured yard and fall back on the cushioned ground.

What am I going to do?

I swirl the tips of my toes in the cool water, as the rainbow of Koi dance within its depths. My head shoots towards the Palace as I hear laughter ringing out. In the distance, I see Elizabeth standing in the center of the reporters. I watch as they converse and the journalists flock around her like chickens to mealworms, and I'm amazed at her composure and grace.

I squeeze my lids shut. I need to face the fact that I will *never* be good enough to be Queen.

I skip a rock across the water, causing ripples along the surface before the inevitable splash. A roll of thunder pulls my attention to the dark clouds building on the horizon, and finches scramble to find safety in the trees. I breathe in the musty breeze and straighten my back as I put one foot in front of the other, until I find myself entering the Palace again.

"Get that thing!" a man yells.

My hand stills on the doorknob as he bullets down the hallway.

"It's going *that* way! Grab it, you idiot!"

I shrug, knowing that it is *none* of my business, until I hear squeaking and see a silhouette of feathers floating to the floor. Curiosity gets the best of me, and my bare feet make soft pitter-patters in the open air of the spacious Palace as I stride towards the bickering.

"No! You go *that* way, and I'll go *this* way!" the man shouts.

Two guards barrel towards me as Snowball darts under my legs. Before I have a chance to confirm that it is in fact her fluffy butt squirming underfoot, I'm tackled to the ground. I see stars as I make contact with the polished

23

floor.

"Great work, genius," one of the males grumbles.

"You were supposed to..."

"Shut up, both of you," I groan.

Two sets of eyes fall on my face. The men both stumble to their feet, as coordinated as a flock of hens fighting for breadcrumbs, and stand at attention. "We apologize, your highness. We were told to collect the animal, but she was more energetic than we thought."

I laugh until my chest hurts and tears warm my cheeks. "Do you mean to tell me that two of the Palace's *finest* can't handle a little pet?" I pound my fist on the ground, finally losing my mind.

They stare, wide-eyed, unsure how to proceed. Then we all cringe as we hear a loud clang and a group of maids squealing.

"Well, boys, follow the screams and that is where you will locate your feathered menace."

They groan and take off, leaving me behind on the floor. Man... Vinny has his hands full if *these* are his new recruits. I swallow at the thought. These boys are replacing Joey.

"Oh, my goodness! Lady Ann? Here, take my hand."

I grasp the small, calloused palm and then rub my sore backside. "Emily, it's nice to see you again. Thank you for rescuing me."

She goes to answer but pauses as a white speck dashes past us, followed by a pair of bumbling guards. "It's my pleasure."

I lose my breath as I notice the box nestled in the crook of her arm. The alarmingly bold tag informs me it contains her husband's belongings. "Oh, Emily." My lip quivers as

24

I meet her tear-stained face. "I'm… I'm so sorry."

"The King is taking care of my family now, Lady Ann. Don't you worry." She runs a hand over my arm. "We will get through this because we are strong women and, well, we have no other choice."

"If there is anything I can help you with, just let me know."

"Well, if you are ever in the neighborhood you could drop by the university and say hi."

"You work at the university, here in the city?"

"Yes, I'm an art professor there. I love my job, but I dread the annual charity ball we throw to help pay for extra supplies and assist students with scholarships." She rubs a hand over her tired face. "There is one tomorrow actually." She pushes out a breath. "I haven't been able to prepare for it with everything going on." Then she laughs and waves her hand at me. "My apologies. You don't want to sit here and listen to me complain, especially with your fiancé down the hall waiting to see you."

Snowball screeches as she slams into my leg and hides behind me. I laugh and collect her in my arms. "You are a naughty girl." Then I turn to Emily. "Tell me when and where. I will be there with cash in hand."

"Oh, you don't have to do that."

I hold up a palm. "Education is the foundation needed to produce strong leaders, and I think it is about time the Palace steps up and helps more in that area. Count me in."

We exchange information and then she saunters off with a wave.

"Caught you! You little sh…"

I scowl at the guards, but it soon dissolves into a smirk as I see feathers and what I *hope* is mud littering their uniforms. "Who caught her, gentlemen?" I arch a brow.

25

"Lady Ann, if you could just hand her to us, we can bring her back to her room."

"I found her fair and square, and when I'm done with her, *I'll* put her back." I turn on my heel and wander towards Christian's room.

"Wait! Please! For the love of God, tell us how you caught her."

The despair in his voice has me pivoting with a grin. "Love, compassion, and a sprinkle of breadcrumbs."

Snowball lifts her chin, and if she could have spat her tongue out, she would have. But instead, her highness turns away from her servants. So, as her loyal subject, I guide her in that direction. I open Christian's door and peek inside.

"I was deliberating over who was out there causing all that fuss. I should have realized it was you two," Christian says with a wave.

I present him with Mistress Fluffy Pants, and he strokes her while she settles in his lap, like that was her intended destination from the very beginning.

"I'm glad you are awake. How are you feeling?"

Christian's smoldering eyes meet mine and I gulp. He's furious… He plucks something off his finger and shoves it in my face. "I wake up and discover *this*," he hisses. "So why don't you tell me *how* I am feeling."

I bite the inside of my cheek as he shoves our engagement ring into my palm.

"So, you're giving up on us, is that it?" he growls.

My eyes shoot to his. "What?"

"Well, you returned the ring, so obviously you are attempting to explain something to me."

"Who gave up on *who*?" I shout, my fists balled at my

sides. "You left me for dead!"

A guard storms in at the sound of our raised voices, but with a flick of his wrist, Christian dismisses him.

My lip quivers as I continue, "How could *you*? I thought..." I suck in a sob. "I thought you loved me."

"I do love you."

"No!" I yell. "When you love someone, you *fight* for them. You *protect* them to the best of your abilities, but what you don't *do* is let them fall into your enemies' hands or pawn them off to your brother." At this point, my lungs are on fire from shrieking and my energy is dwindling. Everything that I have been waiting to say to him spews out like an active volcano, scorching everything in its wake.

Christian looks older than his years as he falls back on the pillows and rubs his stubble. "You have no clue how challenging those decisions were. You have no damn concept of how complicated it is to put an entire country in front of yourself and what *you* desire."

"You are right. I don't. But let me just remind you that I *chose* to leave the protection of the safe room to rescue *you*. I was willing to put myself at risk if it meant just one more minute by your side. And I would do it all over again."

He collects my hands and tugs me to him. "Then what has swayed your choice? I am still here. And I want to be by your side too." He slips the engagement ring on my finger and kisses my palm.

My eyes fill with tears as my heart breaks. So much has happened. Too much. If he only spoke those words on the phone with me, maybe I wouldn't have slept with Ryan. And maybe Christian wouldn't be fighting for his life.

I sit on the edge of the bed and run my hand down his cheek. "You need to shave and get those golden locks trimmed."

Christian rakes his fingers through his hair and nods. Then he opens his mouth to reply but a yawn escapes and his eyes flutter closed.

"Rest and we can talk more later." I pluck the forget-me-not from behind my ear, place it behind his, and try not to notice how frail and thin he suddenly appears.

Just Dance

"Come on, Ann," my dad whispers from within the folds of the darkness.

"Daddy? Is that really you?" I swat the specks of wispy feathers as they glide down my body like raindrops.

"Ann."

"Dad!"

"Hello, sweetheart!" Max shoves me against the wall, wrapping his fingers around my neck. "Did you really think I would leave without you?" Then he squeezes until I struggle for air.

I start awake, clutching my sore collar.

"If you insist on resting here, we should procure a more comfortable chair for you."

I stretch out, glad to see Christian in such a playful mood. His warm tone pulls the chill out of my veins. I glance around and notice Snowball isn't here. That means Elizabeth must have collected her while I was napping. My eyes scan over Christian's freshly bandaged leg and new bag of antibiotics until they land on his smirk.

I shrug and feign regality. "That is a wonderful idea, my King. But I'm afraid the *throne* won't fit."

"Are you already seeking to overthrow me and conquer the world?" His husky chuckle bounces off the walls, masking the beeping monitors.

"You don't believe I can?"

"Oh no, my dear Ann, you misunderstand. I have complete confidence in your ability to change the world and make it better." He kisses my palm. "I just wish you had the same confidence in yourself as I do."

Before I can reply to Prince Charming and his smooth

speech, my pocket starts clucking. I quickly answer the call and palm my face as Emily reminds me of the charity ball. I glance at Christian and bite my lip as I tell her I'll do my best to be there. Once I hang up, I sit on the edge of his bed and run my fingers over his arm.

"What do you think about going to the lake house for a little R and R?"

Christian side-glances all the medical devices at his bedside. "I don't know, Ann."

"Remember when you had the flu and thought you were dying? Then I opened the curtains, made you do some work, and you were cured! Maybe we can do the same thing and see what happens?"

"But this is not the same." He motions to his wound. "Plus, I don't imagine the physician will permit it." My face falls and I look away. Christian grabs my chin and lifts it. "Don't attempt to shift the focus. Who were you speaking to on the phone?"

And I know the subject of the lake house is over before he even gave it a chance to be a genuine thought. But I won't stop fighting this battle with him because he deserves a break, especially after everything that has happened. He needs to breathe in the fresh air and let his body and soul heal properly. I stash the argument in the back of my mind and replay my recent conversations with Emily.

"You are right. We ought to give a substantial contribution to the university. I'll make a note and ensure it is taken care of annually."

I place a hand on his. "Please let me be the one to deliver it." I swallow my emotions. "I know I shouldn't feel indebted to help Emily, but I do."

Christian squeezes my hand before he wipes a stray tear from my cheek. "It is solely your responsibility from this day forward. And it's excellent timing; the statement Vinny gave this morning confirmed that the rebels are in hiding. So, your safety won't be in question."

I climb into his bed and allow him to wrap his arms around me. "Thank you."

"Now that we are passed that, tell me what happened during the attack. From your perspective." I tense and shake my head, wanting to enjoy this moment between us before I crush him with the truth of what transpired in that safe room. He kisses the top of my head. "I'll drop the subject for now, but I anticipate a comprehensive testimony from you tomorrow. No more waiting." He clasps my chin. "No matter what it is you are concealing, it will not change how I feel, Ann. I love you." He rests his forehead on mine.

Does he already know? Surely, he would have said something to Ryan or me. Even if I wanted to tell Christian the truth and seek forgiveness, it would only clear my conscience. It won't help him heal faster. If anything, it will cause him to spiral—send him on an emotional roller coaster—making it even harder for his body to mend. Or have him lose the will to fight.

The nurse appears, whistling a pleasant tune as he enters the room. When his eyes catch ours, he waves me out the door. "Sorry, Lady Ann. The King needs his sponge bath, medications, and rest."

Christian cringes, and I can't help the giggle that escapes me at the thought of Mr. Alpha fearing the help. Christian scowls at my laughter before smacking my butt. "Go and prepare for your ball, *Cinderella*, before I reconsider and require that *you* personally attend to my bath."

"Promise?" I purr, winning me a smoldering grin. I blow him a kiss as I sway towards the door. "Make sure you scrub all the right places." I wink at the nurse as I

31

feel Christian's death glare. The man chortles in response, shakes his head, and snaps on a pair of gloves. Before I cross the threshold, I meet Christian's eyes. "I love you too."

His scowl thaws into a heart-melting smirk. "I know you do."

Once his door closes, my smile falters. What a web I've weaved. The light twinkles off my hand and I raise my ring finger. Then I lift my chin and stride towards the office, a woman on a mission. A quest to talk to Ryan and figure out why he is still ignoring me.

"Oh, I'm sorry, Lady Ann. Prince Ryan doesn't want visitors right now."

I stare slack-jawed at Christian's assistant. "Excuse me?" I draw out.

Tim clears his throat. "I apologize, but he doesn't want to be bothered."

I cock my hip. "Since when does he have the *authority* to turn away everyone and shut himself in Christian's office?"

"Not everyone." He squeaks as the office quiets, and all eyes fall on him. "Just you."

I slap my hand on the wooden barrier and twist the knob. Before Tim can yelp, I slam the door closed and lock it. Ryan leaps from his chair. "What the hell?"

"Well, Tim said you didn't want to be bothered," I purr as I step towards him. "And I know that doesn't include the woman you slept with," I hiss out the last part.

"We can't do this right now."

"And why not? You have been avoiding me ever since the safe room."

"*Why?* Why, you ask! Because while you are *playing* the

hurt fiancée, I am slaving away here, doing the work of *three* employees!" Ryan plops down a stack of papers to slam his point home.

I scan the room and pale as the memories flood me. This is the first time I've been inside Christian's office since Max trapped me within its walls. If I focus, I can see where they scrubbed the blood out of the carpet in the corner. And the safe that Max broke into is repaired, seemingly brand-new.

The knock on the door behind me brings me back to the present, but I ignore the person on the other side and turn to Ryan's red-rimmed eyes. "I'm sorry you've been working relentlessly, but I know your brother would rather you devote time to him in the hospital than sitting here."

"Don't you dare try to tell me what he wants. Because, Ms. Know-It-All, Christian asked me to pick up the slack so he could spend time with *you*."

My mouth malfunctions as his words, each laced with pain, crash into my chest. Why is Christian pushing Ryan away? Does he know what happened? But if he knew, wouldn't he be unhappy with me too?

The door slams open and a man clutches my upper arm. I shriek out of my stupor and jab my elbow into the stranger's stomach, then his nose, in one quick movement. Before my eyes can focus on the crumpling body, blood sprays my chest from his wound.

"Ann!" Ryan circles the desk and hands the guard a handkerchief.

Another guard steps towards me and I narrow my eyes. "Touch me and you'll end up like your friend."

"Enough!" Ryan blares at me. "Hasn't there been enough blood spilt? You will control yourself, Ann. Or so help me, I will kick you out of the Palace, for good!"

33

"You can't do that! Technically, I outrank you!"

"What's going on in here? Oh, my! Ann, are you bleeding?" I drag my eyes over to Elizabeth and shake my head. "Come with me, dear. I will help you get ready for the charity ball." She guides me out, and her tender touch makes me feel like a rabid animal. "Don't worry yourself over him, Ann. Ryan will come around. He is just under a lot of stress. Suddenly stepping into Christian's shoes would take a toll on any of us." She forces a laugh as we pass the other office workers.

Once my bedroom door closes, she sags on my couch with a huff and her confidence fades. In its place, weariness blossoms.

"I didn't mean to hurt that guard, Elizabeth. He just took me by surprise when he grabbed my arm." I swallow back my unease. "Especially in that room."

The Queen's attendee enters and rushes to Elizabeth's aid before she can respond to my apology. "You are looking tired. Should I pull your sheets down for you?"

Elizabeth shakes her head. "Not right now, Adrie. I called you in here to assist Lady Ann. She needs to look amazing for this ball tonight and I only trust one person to do that job."

Adrie's eyes sparkle at the compliment and she nods. "Whatever you need." She strides to my closet and plucks out a few choices. And that's the end of that conversation.

I'm pulled and poked like a rag doll again, and when I'm perfectly remade, I'm guided to my full-length mirror. I gaze at my plump red lips, my perky cleavage now flowing out of the shimmering emerald gown, and silver high heels. I'm going to bust my butt with these shoes. *Again.*

Elizabeth places an emerald crown on top of my head. "What do you think, Ann?"

My fingertips graze the glistening gems. "Why not the red one?"

Elizabeth stiffens. "Unfortunately, that one is in need of repair, but this one is custom-made and handpicked by Christian."

The jewels turn to ice beneath my touch as I remember what happened. I was wearing the crimson headpiece when the jail door was blown off. Of course, it would need *repairs*. Just like everything else around here, it was shattered. My hand quickly returns to my side and all I can muster in the form of a response is a curt nod.

"The color green represents strength and stability. That is exactly what we all need right now. And tonight, you will not be *farmer* Ann but Lady Ann, *fiancée* of King Christian, and our future Queen." Elizabeth half bows. Adrie follows suit, and bile rises up as terror squeezes my heart. Will Christian still want me after he discovers the truth? "Since you are familiar with them, I am having Vinny and Sam escort you to the ball tonight." Elizabeth embraces me before she turns to Adrie. "I'm ready for my nap now."

Vinny is waiting for me at the foot of the stairs. His eyes have bags under them. I question if this is because of the infants or the pressures of the Palace.

"The King would like to see you before you leave."

"Which King?" I mumble, just loud enough for Vinny to overhear as we start walking. "Because it seems that Ryan needs to remember his position. Did you know he asked a guard to escort *me* out of the office? The same office I've been working in for over a year."

Vinny glances around before replying, "I didn't realize that. Elizabeth blames me for Christian's injuries, and I've been kept out of the loop in most things."

I tense. "Do you think they're going to fire you?"

He purses his lips. "They can't right now, but if something happens to Christian, they can legally hold me accountable."

I thought the worst they could do was kick Vinny out of the Palace, but the implications seem far more severe. My heels clicking on the polished floors are the only sound as we weave around the hospital, each lost in our own thoughts. We stop at Christian's door and Vinny waves me inside.

Before I continue, I stare into Vinny's eyes and squeeze his hand. "I'm sure everything will work out, Vinny. I'll always be on *your* side, no matter what happens."

"Thank you." He smiles and stands guard in the hallway.

"Ann, quit delaying and allow me to see your attire."

I roll my eyes at Vinny before turning my full attention to his highness. I twirl and allow the bottom of the dress to flutter around me. Then I hold my hands out and curtsy.

"Magnificent. Now go straight up the staircase and inform my mother that she did far too good of a job, and thus, she must lock you away in your tower."

I press my lips to his chilled cheek. "Wrong storybook, my King." I run my hand down his face. "If you aren't feeling well, I can always stay and keep your lap warm."

"My lap is just fine—*thank you*." He searches my gaze. "I apologize for forcing you into a situation you never chose."

"Christian…"

He holds his palm up. "This attack opened my eyes to what is crucial." He taps his injury. "I've spent too much of my life pleasing others. I need to make myself happy." He swallows. "I want to leave my position as King."

36

His words send me spiraling. Christian, not being a king? "What do you want to do?"

He squeezes my wrist. "I'm going to give Ryan the throne and marry you. We'll move to your farm and have a family. Safely away from all of this mess. If that's what you still want?"

My mind is reeling. I never imagined... *this.*

"I apologize for interrupting, my King." Vinny enters the hospital room. "There's traffic reported on our route, so we need to leave now if you want to arrive on time."

"Consider my proposition." Christian kisses my nose. "Have fun, but not too much. Come and see me when you return."

"I'll make sure I don't kiss any toads." I wink.

"I would hope not, because you already have your King."

"And you are far more trouble than I could have ever imagined." I squeeze his hand. "Christian, can I ask you a favor?"

"You may ask me anything."

"Could you call Ryan and demand that he visit you? Because I know he misses you, but he assumes you don't want him here, and he is too prideful to admit it. Just like *someone* else I know."

Christian leans back and closes his eyes. For a minute, I fear he may have fallen asleep. The emotions playing across his face worry me. Maybe he does know about Ryan and me, and this is his way of punishing his brother? He opens his eyes, appearing exhausted. I lift my chin, resolved to tell him everything when I return. Then I'll let him decide *if* he still wants to settle down on the farm with me.

"Yes, I'll request a visit from him."

"Thank you. And now Cinderella must leave; she can't be late for her ball." I kiss him. "I love you, Christian. I promise we'll talk about everything when I get back. I won't be long. I'll see you soon." I clink towards the door. Before I exit, I pivot and blow him a smooch.

"No kissing toads!" he hollers in my direction before the door closes.

"Ann, you look exquisite! Thank you so much for coming," Emily praises once we push through the horde of press members. "I'm sorry about the paparazzi. I only told the head of my department that you were coming, but word travels fast."

"Don't worry about it. Did you know I wanted to be a journalist in high school? I know. Weird, right? Well, one of my former classmates is a big-shot city reporter, and occasionally he'll get in touch with me, especially when he wants access to a Palace headline. So, I called, asking him to return the favor and to spread the word for your event."

"Thank you so much for your help. We're so full we're actually turning people away. Well, here is your table. I need to make the rounds, but Professor Williams and his wife will keep you company." Emily saunters off as I relax into my chair. Vinny and Sam stand behind me and keep track of the movement around us.

I pivot to the red-haired man and blonde woman sitting across from me. "It's a pleasure to meet you both." I extend a palm. "I'm Ann."

"Thank you for coming, Lady Ann. I'm Kyle and this is my wife, Heather."

When we shake hands, I reposition my sliding tiara. "Do you mind if I slip these heels off? They are killing my arches."

"I took mine off ten minutes ago." Heather wiggles her hot-pink toes in my direction.

I free my feet and stretch my legs. "Thank goodness." I sip my wine, watching the couple from above the rim of my glass. "Aren't you two a little young to be professors?"

"We graduated early and at the top of our class," Kyle replies as if I ruffled his feathers.

"What my husband means to say is that we are young and very blessed to be here." Heather pats his thigh. Kyle smiles at her and they share a moment. I clear my throat and swig my drink, feeling the air heat up around us. "I'm sorry. Earlier today we found out that we're expecting. We're still working through the emotions of being both nervous and excited." Heather grins.

"Congratulations. And if you need any advice, I know just the man." I elbow Vinny. "He and his wife just had twins."

"Oh, my! Twins?" Heather exclaims.

This starts the conversation off on the right foot, as Vinny offers guidance and takes the pressure off me. So I settle back, enjoy the music, and sip my wine.

"Thank you so much for easing some of our worries." Kyle shakes hands with Vinny, before turning to his wife. "Now, if you'll excuse us, they're playing our song."

I watch as he twirls his bride, her dress fans out, and they join the dancers in the middle of the ballroom.

"Anna!"

I cringe at the nickname before spotting the soon-to-be dead man. "You know, when I invited you here, I asked you to leave the nicknames at home."

"I thought *I* was doing *you* a favor?"

As the man approaches, Vinny steps in front of me. "Who are you?"

"Vinny, this is Richard, the reporter I was telling you about."

Vinny nods and steps behind me.

"You are looking elegant. Although I do miss those pigtails you donned in high school. Oh, and those thick glasses! You gave off quite the librarian vibe."

"Pigtails?" Sam smirks my way.

"Oh, yes. This girl fashioned pigtails and braids. She wasn't one to dress up. But now, look at you, marrying the King and playing the part."

"Why are you patronizing me?"

Richard sits and I follow suit. Then he leans in. "I heard rumors."

"You always hear them. They're part of your job." I sip my liquid courage.

"Did a rebel assault you during the raid? My sources say a scuffle was heard over the Palace intercom."

I clench my glass before setting it on the table between us.

"Is this questioning really appropriate?" Vinny steps in again. "Why don't you change the subject, before I escort you outside."

"What else would you like to discuss, Muscles?"

"Have you heard mention of where the Black Rose is hiding?" Vinny asks.

I blink at Vinny, unsure where this is coming from. I thought he wanted to end the discussion?

"You know if I did, I'd have reported the information, like I'm supposed to. Believe it or not, reporters can't just write about anything they want. We are censored in this country," Richard huffs out.

"But have you heard rumors? Do you know the size of the organization? About their history?"

Richard clears his throat and stands. "I'll keep in touch, Anna. Enjoy your evening."

Once Richard has walked away, I pivot to Vinny. "What's with the interrogation?"

"Something doesn't add up. How did the rebels get inside the Palace undetected? Then, when they attacked, they never aimed to kill. Instead, they issued warning shots. Why not destroy everybody onsite?"

"Did you forget the bombs?" I hiss out as my PTSD takes over. "Or how about Max attempting to rape me and slice me to pieces?"

"I'm sorry. I'm just talking out loud." Vinny rubs his face before returning to his stoicism.

His words replay inside my head, but I refuse to believe these rebels are anything but a bunch of murderers. They took so much away from me. Maybe not physically, but definitely mentally. Justice will be served, and while I wait, I'll plaster on my best smile and help raise funds for Emily's charity.

Because *she* lost her husband. The Black Rose may not have killed him outright, but their explosion, their disregard for everyone's safety, took him from his wife and cut short their life together. Proving how evil the rebels really are.

I chug the rest of my alcohol and refuse to think about

41

this any longer. And before the night is over, I dance with every willing body, apart from the busboys. Happy to escape the depressing castle walls and have fun. By the time we return to the Palace, I'm exhausted and eager to take a nice hot bubble bath.

Shock

Chaos.

That's the best way I can describe what is happening in the Palace when we move through the front door. Vinny and I exchange a glance and follow the confusion.

"I need a ventilator—stat!"

The blood drains from my face as understanding dawns on me. "No. Please *no*."

I chuck my shoes and push through the crowd. I skid to a stop as my worst nightmare unfolds. Every nurse is shouting orders over Christian's pale body. The machine's normal rhythmic beeps are blaring and red.

"Move!" The demand erupts from my throat, and I fight my way to my fiancé. "Christian? Christian! You can't do this to me!"

Like a protective mother hen, I claw and kick at the fingers tugging me towards the exit. I couldn't prevent my mom's heart from failing, but I'd make sure it didn't happen to him. Suddenly, through all the yelling and movement, there is a faint bleep. Then the blaring ceases. My head shoots towards the machines and I watch the spike of his heartbeat moving across the screen, erasing the straight line's haunting form. Relief floods me and I drop to the floor, thanking my lucky feathers.

Once everything settles, the doctor informs us that their efforts to eradicate the infection are failing and Christian's body is shutting down. They expect him to have weeks to months to live. I collect Christian's palm as the ventilator forces air into his lungs then out again. I kiss his hand while tears soak his sheet and my heart splinters. The doctor excuses himself—leaving Ryan, Elizabeth, and me inside the ominous hospital room. The Queen slumps in a chair as she processes the information. Her face remains blank, though hopelessness appears to tug her into an endless void.

Ryan rubs his face and continues to pace. "None of this would have happened if you would have just located a safe room like we told you to! If you would have just stayed with the kitchen staff, Max wouldn't have been able to use you as bait!"

The verbal assault hits me square in the chest.

"You are *always* getting into danger, never listening to anyone, and now look!" Ryan glares. "You are a curse to this family! You have done nothing but bring *death* to the Palace!" He shakes his head before storming off.

A slap across the face would have hurt less. I stare after him, my jaw to the floor. The truth behind his words burns through me and I peer down at my hands.

Am I cursed?

I return my attention to Christian. I lean my forehead on his hand. I can't believe I ran out of time. I'll never be able to explain what happened or even apologize. My lip quivers. "Christian, what are we going to do without you?"

Days quickly turn into weeks as I rest by Christian's side. I'm not sure what I'm more distraught over: the situation with Ryan or the fact that I begged Christian not to die and he listened. In the beginning, I thought it was a miracle that his heart started back up, but now... I'm reconsidering, because we have to witness him withering away as the infection takes over his body.

Karen visits when she can, but the babies keep her on a tight schedule. Ryan and Elizabeth come and go, but they're busy transitioning the duties from Christian to Ryan. Jock delivers my meals and sits with me to make sure I keep some food down, but I've lost my appetite. And in turn, I'm dropping weight. Even Dan attempts to call, but I send it to voicemail.

I tuck the sheet around Christian and fluff his pillow. Ryan enters and brushes by me to sit beside his brother. I wish we could get past this. I clear my throat. "It's been a while since you visited. Is everything okay in the office?"

"We can't all fall apart and forget our responsibilities."

The sting of his words takes my breath away. "Ryan, I'm spending time with Christian before…" I let the reality of the situation fall between us.

"While I do everything by *myself*."

"Only because you had guards escort me out of the office the last time I went in there!"

Ryan straightens his suit and strides to the exit. "If you are not going to work, you need to return *home*."

Home. That word slaps me across the face. The *Palace* is my home.

"But what about Christian?" I shout at his back.

"Trust me, he won't even *know* you are gone."

I hurl my shoe at his arrogant head. "Why are you being so *cruel*? What have I done to deserve this?"

As the shoe bounces off Ryan's thick noggin, he pauses. He turns to Vinny and huffs out, "Wait for me in the hallway."

Vinny looks from his employer to me, dips his chin, and follows his order.

"What have you done to deserve this? Why the hell is

45

everything always about *you*?" Venom drips from Ryan's words, and suddenly his resemblance to his father is uncanny.

"No, instead, it's all about *you*, right?"

"If you were really concerned about him." He jerks his thumb to Christian. "You would leave. It's your fault he's holding on. If you go, my brother can die in peace, without these machines prolonging the inevitable."

"What are you saying? That I should leave so he can die?"

"What I'm saying is you should do the right thing and return home. With you gone, the curse will follow, keeping what's left of my family safe."

"You're an idiot if you think that I'm cursed."

"Either way, I don't want you hanging around to find out." He nods as Vinny pops his head in. "I'm late for a meeting. Goodbye, Ann."

Once he disappears, my body goes limp, and I slip to the ground. Tears stain my cheeks, but I'm completely numb to their existence as I wait for the Earth to swallow me whole. If Ryan wants me gone, then I won't cower and beg him to change his mind. He is the next King, and with that, comes the *real* curse. The crown.

I collect my essential belongings, then I tap on Karen's door. She smiles as she steps aside to let me pass. I glance towards the sleeping babies and my heart melts. They seem so peaceful. I tiptoe to Olivia's crib and stroke her golden curls.

Karen leans against the wall as she looks me over. "Where are you going?"

I know once the words are out in the open, there will be no turning back. I close my eyes and take a breath. "I'm returning to the farmhouse. This place only holds pain and suffering for me."

"But what about us? Vinny, the kids, and me?"

"I will miss you all dearly. But this isn't goodbye, right? You guys can visit anytime. My door is always open."

"Are you sure you won't change your mind? I mean, this isn't the first time you've left and then came *right* back."

I swipe at my cheek. "Trust me, Karen, there will be *nothing* here for me to return to."

"Are you taking Snowball with you?"

I falter as I think about the pampered Feathered Queen. She would be absolutely *miserable* in the country. I bite my quivering lip, trying to envision my life without her adventurous spirit. "No, Elizabeth needs Snowball more than I do, especially with everything going on."

A silent tear glides down her cheek, and she nods before she steps away from the exit. "If this is truly what *you* want, I support you, little sister. No matter how much I may disagree with it."

"Thank you." We embrace in a tight hug. "I know I have no right to ask this of you, but please don't tell anyone about what Ryan and I did in that safe room. He has a reputation to uphold, and I don't want to tarnish it. Especially since he has *no* intention of furthering our relationship."

Karen zips her lips, and I slip out as Carter cries for his next feeding.

47

My feet are like cement as I make my way towards the man who changed my life. My fingertips brush his hair. "I know you know already, because you're *you*. But if I don't tell you before I leave, I'll burst with regret. I made a huge mistake and slept with your brother in that safe room. It's no excuse, but I felt abandoned by you, plus the fever and the fear of dying." A heavy tension blankets the room. "I'm so sorry for the pain I caused you and your family. If I could go back, I'd do things differently. But I can't." I brush my lips over his knuckles. "It's time for you to rest, Christian. I love you so much. Goodbye, my King."

Forgotten Gift

I snatch my keys off the pegboard before locating the car Christian bought me for Christmas. I gaze at its shiny black exterior, wishing it were a time machine instead. My reflection echoes my mood, screaming at me with its sunken shadows. Soon my hands glide and tighten over the black steering wheel.

This is it.

I shift the car into drive and begin my journey. The city lights twinkle as they blur by. Once the country views fill my line of sight, my tears push to the surface. I wipe them away while focusing on driving for just *one* more minute, then another. Until I finally arrive at the little farm house. My cute, one-story, three-bedroom, two-bath, brick-exterior home sitting on ten acres of fertile soil.

Mine. I almost forgot. Now that Dad is gone, it's all mine.

Once the garage closes, I gaze at the door leading into the house. I groan as realization hits me. When I enter, a new chapter of my life begins. Or is it just picking up where I left off before I went to the Palace? I bang my head on the car's headrest before dragging my travel-worn body out of the vehicle.

Silver glimmers in the distance and I spot Dad's countless tools littering the crowded work bench in the corner. Every one of them had a purpose. Each just as valuable as the next. Now, here they are, gathering dust and rusting away. I glide my fingertips over their cold steel handles, remembering all that he accomplished with these simple tools.

And where is he now? In the ground, next to my mom.

I rub my temples and chastise myself for the negative feelings swimming around inside my head. "Suck it up, buttercup!"

I snatch my purse, ready to face the music. Then I shove through the entryway before flicking the switch and watching the bulbs illuminate the interior with a brilliance that doesn't match how I feel. I drop my stuff on the counter and take in my surroundings. I hug my suddenly chilled arms as I realize everything is exactly as I left it.

I slide my fingertips over the old beige fabric of my dad's recliner, which is positioned next to mine. This is where my grand adventure began. We were sitting here when my name was called to go to the Palace.

The sunlight from the hallway beckons me with its tendrils of glitter. My body has a mind of its own as my feet stroll to my dad's bedroom. Even though he has been gone a while now, I never went through his belongings or got rid of anything. I just couldn't bring myself to do it. As I peek inside, my knees grow weak.

The space still contains his soft, woodsy musk. His flannel shirts tickle my fingertips as I beg them to bring him back, even for just a moment. My gaze settles on his dresser, and I choke on a sob as I lift the picture of my parents on their wedding day. I rub my thumb over the cold glass while I admire their grins, so full of dreams. I settle it back in its place before tilting my head when I notice something odd.

On the worn nightstand is a brown paper bag. I peek inside. There's a bottle of whiskey and a sealed envelope addressed to me, written in Dad's chicken scratch handwriting. Biting my lip, I consider leaving it be. But curiosity gets the best of me, and I tear it open. My brow shoots up when I realize it's a congratulatory wedding card.

The glittering cardstock toasts Ryan and me on our big day, the contents explaining how proud and happy my dad was. It also says he knew this day would come ever since I brought Ryan home with me.

I crumble in a heap of exhausted limbs. This must have been before he died, when Ryan and I were talking about setting down roots. I can't stop the scream that rips through my body before I hurl the object of my contention.

Before my dad was murdered by Max, Ryan and I were planning our future together. We knew we wanted to live here at the farmhouse with constant visits to the Palace. We dreamt of having two children, tons of chickens, and maybe even some ducks. And Karen and Vinny would be right around the corner, so our aunt and uncle duties would never falter.

Now they're all *broken* dreams.

I side-glance the whiskey. Why would he gift us alcohol? Maybe it was for him? I mean, he was finally able to celebrate a job well done because he discovered someone who loved his daughter as much as he did. I rest my back against the wall, open the bottle, and sniff.

What the hell is this? It's definitely not anything like the sweet wines the Palace serves.

If it was good enough for Dad, it's good enough for me. Too lazy to get a glass, I position my ruby lips over the rim and tilt the brown liquid down my throat. The sudden burn instigates a coughing fit. I scowl at the bottle. Why would anyone drink this?

A warming sensation washes over my numbness before I take another swig. The more I drink, the easier it is for my mind to release my woes, and my heartache becomes less noticeable.

Eventually I stagger towards the living room. In passing, I giggle at the photographs hung in the hallway. Pictures of my lost family and past friends. I halt at the one of Christian's wedding, when he married the all-too-perfect Mary. Before we discovered she was helping the Black Rose.

That two-faced little brat!

My arm pulls back and I punch her in her pretty face.

Ha! Take that!

Glass shatters and distorts her painted visage. Soon *all* of the images depicting Mary or Ryan end up on the floor.

Yes, that feels better. Maybe breaking glass can destroy that alleged *curse*?

Or maybe I'm not the problem to begin with! Maybe it's really *them*? I should have stayed home after King Mark sent me back, then my dad, Suzie, and Christian would still be healthy.

All this thinking causes my head to swirl, and I stumble before letting the wall catch my clumsy frame. Then I slide to the floor, cackling at my realization. My little world was great before them. *They* are the ones who ruined *my* life. I lean my overheated head against the cold plaster as the white popcorn ceiling sparkles in the distance. I quickly pinch my eyes closed and groan when everything spins like a kaleidoscope.

I jerk up as something strikes my cheek. "Dan? Where did you come from? Did you just hit me?" I growl at my supposed friend and contractor, who helped me rebuild the chicken pen at the Palace.

"Don't you remember? Christian hired me to take care of your house. And when he bought Suzie's property, I moved in there. Ann? What happened? Why are you bleeding? And why is there glass everywhere?" Dan kneels, his green eyes examining my fingers.

I hiccup. "Dan, it's the *curse*."

He arches a brow and seizes the half-empty bottle of whiskey. "All righty then. How about we get you to the hospital? I think you may need stitches." He wraps an arm around my waist and lifts.

"I'm not going anywhere but to my room."

Dan tugs me towards the front door, over the battlefield of glass littering the floor. "No way, Ann, you need *medical* attention."

"Stop belittling me!" I hiss. "You're not listening! I *am* a curse! You need to leave while you still can!" I pull away from him, stumbling over my own feet.

Dan growls as he clutches my wrist. "Are you hearing yourself? You are not some plague. Who the hell put that idea into your head? Was it that pink Godzilla chicken from your dreams?" He wraps an arm around my waist again and tugs me to the front door.

"First off, I'm never telling you about *my* dreams again. Second, that nightmare was horrific! It was eating my brain and its feathers were ninja stars." I shiver as I remember, then I dig my feet into the carpet. "You still aren't hearing the words coming out of my mouth." I shove him back against the wall with such force a few more picture frames fall and shatter. "Leave me *alone*." I stride to my room.

He pinches my shirt and yanks me to his chest. "You listen to *me*. Right. Now." I turn my head away, but he plucks my chin and lifts it roughly. "You are a beautiful, intelligent, and compassionate woman. And *anyone* who says otherwise is an idiot." He stares into my hazel eyes and wipes away my tears with his thumbs. "Now. *Please*, let me take you to the hospital."

"You're the idiot." I rush to my room, before we start our tug of war again, and fall onto my bed. I snatch my pillow and hold it to my face.

"Tell me who told you this so I can kick their ass."

"Your soon-to-be *King*—Ryan."

He arches his brow as he ambles over. "Ryan? But he loves you? Why would he say that?"

I snort laugh. The whiskey burns as the acid rises. "Love. He never loved me. He got what he wanted."

"Get some rest. We'll talk when you're making a little more sense." Dan lowers himself next to me before tracing slow circles on my back. His gentle touch quickly puts me into a soothing slumber, and I silently pray that the pink fluffy Godzilla chicken keeps its talons out of my dreams.

Sweet Peaches

The sunlight glares it's perky little head at me. I roll and burrow into my pillow. I reach my hands out to swat at my bright offender, but my palms strike a warm body. My eyes shoot open, and my head flings up. I squint at a man's back and try to remember where I am.

Well, it's too sunny to be the safe room. And there are no maids or fancy furniture, so it's not the Palace bedroom. My eyes drift to Dan's dark hair and slow-moving chest. Oh, no! My palms spasm over my body. *Phew.* My clothes are intact. I sigh with relief, rubbing my hands over my face. The movement sends sharp pains up my arms. Ugh, that's right. Now I remember. After my drunken rage, my fingers were sliced by shards of glass.

I tiptoe to the bathroom and reach under the sink for the first aid kit. I brush the dust off the lid and cough. Well, there's no mold or fungus growing. That's a good sign, right?

I slap my hand over my heart, my eyes meeting Dan's in the mirror as he stands in the open entryway.

"How old is *that*?" He aims his thumb at the container.

"I can't remember the last time I used it."

"Do you think it's safe to open?"

"Why wouldn't it be? I'm pretty confident bandages do not expire."

"Sit." He motions for the top of the counter as he flicks the light on.

"Can't we just do it in the living room?"

"Ann, there's glass *everywhere*. Let's just get you cleaned up." He places his hands on my hips and lifts me up on the counter. "Then we can work on cleaning the house."

55

"You don't need to do this."

Dan removes tiny crystals out of my palms and sweat drips down my chin as I contain my agony. Then he applies liquid to the sores and I all but scream out.

"I'm sorry. But maybe this will *remind* you why you don't drink." He affixes the bandages to each of my wounds. "All done. Now, how about you buy me some lunch?" He pats my knee. "I know the perfect place."

I scoot to the edge to jump off, but he lifts me up and sets me on the floor instead. Then his fingertips linger on my sides as he smiles. I scan his emerald eyes, unsure what he's thinking, but as quickly as he touched me, his hands are gone and he is striding to my bedroom door.

"You get dressed, while I make a pathway through the house to the front door," Dan throws over his shoulder.

"I'm not going to the doctor!"

He waves me off. "Yeah, yeah, yeah. I get it. Stop whining and change into something else... preferably something that *doesn't* smell like you swam in a pool of whiskey."

I narrow my gaze, and as he turns the corner, I lift the hem of my shirt and gag. I guess clean clothes and a *shower* wouldn't hurt. I roll my eyes at my bandaged hands and grumble. Well, I guess clean clothes will have to do for now. I wiggle my wrapped fingers. I feel like an idiot. No, an irrational mummy is more accurate. Changing my outfit proves far more challenging than it *ever* should be. Mental note: Don't drink whiskey... ever. Drunk Ann is worse than an angry cockfighter.

"Come on, slowpoke, before you're buying me lunch *and* dinner!" Dan shouts from the hallway.

I stomp to the front door. "There is nothing wrong with combining two mealtimes into one big one. You know, they actually already have a name for it. It's called: *dunch*. And before you ask, *yes*, you can include breakfast into that and get ba-dunch." I brush past him and walk outside into the crisp air. "Now look who's *slow*."

"What kind of made-up word is ba-dunch? That sounds like a German rock band."

"Oh, you mean 'Du Hast'? That's a *song*, not a band."

"I don't even want to know how you know that." He chuckles as he opens the door to his truck for me.

"What? You don't think the Palace teaches *that* to its ladies?"

His roar of laughter echoes around the cab of the truck. "Heaven forbid they actually educate you in other country's affairs, especially music. I mean, could you imagine King Christian head-banging at a diplomatic rock concert?"

The air around us turns frosty at the mention of Christian. I nibble my lip and watch the gravel road turn to asphalt. I tap the windowpane as we pass Jessica's Memorial Library where I volunteered. I get lost in happier memories—when I taught children that books are grand adventures while we read, made crafts, and played games.

Dan pulls into a parking lot and clears his throat. "How is your fiancé doing? I mean, I saw the news report and you stated that he wasn't doing well. But I get the feeling it's more serious now that you've returned home."

I can't meet his gaze. "How do you know I've *returned* home? Maybe I just came to visit my dad's grave?"

"If you don't trust me with the information, I understand."

I lift my head. "The Palace doesn't want word to get around yet, but Christian's time is limited." My lip quivers, and he tugs me to his chest before I continue, "It's horrible, Dan. He is on a ventilator and…" I suck in a sob. "It's all my fault, because when his heart stopped, I begged him to come back. *Begged*! Now his body is only functioning with machines." I stare into his eyes. "He wouldn't be suffering right now if it wasn't for me. I left so he can finally find peace."

Dan kisses the top of my head. "Oh, my sweet Ann, you are not powerful enough to stop death. Christian is stubborn; that's why he's still around." I want to believe his words, but he wasn't there. He doesn't know what really happened in that hospital room. "Now wipe those tears and let's get some grub. You'll feel better after you soak up the rest of that alcohol with some fluffy pancakes." Dan leads me to the restaurant, and I grin up at the sign. It's not a fast-food chain type of place, but a locally owned and operated diner, nestled next to a mechanic's garage and gift shop.

The bright-blue paint on Justin's Tire and Lube is welcoming but rugged, with a constant flow of customers. A thin, tattooed man curses and tosses a shop rag as we pass. Then he runs his hands through his hair, smearing grease on his military cut strands. Suddenly he stops and squints at us. "Well, look who finally graced us with her presence!" The blue-eyed mechanic stomps in our direction.

Dan freezes but I place a hand on his arm. "Justin is a family friend."

The man in question collects me in an oil-smudged hug and swings me around. "What are they feeding you at that Palace? Tea and crumpets? You've lost weight." He sets me down. "Your dad would be fuming. Now go inside Sarah's and get yourself some of her country fixings. You'll be rounder than a potbelly in no time." He shoves a twenty into my palm.

58

"Justin, quit it! You worry too much." I force the bill back into his hand.

He wraps a corded arm around my neck and rubs his knuckles over my hair. "Oh, look who grew a pair while she was off playing Pretty Princess." I slam my foot on his steel-toed boot before shoving him back. When he stumbles, his face lights up with pride. "And you took *my* advice and learned some defensive maneuvers."

I flip him the bird and roll my eyes. "I'm not a little kid anymore. Stop treating me like one."

"Oh, what manners." His laughter rings out before he bows. "My *Lady*, please forgive me."

We glare each other down until we finally burst into laughter. It's nice to be around someone I knew as a child. Growing up, this little plaza was a great escape from the farm. Plus, when I learned how to drive, it was the best place for an oil change. Especially since Justin would give me the family discount, and in exchange, I would bring him eggs and produce.

A gruff male voice shouts over at us and Justin grumbles, "Don't be a stranger, Ann." Then he walks off.

I clutch his wrist and gasp. "What? Could it be?" I tug at a wedding band. "Who in the world would be dumb enough to keep you around?"

Justin yanks his arm away. "If you decide to come around more often, I might introduce her."

His teasing words make me cringe. He's right. I haven't been around. Even when I came back last winter, I never visited because I was too busy with the library.

"I'm sorry," I whisper.

"Hey, I get it. You got your *fancy* Palace pals now." He pinches my cheek. "You don't need us poor folk anymore." He pulls out a business card and hands it to me. "Her name is Suzanne, and she is three months pregnant with our second child. Now here is my cell number. Call and catch up when you aren't too busy primping your feathers, okay?" He saunters off to his maintenance bay.

Dan guides me to the diner, but as we pass the gift shop, I tug him inside. The little bell above the door jingles, and a dark-haired man pops his head over the counter. "I'm sorry, the diner is packed and I'm running both today. All the canvas and clay sculptures are twenty percent off and made by our talented local artists, Paul Putzer and Brittney Bornemann. The beautiful dream catchers are handcrafted by another local, Courtney Jeffcoat…" As his mocha eyes rest on me, he stops. "Listen to me blabber on, when you already know all of this."

"Hey, Frankie, how have you been?"

"As good as I can be, considering." He rubs his neck. "I'm sorry to hear about your dad and Suzie. You must be going through a rough time too."

My breath catches as I look around the shop. Normally there was a beautiful blonde behind the register. She was what kept people coming in, with her contagious laughter and generous heart. "Where is Sarah? Did she go to the diner?"

Frankie frowns. "No, she actually passed away last year."

"Oh, I'm sorry to hear that."

"Yeah, business hasn't been the same since. I was hoping to keep it operating, at least until our daughter, Aurora, was old enough to take over, but I don't think I can keep it afloat that long."

"Excuse me, sir. But we're having a problem with the broiler, again." A cook comes over.

60

"It's never-ending." Frankie offers a sad smile. "Let me know if I can help you find anything." His slumped figure strides to the diner through the adjoining door and my heart sinks. This place was thriving; surely it won't close.

"All right, quit stalling. I'm starving." Dan guides me towards the diner, and we find a booth in the back.

I look around at all the cute western memorabilia adorning the walls. Soon, the waitress pulls me out of my thoughts as she jots my order of chicken and waffles and Dan's cheeseburger and curly fries. Then she saunters off, leaving behind two sweet teas and a bowl of lemons.

"You know, I always wanted to work here," I say as I squeeze a lemon into my glass.

"Why didn't you?"

"Because my dad needed me on the farm."

"Well, what's stopping you now?" Dan counters as he stirs his tea with his straw.

"What? Go from a Palace Princess to a diner girl?"

"Technically, you were almost a Queen." Dan smirks. "No, what I mean is: why don't you buy this place? Or become an investor to keep it afloat?"

"I would be lying if I said I haven't thought of doing that. I mean, I love my farm, but I could turn the shop into a little book nook and sell chicken stuff on the side. Plus, my eggs and produce could supply the restaurant."

"Then why don't you do it?"

I dangle my engagement ring. "Because this is a ball and chain. It means the Palace can call me back at any time—day or night." I rub the band. "It means I will never be truly free to do what I want. At least not until…" I let the words fall between us.

I can't force out the reality that Christian is dying. With

him gone, I won't be needed or wanted; Ryan made that very clear. And if I'm truly honest with myself, I can never be completely happy doing office work and meeting with the press. That's not who I am.

Our food arrives, and the smell of the grease burns my nose and makes me queasy.

"Is everything okay, darling?" The waitress draws out as she smacks her chewing gum.

I stumble out of the booth and down the hall to the bathroom. I make it just in time to hurl into the porcelain. As I splash cold water over my hot face, I groan. Once I get my bearings, I pat my stomach and then trudge back to our table. Jock has spoiled my country-eating habits. I've spent too much time surrounded by healthy fixings at the Palace.

"Are you okay?" Dan questions as burger grease slithers off his chin.

"You know what? I'm going to stretch my legs and walk back."

"What?"

I put up a hand. "I want some time to myself, to clear my head. Don't worry, I'll pay on my way out."

"Okay." Dan raises a skeptical brow. "But if you change your mind, call my cell and I'll pick you up."

I pay the waitress, leaving a hefty tip, and finally get out into the fresh air. I send a wave towards Justin as I stroll past the shop, before he disappears under an SUV.

Though summer is still in full swing, the wind sweeps my hair back with a hint of iciness and reminds me that fall is right around the corner. I shove my hands in my pockets as I admire the beautiful foliage. I breathe deep and take in the miles of open fields dotted with dairy cows. My presence doesn't disturb them; I blend right into their world.

My fingertips graze the rough bark of a peach tree. I pause to assess the enormous orchard. My eyes drift over the countryside, and I notice that there are no fences surrounding most of the lush fields. And nobody is rushing around with guns strapped to their sides.

I snatch a plump peach and wipe it on my jeans. Then I sink my teeth into its flesh, enjoying the juices rolling off my cheeks. *This* was tastier than that fried food.

My summers were spent in high trees, with a book and snack as company. A grin spreads across my face as I pull off my bandages and clasp branch after branch, until I'm six feet in the air. I ease between tree limbs and settle against the trunk with my legs swinging freely in the sky. I observe bees and butterflies twirling and buzzing around me, intertwined in a dance with the wind.

This is home.

As I reach for another peach, my phone clucks and I answer it, "Hey, Karen!"

"Hey, girl, thought I would check in with you. What are you up to?"

I spread my arms into the breeze and close my eyes. "I'm finally *flying* free."

"Oh, man, whatever you're taking, give some to me." Karen chuckles. "I'm elbow-deep in dirty diapers and my boobs are killing me. What was I thinking, trying to feed *two* kids with just *one* set? Would you be interested in lending me yours for a few months?"

"Uh, no. I can't imagine letting anything suckle on me."

Before she can answer, I hear grumbling and shuffling. "Not again! I'll be right back."

"Are you talking to me?"

63

"No, sorry, Ann. I bled through another pad, and I need to clean up. Ugh, this bleeding is ridiculous! It's hard enough taking care of two tiny humans without worrying about switching out *my* diaper. I mean, don't get me wrong, I love the fact that I was period-free for eight months, but now it's like months of flow catching up with me."

My fruit slips from my fingertips and bounces off several branches before it explodes on the ground. "Ka-Karen, I need to go."

"Did I give you too much information? I have such a big mouth sometimes."

"Yeah, I mean, no. I just need to charge my phone. I'll talk to you after it charges."

"All right, call me soon."

I jump down, sending tingles up my toes from the impact, then take off towards the house at a brisk jog. I mentally chastise myself for not being more careful, but I was always on time! It was like clockwork with my body!

The tears stream as my feet pound the untilled earth. I was free as a bird for a whole five *minutes*. It's okay. I had a serious infection—surely the doctors checked my bloodwork for a possible pregnancy? Yeah. That's right. My cycle is just late because of all the stress my body has been going through. I'm sure my period will arrive any day now.

When I return home, I'm surprised to see Sam talking to Dan on the front porch.

"Hey, Sam." I brush past them to grab water from inside the house.

"What the hell happened in here? Did someone break in?" Sam questions as she follows me.

"Ann got a little drunk and broke some picture frames,"

Dan explains.

"What? Ann did this?" She inspects my hands.

"It's a long story," I reply. "Shouldn't you be at the Palace?"

"Ouch. I thought you'd be happy to see me. Well, Ms. Crabby Pants, I'm off for a few days, so I decided to come hang out with my man. Maybe see a movie? Or just snuggle under the covers for a while."

I finish my glass of water and walk back to my room, with Sam in tow and Dan fiddling around in the kitchen. "That sounds like fun."

I settle on my bed before snatching my romance book, *Expecting Moore,* from my nightstand. Eager to continue Robbie and Cassie's love story and escape for a few hours.

"Do you want to talk about it?" Sam interrupts.

"Nope." I turn the page with finality, hoping she gets the hint.

"Ann…" Ms. Persistent continues.

"I said I do *not* want to talk about it."

Dan comes around the corner with sandwiches. "I thought you would like something to eat. Since you didn't have anything at the diner."

I slam my book down with a grunt. "I appreciate all of your help, but you are a couple, so go and have fun. I'm fine alone."

They look at each other with arched brows.

"Go—that's an order." I try to use my old title to scare them into action.

"Come on, we're your friends. You can talk to us about anything," Dan offers.

I bite into my sandwich. "Yum," I mumble with peanut

butter stuck to the roof of my mouth.

"Come with us to the movies and get out of this stuffy place. I'll pick out an outfit for you." Sam bounces to my closet.

"I'm dressed."

"Girl, I'm not going out in public with Cowgirl Ann. You are going to look nice." Before I can respond, Sam's phone rings. "Yes, sir... No, I completely understand... Yes." She pouts as her gaze falls on me. Then she saunters over and hands me her device. "It's for you." Then mouths, "Sorry."

"Hello?"

"Ann, we have a situation, and we need you to return to the Palace."

My heart clenches. "Is Christian okay?"

"There hasn't been any change in his condition since you left."

I let out a breath, but then anger boils up as I hear Ryan in the background. "Is the Prince standing right next to you, relaying the information instead of talking to me himself? Why didn't his *highness* call me directly and ask *nicely* for me to return?"

There is a pause as Vinny stumbles, "Does that even matter..."

"If he needs me to come, he can ask. Now hand that *chicken* the phone."

There is rustling and muffled voices, then Vinny replies, "Prince Ryan doesn't wish to come to the phone at the moment."

I rub my temples as my stomach rolls. "Ryan sent me away to begin with. If he wants me to return urgently, he can ask me himself. Because the only reason I'd return willingly is if it's for Christian. Goodbye, Vinny!"

I toss the phone across the room. I put my shaking hands to my mouth and sprint to the bathroom, where I violently release my brunch into the cold ceramic. Suddenly, my hair is swept out of the way by gentle fingertips. When I'm done, someone shoves a towel in my face and I wipe the sweat off my brow before leaning against the wall with my lids pinched, willing my stomach to stop churning.

When I catch my breath, Dan is staring at me, still holding my hair back. I force a smirk. "Are you trying to poison me, evil stepmother?"

"Sam ate the same thing and she's fine."

On cue, she plows through the entryway. "Thanks a lot, Ann! Now Vinny is taking his annoyance out on *me*! Why did you have to hang up on him? He may be your friend, but he is my *boss*!" She plants her hands on her hips, but then her emerald eyes soften as she sees me leaning against the wall. "Are you okay? Why don't I call a doctor?"

"It's just stress." I turn to Dan. "You can let go of my hair."

"Sorry. I wasn't sure if you were going to pull another *Exorcist* move." He smirks at me before he turns to Sam. "What exactly did Vinny say?"

"He's demanding that I bring her back as soon as possible."

I cross my arms over my chest. "Like hell you are."

"Hey, I'm not the bad guy here so don't make me whoop you. I have my orders."

"Well, technically, you're off for two days, so I have some time."

Sam picks at her nails. "Please don't make me choose

between my friend and my job."

I stand straight. "I have survived a lot worse than the wrath of you, Vinny, or his highness!" I ball up my fists. "I have lost my mom. My dad. And my fiancé is wilting away in a hospital bed!"

"Ann, you're not the only *one* with troubles! We have all suffered in our lives."

I brush past her but she grabs my arm. "Sam, this isn't a cock fight. I'm not trying to pinpoint who has the most pitiful life! Now. Let. Me. Go."

She returns my glare. "It's my job to take you back to the Palace."

I shake my arm free. "Call Vinny and tell him I refuse. Explain to him that I'm not some *yo-yo* the acting King can yank back on a whim."

She throws her phone at my chest. "You do it. If not, we leave in an hour." Then she stalks out of my room.

Dan leans on the wall with his hands in his pockets. "Well, look who's sticking up for herself."

"Shut up, Dan."

"I mean, you have always *allowed* everyone to manage your life. So, good for you. But can I make a suggestion?"

"No."

"Keep Sam out of this, please. She has enough problems."

"So, you're taking her side?"

He places his hands gently on my arms. "Hey, no one is taking sides." He brushes my hair off my shoulder. "I mean, I would love to see you girls wrestle on the floor. It's a real fantasy of mine." He chuckles, then grabs my chin. "Returning to the Palace doesn't change anything."

"It does! It means I have to sit there and watch Christian fade away. Just like my mom," I whisper.

He coils his arms around me. "I am sorry." He takes Sam's phone out of my hands. "Let me call Vinny and attempt to smooth things over."

"No, I should do this myself."

"Okay, if that's what you want." He places the device in my open palm. "I'll go check on Sam."

I plop on my bed, take a deep breath, and dial.

"Hello?"

"Hey, Ryan."

There is a short pause. "Ann."

"You made it clear that you do not want me at the Palace." The silence causes hot tears to wet my cheeks. "So, why the sudden change of heart?"

"Because Mom asked me to call you back."

I should have known. Elizabeth is all about appearances. And what does it say when I leave the Palace while Christian is sick?

"Well, you should have thought about that before you told me to leave." I squeeze the bridge of my nose. "Is this how it's going to be between us?" Silence. "Fine, I will call your mother and explain the situation."

His annoyed sigh says enough. I squeeze the phone against my ear, and I hope that he will say something, *anything*. But the line goes dead. The phone slips from my grip as my head falls in my hands. When did he morph into this monster? How did it get this bad?

"Ann? What did he say?" Dan asks.

"He doesn't want to see me."

Dan sits next to me with tissues. "*Who* doesn't want to

69

see you?"

"You know what? It doesn't matter because I'm not going to listen to him. He conned me into trusting him once before, but never again." I blow my nose with finality.

Funky Monkey

Dan pulls my comforter to my chin. "You'll feel better with some sleep. I'm going to speak with Sam and attempt to talk some sense into Vinny before he decides to fire her."

My lids lower as I nod, wishing I could sleep my *life* away.

The red and orange leaves flutter like fluffy feathers, obscuring my vision. I clutch a bundled blanket protectively to my chest but freeze as a shadow approaches. Suddenly, the figure shoves me, and I tumble off the edge of existence. As if on instinct, I release my treasure as I attempt to save myself. But before I plummet, agony clenches my heart as the package is caught by the stranger.

The sensation of falling jolts me awake. Sweating and breathing in rasps, I toss back the suffocating covers, not wanting to go back to sleep. I pad through the quiet hallway. My breath catches at my rage-induced mess decorating the kitchen table. Dan did his best to sweep up the glass but there are mangled picture frames everywhere.

What is wrong with me? I never drink like *that*. Maybe I'm going through an early mid-life crisis?

As I turn the corner, I silently watch Sam and Dan in the kitchen. They are sitting on the bar stools laughing while sipping coffee. Enjoying each other's company. Offering little sweet touches of affection. The smell of the glorious liquid squeezes my stomach and I feel myself pale with nausea. I attempt to hold back my groan but it presses out, ruining their alone time. Dan's eyes meet mine before he stands, offering me his seat.

"No, please sit. I'm fine."

Hesitantly, he does what he's told. "Ann, I explained

71

to Vinny that you have the flu and need to rest before traveling. So, I bought you a few days."

"Thank you. And I will call Elizabeth. Apparently, she is the only reason the Prince is making such a big deal about me returning."

"Vinny wants us to stay here with you for the time being, providing updates throughout the day," Sam slips in.

"Of course, Mr. Control Freak wants you to babysit me on your days off," I huff out. "But you know, that doesn't have to completely derail your plans. We can send Dan to the store to buy movies, popcorn, and candy and we can have our own movie night in the comfort of the living room."

"Maybe."

"Come on, it's my treat. You can think of it as babysitting money."

She embraces me. "Listen, I'm sorry about earlier."

I rub her back. "I still think I can whoop you."

She laughs as she tosses her hair over her shoulder. "Keep dreaming, sweetie." She turns to Dan. "I will make a list of movies and snacks for you." Then she skips off.

I look at Dan. "You have your hands full with her."

"You have no idea."

Dan continues to watch her as she settles on the couch. When his eyes meet mine, I bite my lip. "Dan, can I trust you?"

"Is this a trick question?"

"No, I am being serious."

"You can trust me, with anything."

"When you go to the store, I need you to pick up

something unusual."

He pats my shoulder. "Trust me, I have a *huge* family, full of women. What is it you need? Some pads or tampons? Or that funny-looking cup? I mean, I don't understand why you would want to shove something like *that* in your…"

"I need a pregnancy test."

My words throw him back a step. He shakes his head. "Very funny. Is this a late April Fool's joke? Is Sam in on this too?" I clutch his shoulders and move him farther away from his girlfriend. He blinks, dumbfounded. "*What* did you ask for?"

"Shh, you heard me, and I'm not repeating it. *Please*? I would get it myself, but now I'm under house arrest. Plus, with my popularity, somebody might start an unnecessary rumor if they see me buy one."

He paces the kitchen, acting as if ants are crawling up his pants. He rubs his hands over his stubble before he pivots on his heels. "Whose would it be?"

Sam comes around the corner waving her list triumphantly, saving me from having to explain. She hands it to Dan, but then she quirks a brow. "Is everything okay?"

"Yes, Dan was just trying to get me to eat something, but I told him no."

Sam arches a brow at the culprit. "I'm sure Ann will eat when she's *ready*."

"Yes, of course. You are right." He raises the list. "The errand boy will return." Sam gives him a quick kiss. Then he brushes past me, whispering, "With *everything*."

After what Karen said the other day, combined with that nightmare that felt so real, I'm freaking out. I know my cycle is late, but with all the stress and my infection…

I'm confident it'll make an appearance soon. My gaze lands on my chipped toenail polish as I hear the front door shut. What am I going to do?

"You are the best! What a great idea to have a movie night together!" Sam wraps an arm around my waist and guides me to the couch. She helps me sit, grabs blankets, and works on setting up the TV. "This will be so much fun!"

My phone clucks from my pocket and distracts me. "Hello?"

"Ann?" Elizabeth asks. Oh boy. Now I'm in trouble. My mind buzzes a mile a minute. What if the doctors took blood while I was recovering, and Elizabeth knows something? No. She would have told me. Or, at the very least, the medical team should have. "You never called me last night, so I wanted to see how you were feeling."

"I'm sorry. I meant to call but I fell asleep." I wipe my brow.

"It's okay. Vinny informed us you were ill."

"Us?"

"Oh, where are my manners? Ryan is on the line too. Say hello, Ryan."

"Mom, this is completely unnecessary," he grumbles.

"Stop it, Ryan. Now, Ann, how are you feeling?"

"I think I have the flu."

"Well, it's a good thing Dan is there to help you, *again*," Ryan mutters.

My mouth falls open. "Dan is with Sam!"

"For now."

"You..." I blare.

Elizabeth clears her throat. "Enough. Ann, Vinny gave

74

us his word that Sam is taking good care of you. Is she with you now?"

"Yes, she is babysitting me," I scoff.

"And, afterwards, are you coming back to the Palace?"

I take a steadying breath. "I don't see the point. Christian is..." Tears choke me, and I cough. "He isn't in the best shape. And your *other* son has made it clear he doesn't want me around."

"Ryan?" Elizabeth questions. There's a click as Ryan ends the interrogation.

"I'm sorry, Elizabeth. Ryan told me how he truly felt. That is why I left the Palace to return home."

"Ann, he doesn't mean it. Whatever he said..." She trails off.

"He knows where he can find me to apologize."

"I can reason with my son—make him see the error of his ways. He is just a mess right now. We all are. Our family is being torn apart by grief yet *again*. I am going to speak to him and then get back to you. Get well soon."

I hang up and wrap the fleece blanket around my shoulders.

"Who was that?"

"Elizabeth and Prince Ryan." I tug at the loose threads on the cover.

Sam sits down next to me and pats my leg. "How about we see what's on?" She flips on the TV and we watch a cartoon until we hear Dan return with his hands full. "I'll help you unload." Sam jogs to his truck to grab more goodies.

I push off the couch to follow her, but Dan steps in my path. "Grab *it* out of my pocket," he whispers.

I smirk at the bulge in his front pocket. "Oh, Dan. You shouldn't have."

As Sam approaches, I snatch the pregnancy test and shove it in my shirt. I hold my breath and pray she didn't notice my hands on her man. Thankfully, she walks around the corner with an armful of bags. "Honey, you are too good to us! You bought everything and more!" she sings as she places the items on the counter.

Dan looks at me with a sad smile, then trails behind Sam. "I even bought you Funky Monkey ice cream."

The voices drift off as I tiptoe to my bathroom and shut the door. I gawk at the ominous pink box, and my hands shake as I rip it open and follow the instructions.

Moments later, I set the test on the counter and *wait*.

Chick on Board

I settle at the end of the couch, wrap my body in my blanket, and cocoon myself from the rest of the world. I force an engrossed look as we watch a romance movie. Then a comedy. My mind is numb. Not even an attack ninja chicken gets a giggle out of me. I stare at the screen and wish I could dissolve into this fictitious world. Every now and then, I catch Dan peering over, but I can't meet his gaze. It was humiliating that I had to ask him to buy the test to begin with.

When the second movie ends, I don't even notice until Sam stretches out like a lazy cat and grins at Dan. "Are you ready for bed?"

He squeezes her hand and nods. "Why don't you take a nice hot shower and get comfortable while I clean up?"

A childish pout plays on her plump lips. "You aren't going to join me in the shower?"

He blushes and clears his throat. "No, thank you."

Sam wraps her arms around his neck and presses her body into his, before she whispers in his ear as she strokes his hair, "Maybe next time." Then she sways her ample hips and saunters off.

Once the bathroom door is closed, Dan turns to me. I open my mouth to explain the test results, but the ringing of the phone interrupts us. Saved by the bell! I leap up and run to answer it. Dan's laughter follows behind me. "You are saved, for now." Then he starts clearing our movie mess.

"Hello?"

"Ann, dear, how are you feeling?" Elizabeth asks.

"I snacked on some popcorn, and so far, it's staying down."

77

"That is wonderful news. And how are Dan and Sam doing?"

"Great. They are getting ready to go to bed."

"Oh, my. It's late, isn't it? I am sorry."

"Elizabeth, you know you can call me *anytime*. It is never a problem."

"Thank you. That's very kind of you, dear. Oh, before I forget, Ryan said he is okay with you remaining at your house. *If* that is what you want. He is just being stubborn. He doesn't want to say it out loud, but he misses you."

I swallow and squeeze my eyes shut. Or maybe Ryan really doesn't want me around? After all, he did say I was a *curse* to his family. I clear my throat and decide it is safer to shift the subject. "How is Christian doing?"

"I'm afraid there hasn't been much change since you left. I am actually at his bedside right now. I find it comforting." My words cannot form at the image. No parent should have to watch their child fade away. "It's hard seeing my *strong* boy like this. I mean, never in a million years would I have thought…" Her voice fades and I hear her blow her nose. "I'll let you go back to your friends."

"Have a good night. Sleep well." We hang up and I glance around the corner to see the living room empty. I sigh as I tap my head on the counter a few times. "What am I going to *do*?"

I stand straight and decide to call it a night. I walk to my room, change into comfortable pajamas, and slide under the covers. The darkness offers me comfort, but I can't stop thinking about the turn of events today. Out of the corner of my eye, I see my door crack open and close quietly. I rub at my face and sit up. I feel my bed dip down as I make out Dan's silhouette. "Okay, Ann, spill it."

"Where is Sam?"

"She falls asleep fast and hard." He elbows me. "Come on, don't keep me in suspense." My silence fills the room and blankets us in tension.

I place my head in my hands and my barriers crumble. "I'm so *stupid*, Dan. So foolish."

He collects me in his lap. "Ann, stop belittling yourself. Tell me what happened so I can help you fix it."

"Instead of me saying it out loud, how about you guess?"

"Well, I heard rumors that Max… and, well, he was pretty public about his intentions."

"It never got that far. Close. But no."

"Well, my second guess would be King Christian." He strokes my hair gently. "You two always had a more… physical relationship."

I groan and shake my head. Dan couldn't even guess in two tries! How loose am I?

He tenses. "Oh, Ann. *Not* Prince Ryan. Please tell me you didn't."

My hormones get the best of me, and I start to cry again. "See? I am *stupid*!"

He rocks me gently. "Tell me what happened."

"I'm sure, with your level of intelligence, you can *figure* it out."

"Did he use his title and force you?"

"No, nothing like that. Ryan made me a lot of promises in the safe room. Specifically, that he was going to demand that Christian let him marry me." I put my hands over my face again. "So naïve of me to believe him."

"Ryan doesn't have a damn backbone! And yet, he

pledges that he's going to stand up to his brother? And while you are scared for your life and in pain. He knew what he was doing, the slimy little prick. *He* should be the one who feels guilty."

"Really? How does it look? I mean, honestly! Here I am, engaged to Christian, and I sleep with his *brother*! I'm the family trollop. You know what? Maybe I should hit on Elizabeth next?"

His laughter vibrates against my neck. "Stop. It was never a secret that Ryan and you were planning a future together. And it wasn't your fault that Mary turned out to be a murderer, forcing you into her place beside Christian. You and Ryan love each other and that is hard to turn off." He leans back against my headboard and sighs.

"Dan, you never asked if the pregnancy test was positive."

He arches his brow. "Ann, I have known you long enough to know you would never be acting like this if it was negative."

"You know, this is a good tale for your next book, and I bet the dumb blonde could fill my shoes perfectly."

"No way! I can create better narratives than some *dumb* romance."

We laugh together as he caresses my arm. I lean against his chest. "Dan?"

His yawn resounds throughout the room. "Hmm?"

I swallow the lump in my throat as I listen to his steady heartbeat, imagining it's my child's instead. "Do you think I will be a good mother?"

"There is no doubt in my mind that you will be a great mother." He smiles at me. "I will call my mom first thing tomorrow and get some morning sickness remedies for you."

"But what will Sam say?"

He shrugs. "She will know sooner or later, right?"

He's right. Soon the whole country will know. Sweat beads across my brow. What have I done? Not only did I sleep with my fiancé's brother, but I'm now pregnant with his child. My parents would be so *proud*. I retrace the history of the last several kings. All died young and the previous two were murdered. I claw at my belly button. Will this be my child's bleak future?

"What do you think will happen when word gets out that I'm pregnant with the next *heir* to the throne? This innocent baby has no hope for a happy future. No chance for a real life." Tears escape down my chin. "I mean, think about it! Its father doesn't even want to be *around* its mother."

"We will figure something out. But it can't be all that bad, right? I mean… they'll want for nothing. They'll have access to money, the best education, and amazing food."

I jab a finger into his chest. "At what cost, though? What happened to King Mark? Murdered. King Christian? Shot and currently dying in a hospital bed. This child will have no choice but to step in after whatever tragedy happens to Ryan!"

"Ryan is strong and *sometimes* intelligent. He will be more careful than King Mark or Christian. And since the rebellion is close to extinction, Ryan won't have to worry about them attacking anytime soon." He grabs my chin gently. "Ryan has a right to know about this child. And after everything that has transpired over these last few years, he needs this news. Heck, the country needs it too. A child stirs hope and renews life."

"Are you telling me you'd rather put my child in harm's way to make the country and his highness happy?" My hands go to my belly. "It's my job to protect this baby from the monarchy's cutthroat world. I'll never subject them to the curse of the crown." The dark figure from my nightmare incites a new wave of moisture on my forehead. "They will find out and take it away from me! Then they will force it to marry and die like the rest of them. Can't you see! The only way to protect it is to keep it away from them."

"Why don't we just take it one day at a time? I will call my mom and ask her for some remedies for morning sickness and sleep." When my brows shoot up, he lifts a hand. "I will just tell her its research for my next book."

"Thank you," I squeak out. He nods, pushes to his feet, and quietly closes the door behind him.

"Ann? I made you something to drink to calm your nerves." The bed dips and I rub my eyes. "It's been proven to work, according to my mom, and it's all natural and safe." Dan hands me a warm mug.

The sweet steam encourages me forward and I sip at the unfamiliar liquid. "Thank you."

He runs his hands through his hair and glances at my door. "Hey, Ann?" His tone tells me I'm not going to like what he's about to say, so I bite my lip to keep it from answering. He pivots to meet my gaze. "If all that's stopping you from having the baby is that someone will find out and take it back to the Palace to be the next heir…" He swallows and pinches his eyes. "Then tell everyone that the baby is mine."

My brain takes far too long to register what he is

saying; even after his words sink in, I think I've heard him incorrectly. "What?"

He collects my hand in his. "You know I've always had feelings for you. And if you asked, I would stay here and raise this child as my own. Nobody will ever know the truth." His thumb tickles my palm. "We can do this, together."

"We? You know just as much about infants as I do." I burst into a fit of laughter as my sanity splinters.

"We can travel to my family home. They can help us raise and protect the baby."

I tug my shaking hands away from this madman's grasp. "Dan, I don't understand." I rub my palms down my face. "What about Sam?"

He takes a deep breath, and I can tell that he's choosing his words carefully. "I love Sam, but I'm willing to overlook that, because I loved *you* first." He places a trembling palm over my belly. "Just promise me you'll think about it." He kisses my forehead, then stands. "We can talk more tomorrow."

The door clicks before my mind can stitch together everything that just transpired. Dan is willing to leave the woman he loves to be with me, so he can play daddy to Ryan's child? I massage the confusion out of my temples. What am I missing?

Different Beans

Dan's mom is a genius. Whatever I drank has me slipping into a dreamless deep sleep. If only it could cure my current predicament...

The feather necklace draped over my neck heavies as I think about my dad. What would he tell me to do? I rub the metal, begging him to send me some insight. My eyes burn a hole into the ceiling as I demand his guidance, and my cheeks moisten when I think about my mother. Her laughter rings out in my memories. My vision blurs as I glance at my flat stomach. I made this. Or really *half* of this. I agreed to sleep with Ryan and I knew the potential consequences.

I notice a cup on my dresser with a scribbled note beside it. Dan's chicken scratch informs me that the liquid will help my queasy stomach. The aroma makes me cringe, but I sip it anyway. There's a large serving of peppermint with a hint of cinnamon. It's not bad. I think about what Dan said last night. He is willing to give up everything to raise this child. He is a great friend. But this isn't his problem to solve.

I need to take this pregnancy one day at a time. Miscarriages are common during the first trimester anyway. My mom had three of them after I was born. Not that I'm wishing that on myself, but there's no reason to send baby shower announcements either.

The memories of my mother sobbing while she cradled her stomach clench my heart. Each loss took its toll on her. She'd mourn for months after the bleeding stopped. Then she'd pack away the tiny clothing, toys, and bedding and tuck them in the attic.

My lip quivers. The last pregnancy was the toughest. We found out she was with child at the same time we discovered her cancer was back. She refused treatment until the baby was born. So, when she lost it, her body was in no state to win the war.

My eyes drift to the attic entrance in my room. How long has it been since I went up there? I shiver. It's probably full of spiders or rats. But maybe Dad packed Mom's baby books amongst my old clothes. My crib might even be up there collecting dust.

I set the empty mug down before making the climb up the rickety wooden stairs leading to the darkness. I wave the cobwebs away. That's when I notice the wooden chest. Dad made this for Mom when her best friend Sal moved. I don't remember why he left, but he and Mom were neighbors even as adults; then one day the whole family disappeared. I open the lid and peek at the contents. Excitement bubbles in my chest. I was never allowed to open this wooden box. Dad said it was just for Mom. Then, when she died, I couldn't even look at it without thinking about her and what I had lost. Inside there's baby clothes, birthday cards, and pictures. I sift through everything until a tiny piece of notebook paper catches my eye. I unwrap it and notice I don't recognize the penmanship.

Dearest AnnaBelle,

Never forget how much I love you.

Always and forever,

Sal

When did he write this? I look for a date, but there's nothing but a bunch of scribbled numbers on the back. I chew my bottom lip before pulling out my phone. I type the digits into the search engine and wait. I squint at the results. They are coordinates to an empty field. Weird. I sort through the rest of the items, but there's nothing that can explain what I found. Why would her best friend give her these?

My stomach rumbles, reminding me I'm neglecting it. The mystery will have to wait. I brush off the debris and stuff the paper in my pocket. Before heading down, I compose a mental note of the baby furniture littering the attic, realizing that most of the clothes have holes in them from moths.

I squeal as a mouse scurries over my toes. I dash to the exit. Even though it was a little critter, I can't help but feel like there are bugs crawling on me. So, I jump into the shower before heading towards the kitchen. I walk to the coffee machine and frown.

Dan comes in from outside, smiling at me. "Good morning, Ann. Were you able to sleep better?"

Before I can answer, Sam strolls in behind him and waves.

"Yes, I did sleep better. Thank you." Then I point to the problem. "Where is my regular coffee?"

"Oh, I bought you some decaffeinated grounds." Dan gestures to a bag on the counter.

"But…" I pout.

"It's easier on the stomach." He gives me a pointed stare.

I scowl at the offensive item. "Fine."

He smirks as laughter sparkles in his eyes. "It's just temporary."

Sam sighs before adding her two cents, "But it tastes funny." She settles on the bar stool. "Vinny called earlier to check on you."

"Did you tell him I was dead?" I smirk.

"Yes, and he will be right over to collect your body and *kill* me." She rolls her eyes.

"Sounds like Vinny," I grumble.

I miss Karen, and I could really use her expertise. But then I question if I *should* tell her about the pregnancy. I don't want to force her into keeping yet another secret for me, especially with her and Vinny's positions at the Palace.

"I informed Vinny that you were still recovering, and he said to take your time. I guess your phone call with the Prince has Ryan in a mood, and he no longer cares *if* you return." Sam snorts. "I wonder how long it will last though."

I sip my coffee, then spit it back into the cup. "This is disgusting."

Dan grabs my regular beans and brews me a fresh mug. "If you throw up, don't say I didn't warn you."

"I'll make sure to aim for your shoes when I do." I wink.

He ignores my banter. "I took care of your chores, and now I'm returning next door to shower and get ready for work. I've got a long drive ahead of me."

Sam snatches his wrist. "I'll walk you home. Then I have some errands to run before I return to the Palace."

"Give Vinny a kick in the butt for me, won't you?" I smirk at their departing silhouettes.

Vacation

The silence is deafening. The house feels too large without anyone else occupying it. I tap my fingernails on my cup. What am I going to do now? It's only a matter of time before his highness calls me back to the palace for one reason or another. Plus, I'll have to face the music about this pregnancy and what I'm going to do about it. I cringe. I bet when Dan returns, that's what he'll want to discuss. Especially with Sam back at the Palace because we'll have privacy to talk more openly about the situation.

I tap my forehead on the countertop. "Come on, Ann. For once, ask yourself what do *you* want?" I chastise myself. "The chickens are at the Palace so you don't need to care for them here. And you have a nice chunk of change in your bank to cover a fun time."

Should I go on a vacation? Isn't that what Karen did before the babies were born? I pull out my phone. When I unlock it, my search history pops up. I nibble on the inside of my cheek. Is this fate telling me I should travel to these coordinates? I zoom out and arch a brow at the grassy field. There's nothing here. Why would my mom's best friend leave them for her? Maybe it was by mistake? I could be wrong altogether. What if they aren't coordinates at all?

I tug the note out of my pocket and look it over. No. There's something there. I can feel it.

What's the worst that could happen? The field is nothing more than a valley and I waste hours of driving. But in leaving, I'm also putting off talking to Dan and Ryan. I shove back the bar stool with finality. I know it's not right to run away from my problems. But I need time to clear my head and decide for myself what I want to do before it's dictated *for me*.

So it's settled. I'm going on a road trip.

My legs cramp as I drive down the deserted highway. I massage them with one hand while I steer with the other.

"How much longer?" I yell at the GPS for the hundredth time. "I have to pee and I'm starving."

The phone ignores me and I don't blame it. I've been whining this whole time. Probably because I'm so nervous. I've never been big on adventures. I'm a homebody. Well, except when I was filled with adrenaline and went on a hunt for Dad's murderer. I hate the unknown. Yet, for some dumb reason, here I am, going to a weird place on my own. Does pregnancy cause a sudden lack in judgement?

No. It's just me. When things get bad, I run so I won't get hurt or disappointed. I hate being this way, but there it is.

"You've reached your destination," the cellphone snips at me.

I pull into the field and put the car in park. It's exactly what the map showed me. I step out and spin in a circle. There's no structures for miles. I bite my lip. And this pregnancy bladder is not happy. If I don't find a bathroom soon, I'll have to pop a squat.

"Hello?" I shout to the vastness. "Anyone here?"

Of course not. I dig my knuckles into my eyes. Should I head back home and face the music or find another vacation destination?

I kick the tall grass. Why did I put so much hope in this? What did I think was going to happen? Sal would embrace me upon arrival and share all of my mother's stories? A tear wets my cheek. Or maybe I was hoping to find comfort and advice from one of the only people my mother trusted intrinsically? Someone who could give me some parental insight. A close family friend who knew my mother and could pass along that information to me.

Because I'm drowning in self-doubt.

I sink to the ground. I don't want to screw this kid up. I want them to enjoy life, without constantly being in the public's eye. They deserve that and so much more.

A click sounds by my ear and I freeze as I notice a large shadow. "Don't move," it hisses. "Who are you?"

"I'm Ann," I announce.

"Why are you here?"

"Please don't hurt me. I'm looking for someone. Maybe you could help?"

"Who are you looking for?"

"Stop! Put your weapon down!" a spot in the distance commands. That voice. I know the man running this way. "Don't hurt her."

I rub my eyes and blink. "Dan? Do you work out here?"

"Ann, what the hell are you doing here?" He grabs my arm and pulls me up. "You shouldn't be here."

I can't speak. What's going on? Instead, I fish out the tiny note from my pocket. The shadow behind me roars and aims his weapon. I yelp and wave the paper around like a white flag of surrender so he can see I mean no harm, unless he wants a paper cut.

Dan takes it and reads it. "Shit," he declares before

90

running a hand through his hair. "This complicates things." He nods to the person behind me. "Don't hurt her."

Suddenly, I feel a sting in the back of my arm. I open my mouth to scream, but my world goes black.

Leverage

"What the..." I rub my eyes until they focus on my drab surroundings. As everything becomes clear, my heart races. The light-blue room looks like a little studio apartment. There is a tiny kitchen, a compact bathroom, a love seat, a scratched-up coffee table, and a lumpy twin bed. I stand quickly, trying to get my bearings, but the world spins and I fall down on the mattress. I look at the back of my arm and see a needle prick.

This is definitely not the Palace. There are no windows, maids, or even clocks. I tilt my head and carefully step off the bed. I lean my ear against the cold wooden door but I can't hear anything. I twist and pull on the silver handle.

It's locked.

I bang my fist on the paneling. Stop. And listen. "Let me out! Hello?"

My heart pounds in my ears and I try to catch my breath. Memories of Max's abduction swim in my head. My knuckles go white as I clutch my temples and scream to keep the painful flashbacks locked in their cages.

"I am safe. I am safe," I repeat the mantra my therapist taught me. But the lie doesn't fool anyone. I'm someone's prisoner, again. And this time, Christian won't be coming to my rescue.

I curl in a heap on the bed and black out.

Whispering voices surround me and my eyes fly open. I'm in bed. Under the covers. I toss the blanket aside and dash to the door. I spot a piece of plain white paper on the grey countertop. It's a note, letting me know there's water and food in the fridge. I crumble it up and toss it at the wall.

Where am I? Who the hell wrote this note? The

questions wait in the back of my mind as I sprint to the bathroom. I glare at myself in the round mirror and wash my hands. Dark circles and ashen skin stare back at me. I'm a mess.

On the brink of starvation, I rip open the fridge. There's fresh fruit, water, and a few lettuce wraps. I hastily grab everything, kneel at the coffee table, and eat my fill. As I lean back against the sofa and rub my full belly, the doorknob rattles. I frown as an older woman shuffles in, dressed in tactical pants and adorned with a gun holster.

At the sight of her weapon, I jump and back up against the wall like a caged animal. "Stop right there. Who are you?"

She deposits some pills on the counter. "I'm just dropping off some prenatal vitamins, omega 3s, and ginger capsules." She turns to leave.

The only person I've been able to communicate with is leaving. "Wait!" I take in her emerald eyes. "Are you Dan's mom?"

"Why do you think that?"

I look down at the capsules. "Because it was you who recommended the drinks for nausea and sleep, right?"

"Anybody could have done that."

"Your eyes give you away."

"I can see why he likes you." She walks to the fridge. "You are intelligent, beautiful, and stubborn." She hands me a bottle of water with an arched brow. "The way he talks about you. The way he keeps the books you edit close by, on his bookshelf." She tilts her head. "The way he begged us not to hurt you when we raided the Palace."

I step back and pale. I hear her words, but I can't believe them. "No."

She crosses her arms over her chest. "And he was

right. You are valuable to the cause. Now we have the leverage we need to get to the King." Her eyes drop to my midsection.

I throw my hands over my abdomen. "No. You can't."

"We will." She shrugs. "Either you, or the baby, will get us where we need to be with the soon-to-be King Ryan. We have fought too long and lost too many good people in this war. The government *will* be changed. By any means necessary." She taps her nail on the counter. "Now please take the vitamins."

Bile rises in my throat and I make a mad dash for the bathroom. I release all my hopes of finding a friendly face down the toilet. I lean my head on my shaking hands. "This must be a nightmare." I pinch my cheeks.

"Welcome to the Black Rose Rebellion, Ann."

"How long has Dan been a part of this?" I stare into the toilet, my stomach rolling again.

"Our family has always been members of the cause."

"You mean he's been with *them* this whole time!"

"Yes, mostly with hidden objectives. The contractor job at the Palace to build your chicken pen was his idea and it has paid off well. Then he got intel from his girlfriend. What's her name again?" She looks to the ceiling.

"Samantha?"

"Sam, yes. That's how we knew about the servant's entrance and the guard rotations."

"So Sam knows?"

She rolls her eyes. "That girl is wrapped around Dan's finger. She voluntarily gives him information."

I pull myself off the floor and splash water over my face. I stare at her in the mirror. "What do you plan on doing with me and my baby?"

94

"It's simple. We want to trade you and the child for the King's signature. A signature to change the government back to how it used to be. One that truly represents its people with real voting rights and equality."

"You are murderers! He'll never do what you ask!"

"Who're the murderers? Us? They started this!"

There's a knock on the door. "Mom?"

My head shoots to the voice and I stomp towards it as Dan enters the room. "How dare you!"

"Calm down. I was always on your side."

I shove him backwards. "My side? Who are you kidding? You're a selfish jerk!"

"That's not fair. I've done nothing to deserve that." He grabs my wrists. "You know I've never hurt you or anyone else."

"Liar! What about my dad? Huh?" I tug at his hold. "He trusted you! You were like a son to him!"

"I loved Jack! He took care of me when I needed him! I would never hurt him!"

"Look around you! You are part of the same group that murdered him. You may not have pulled the trigger, but you are still responsible." I jam my knee into his groin, and he releases my wrists. "You are dead to me."

Dan groans and doubles over.

"I think she needs some time to ease into this, son." His mom helps him upright. "We'll be back later."

The door closes before I have a chance to protest. My head is reeling with all the new information. How can Dan be with the Black Rose? He's a family friend! My dad personally vouched for him, even wanted us to date. How could this happen? I run my hands through my hair as I pace.

At least I know I'm safe. *For now.* Because they need to keep me healthy so the child grows. Maybe I can escape during that time? Or I can convince them to change their minds?

I huff out a breath. Great. I traded one prison for another. I regret ever leaving the house. That's it. When I get out of this mess, I'm never stepping foot outside again. It's safer that way. People suck.

But, the note that led me here…

I pat my pants. It's gone.

Mr. Sunshine

The next time I wake up, I groan and turn. When I open my eyes, I squeal and back away. And end up on my butt on the floor. "Dan! What the hell!"

He mumbles and then looks over from the tiny couch. "What are you doing on the floor?"

"What are you doing sleeping in my room?"

"It was mine before it was yours," he grumbles, then goes back to sleep.

I resist the urge to suffocate him with a pillow because I have more pressing matters to attend to. When I close the door to the bathroom, I find a towel and fresh clothes laid out. I finger the pink sundress. It's definitely not my favorite color. I bite my lip as a assess my dirty clothes. Pink will have to do. I start the shower and take my time with the bar of soap and floral shampoo and conditioner. When I turn off the water and pull on the clean clothes, I feel more human. However, as I exit the bathroom, I collide with a chest and my hand goes to my rapid heartbeat. "Dan!"

"I have to use the bathroom." He shrugs. I settle on the couch. Dan comes out and looks over my outfit. "That color looks nice on you."

"Why are you down here? I meant it when I said I never wanted to see you again."

"We have a limited amount of space, and since I don't technically live here, I stay in this room when I visit. It's the only guest room available."

Even though I don't forgive him, I need answers. "Where does Max and Mary fit into this group?"

"Their family consists of our founding members, and Mary was a field operative and Max was logistics. Each with their own set of skills." His explanation is delivered without emotion—as if it's just simple fact. I bring my knees to my chest as I sit on the couch. "What are you thinking about?"

"How my whole life has been a lie." I shrug. "I was so happy on my farm, then this stupid selection had to ruin everything."

"*Your* life may have been happy but think about all those branded rebels trying to survive."

"What do you mean by branded?"

"When individuals help or are thought to be a part of the Black Rose, they are rounded up like cattle and branded with a 'R' using a livestock brander. So that others know to stay away from them, or suffer the same consequences. They are then outcasts in their own country: they are forced to eat out of dumpsters, they can't find good jobs, and most are found murdered on the side of the road."

"That is barbaric."

He lowers himself next to me. "Men, women, even *children*, Ann. No one is immune to the King's wrath."

"Wait. Are you telling me *Christian* knew about this? That he hurt these people?"

"Do you really think your fiancé was any different than his father?"

I sit straighter. "Yes. I mean, he gave Mary and Max a fair trial, even after everything they did."

"They were never branded, so Christian didn't know they were part of the rebellion until it was too late."

"He would never condone this sort of behavior." But, as the words leave my lips, Ryan's warning about Christian's dark side blares in my head. Is this what he meant? Images of when Christian interrogated the Black

Rose suspect and returned with blood-stained sleeves flash behind my eyes.

"You don't have to believe me. I've seen it happen. But if you have any doubts, the next time my mom comes in, look at her hand and ask her to tell you her story."

"I sat in that *office* with everyone. Every day. Not one thing that passed over my desk suggested such horrors."

"Oh, I'm sure they censor their documents. But I promise you, it's happening. And since your little speech, those who were branded and ignored for years are being persecuted in the streets."

My head jerks up. "*My* speech? You guys attacked the Palace!"

He stands. "And how many of us had to *die* before that happened? Hundreds. Thousands."

"But you knew what you were getting yourselves into when you wanted to rebel against the government!" I spit back.

The door opens and we both turn. Dan rubs his face and nods towards the stranger. "Ann, this is my brother, Jeremy."

"So, *this* is her?" The stranger sizes me up, and I feel an icy chill crawl across my spine. His tough exterior and clenched jaw scream trouble.

Dan frowns. "Let it go, Jeremy."

The man crosses his arms over his chest. "Mom sent me in here to let you know that Sam is worried and wants you to call her."

I swallow as he stomps out with a look that could kill. "I'm guessing he's one of the individuals who *doesn't* like me."

"It's more complicated than that with Jeremy, but long

story short: Mary was his wife."

I nearly break my neck as it snaps to attention. My mouth opens and closes, but I can't vocalize anything because my brain is frying from information overload. The rebels were good but turned evil by mistreatment. Dan is a backstabber who's also keeping me safe. And now Mary, the Queen B herself, was married to a rebel. It's too much. It might be a mind trick, but I can't help but fuel this dumpster fire. "Mary couldn't have been married to *two* people at once; it's against the law. Plus, the competition forbids it and she never would have made it as far as she did with Christian."

"Technically, rebels aren't legally able to get married. But, in every way that matters, she was Jeremy's wife. Then, when Christian's selection came up, she put her name into the running, along with several other women who supported the cause. We needed to get in as many as we could, because our goal was to change the government from the *inside*."

His words sink in. If they were true, that meant they didn't want blood spilled, at least not at first. So what changed? Why did they suddenly attack the Palace?

"Do you believe me, Ann?" He kneels at my feet. "That I never meant to hurt you. If it helps, I'm sorry you found out like *this*. I was hoping you'd let me help raise the child and we could move here, together."

"Dan, I wasn't going to let you give up Sam to help me. Because, from what I've witnessed, you do love her, right? Or were you always just playing her for information?"

"No. I love her." He rummages in his pocket and hands me a velvet box. "I've been waiting for the right time to give her this."

I pop open the box and smile at the princess-cut diamond ring. I snap it shut, locking away his false hope.

"She'll never agree to this, if you don't start telling her the truth. You can't build a marriage on lies."

He shoves the ring back in his pocket. "It's a mess."

I know he has an interesting tale to share, but now's not the time. At least not until I know I can trust his words again. "I don't hate you." His eyes meet mine and I lighten the suffocating atmosphere. "I mean, I did save you from a falling hammer." I rub the scar on my scalp. "If that doesn't prove it, I don't know what does."

He wraps his arms around me and squeezes. As much as I wish he'd suffer for all the lies and deceit, Dad trusted him for a reason, and I intend to find out why.

When we separate, his eyes trail down to my chest. "Why aren't you wearing undergarments?" I narrow my gaze and shove him away. "What? I just noticed!"

"You are a pig! I give you a friendly hug and you turn it into something dirty!"

"It was just a question, Ann." He holds up his hands in defense.

"I didn't realize I was going to be kidnaped, or otherwise I would have tucked some underwear and a spare bra in my pocket. And no one left me *any* to change into. So blame the genius who didn't do their job!"

"Not that I'm complaining about the situation, but how dirty were the ones you had on?" He chuckles.

"It depends on how long I was *knocked* out. I don't have a watch or even a calendar in here."

"Is there anything else missing?" His lip twitches and I know he's baiting me.

"Actually, yes. I require some books, a clock, a hairbrush, and maybe some things to keep my hands busy," I demand with false authority.

His laughter brightens the room, and I can't help but join in. I blame sleep deprivation and my stellar emotional health.

"Looks like I'm late to the party." Suddenly the light is sucked out of the room as *he* stomps in. Mr. Sunshine-and-Rainbows.

"Is it babysitting time already?" Dan elbows me out of my terror. I glare at him and sit on the couch, crossing my arms and legs. Dan eyes Jeremy's stern face. "I know that look. Whatever you're thinking, *don't* do it." He pats his brother on the shoulder, then turns to me. "I'll be back soon."

I assess my prison guard. He must be older than Dan. He's tall with short dirty-blonde hair. His eyes are hard to see in the distance, but they appear grey. Tension fills the room as we stare each other down.

"I didn't know Mary was married." I attempt to break the silence.

"Would it have mattered?"

"Yes, because then she wouldn't have been allowed in the selection to begin with."

His boots thump as he closes the gap between us and kneels. I suppress a gasp as I notice his eye color is the *same* shade as Christian's. My heart aches and my world tilts, as I desire nothing more than to be *safe* with in the Palace walls with the King (or even Ryan). Instead, I'm here with the Terminator.

My chin is snatched, pulling me out of my despair. "Listen, little girl. I'm here to make sure no one slips in to jam a knife into that cold heart of yours. That's it. I'm *not* here for your entertainment or for your pathetic small talk. So zip it."

My backbone straightens. This *jerk*. I lean towards him,

our noses touching. "I would appreciate it if everyone would stop blaming *me* for their crimes and learn to take responsibility for their *own* actions."

The roar of laughter he emits has the hair on my arms rising. "You love to hear yourself talk, don't you? Well, your rank in the Palace means *nothing* here." His glare sends chills to my toes. "I'm a god within these walls, second in command of this army, and I outrank you. So do what I say, and you might survive."

"I'm *not* the enemy. I had no prior knowledge of the Black Rose before they killed my father!"

"Liar," he spits the insult.

I lean back, away from his hot breath. "Believe what you want. But tell me this, what do I have to gain by lying to you? I'm stuck here." My traitorous lip shivers as my predicament finally sinks in. I throw my hands up as tears well in my eyes. "My fiancé is dying, my baby's daddy has no idea where I am, and I just found out my friend is part of a rebellion group that murdered my father, my neighbor, and put my fiancé in the hospital."

"I did it." He rocks on his heels.

I wipe my lids. "You did what *exactly*?"

"I'm the one who shot your pathetic King." My hands go to my mouth as he continues. "I watched as Mary's limp body was carried out of the chaos. Then I saw *him* walking *away* from his fellow comrades, letting them fight *his* battle. All the sins of his ancestors, just slipping away, unpunished. He's lucky it was just a warning shot. The bullet only grazed his leg, so he could never again walk away from his family's messes, without the reminder of the war they caused. That little bit of spilled blood was nothing compared to the volumes he's taken from us."

My heart splits along with the remnants of my sanity. I snap. A war cry rips through my throat. I dive at Jeremy with all intentions of tearing his pretty little head off. We tumble onto the coffee table, shattering it into pieces. Before I know what's happening, I tug his knife from his holster and press it to his throat. His pulse quickens under my fingertips.

"How could you shoot him with his back turned? You coward!"

He leans into the blade. "Just do it. We all know you're capable. The Palace trained you well, didn't they?"

A trickle of red coats the blade's edge and my mind goes back to the carnage from the raid at the Palace. The mixture of pale, dead-eyed rebels and Palace members. As the blood drips on the floor, I shake my head. This isn't who I am. How this man can get under my skin like this is beyond me. I throw the knife across the room, and my resolve melts as I pound my fists on his chest. I wish I could avenge Christian and those who have lost their lives to this ruthless group. But I'm too weak.

I hit, cry, and scream at my new punching bag until my throat is hoarse. Once my rage is released, I roll off his body and stare at the dirty ceiling, begging it to swallow me whole.

"Why didn't you kill me?"

"I already told you I'm not the enemy. I'm not a murderer. As much as I would like to be right now," I grumble the last bit to myself.

He leans on his elbows. "Well, don't expect the same courtesy from me."

"How did you know I wasn't going to kill you?"

His smirk is disarming. "I didn't." My mouth falls open. This cocky rebel. Was he really going to *let* me hurt him? He moves his hand to his neck and examines the moisture coating it. "Not many people can say they've

104

caught me off guard." He stands before offering me a hand.

I arch a brow as I look at his wrist. Maybe this can be the start of us trusting each other? Maybe we can build an understanding? I just need to make the first step. I suck in a breath before placing my palm in his. The wind is forced out of my lungs as he slams my back to the wall.

"Believe me when I say this," he sneers. "I won't make the same mistake twice."

With all my strength, I shove him back. "I have *nothing* to lose. Your group made sure of that!" My chest rapidly rises and falls. I lift my chin high. "You know what? I'm done being lied to, being treated like some kind of pawn. So go ahead. Kill me. Let someone sneak in here and end my meaningless life. Continue to prove to the world that you are *exactly* what they think you are."

The door opens and Dan returns. "What the..." His jaw falls open. "Jeremy, what did you do?"

The rebel leader strides over to Dan. "*That* had nothing to do with me. You can thank her for the mess. What's going on with Sam?"

He rubs his face as he leans on the counter. "I might need to move my plan up a few weeks."

"When are you leaving?"

"I need to talk with Mom first." He glances towards me. "Or should I wait?"

The door slams open and a panicked man yells, "Medical bay. Now!" Then he disappears, leaving the door wide open. The two brothers look at each other and run out.

Bloody Truths

I'm not sure what I was expecting to see when the door opened. I guess maybe Hell—with a bunch of horned demons running around—would have been close.

"Please save my baby!" a woman sobs.

My feet have a mind of their own as I follow the anguished words until I'm staring at a bloodbath.

"Someone apply some damn pressure… he's bleeding out!" a man shouts before he grabs the closest wrist and pulls it to a gushing wound.

I yelp as warm liquid soaks the cloth under my hands. "But I'm not qualified for this!" I start to protest. But my remarks fall on deaf ears as people scramble around me, all barking out orders. The body beneath my palms twitches and my head shoots to my volun-told job.

"Stop!" The boy grabs my arm. "It hurts!"

One look at the man next to me tells me not to move or else.

"Shh, baby. Just lie still. They are here to help you." The woman runs her hands over his sweat-soaked locks.

"I'm sorry. I don't…" I push out as my lip quivers. What I'd like to explain is that I don't want to be standing here in the middle of a damn warzone. I just want to return home and forget all of this. Pretend it doesn't exist. But when I meet the boy's eyes, I can't get the words out. He is so young, not even ten years old.

"What happened!" Jeremy blares as he inserts an IV.

"The enforcers found us leaving the city and they branded Billy." The woman sucks in a sob as she rubs a scarred R on her own hand. "I knew it was getting infected, so when the coast was clear, we made our way here. He was shivering with fever, so I begged a store owner for some medicine. But they feared they would get caught, so they fired a warning shot, the bullet hit a window, and the glass shattered everywhere."

Even if I don't understand, I can still offer sympathy in her time of need. "We will do whatever we can for your son."

Her big brown eyes lock on to mine and she nods. "Thank you."

Jeremy narrows his gaze as he finally realizes who is standing next to him. "Go back to your living quarters. You aren't authorized to assist in the medical bay."

The boy's body starts thrashing wildly and it takes three of us to hold him down. As everyone shuffles around me, I bite my lip. These same people raided the Palace with bombs and guns. And yet, here they are, trying to save a child's life. This doesn't make sense.

My skin is red, but I don't care. I scrub and scrub.

A knock on the doorframe pulls me out of my sorrow.

"We did all we could." I continue the attack on my arm, wiping away the life fluid that seeped from Billy's body. Dan places a hand on mine.

"Why would enforcers do that to him? They're supposed to protect, not cause harm. He's just a kid! What if he doesn't survive?"

He collects me in his arms, as I fall apart in exhaustion, and kisses the top of my head as he tucks me under the covers. "Get some rest. We can talk later." He sits on the edge of the bed. I lay my head in his lap and he strokes my hair while he hums a song that's familiar and comforting, but the words are lost. My lids flutter and I drift off to nightmare after nightmare as my brain tries to comprehend each new horror.

I slip out of the bed and go to the fridge for food. As I munch, I stare down at my dirty dress, wishing I had another set of clothes to wear.

"Oh man." Dan rubs his neck from his spot on the sofa. "I slept like crap."

"And you totally snore."

"I do not." He ruffles my already crazy, unbrushed hair as he strides over.

The door opens behind us and we both freeze as Jeremy enters. He hands me my vitamins and I can tell he had a rough night too. Everything happened so fast, but one thing is for sure: he cared about that kid and his mother.

"How is Billy?"

"He's critical but stable. He's resting now. How about we go for a walk?"

"Is this another sick trick of yours? Like when you offered me a hand up?"

"Only one way to tell." He offers me his arm this time.

I smack the offensive limb. "Keep your hands off me. I'll follow behind you. It's better than being locked up in here. I mean, what do I have to lose?"

"Smart move."

I'm amazed by the number of people and various activities surrounding us. It's a whole community of men, women, and children with smaller buildings, countless rooms, stairs leading up to another floor, a dining hall, and even a training arena with a small gun range and track.

"Not what you expected to see?" Jeremy asks.

"I was expecting fire and brimstone."

"No, you're confusing us with the Palace." He rolls his eyes.

"We have been hiding for a long time. Most of the children were born here, or near here, while some were rescued when their parents were killed," Dan explains.

A woman with red hair approaches, though a scowl darkens her features. "We have acquired what you asked for."

Jeremy signs a sheet of paper. "Tammy, this is Lady Ann."

She crosses her arms over her chest. "I know who she is."

An uneasy chill sweeps through the room as my name is announced. Everyone pauses their activities. A man in tactical pants stomps over. "Ann? Daughter of Jack Gable?

Dan warms my unguarded side as I respond with a nod. "Yes."

The stranger removes his gloves and offers me a hand. "Your father dug my son out of six feet of snow last year during that blizzard. I never got to thank him."

"My... father?"

"Yes. I owe him a great deal." After I shake his hand, he continues. "I'm sorry to hear what Max did to your dad. Jack was a good man and never deserved what happened to him."

I can only nod past my shock. My dad knew about the Black Rose and helped them? Or maybe he just helped this man's son?

"See? We aren't *all* monsters." Jeremy's lips twitch as the other guy walks away.

"Neither is everyone in the Palace," I snip.

He ignores me and returns to Tammy. "Thank you for informing me."

She nods and heads into the shadows, glaring over her shoulder.

Dan scoffs, "Maybe that will keep Tammy off your back for a while."

I tilt my head. "Aw, Mr. Macho is afraid of a woman. How shocking."

"I just don't have time for relationships." Jeremy pats me on the head like I'm some subservient dog. "You are the perfect woman deterrent for me." He elbows Dan. "Stop pouting. You knew the moment Ann arrived she was never going to choose to be with you. And she has no interest in me either, right?"

"I have enough problems to deal with without adding you two idiots into the mix."

"Plus, she is engaged to be married." He fingers my ring.

I tug away at the sting of his words. What I wouldn't give to go back to those simpler days. Before I got mixed up in this war. When my dad was only a phone call away and our neighbor, Suzie, would insert herself into my dating life. I swipe at my eyes before Jeremy can see

110

my tears. I stand tall. This ring is a reminder that I *will* be rescued. Then Jeremy can rot away in prison for his crimes. But what about Dan? Was he telling me the truth about everything? And what about the other rebels?

My eyes scan the rusty staircase in front of me. How long has this place been here? And why hasn't the Palace discovered it yet?

Jeremy waves me forward and I start the climb. Eventually I reach a metal door and push forward. The bright sun assaults my eyes. I hold my hand in front of my face as my feet crunch on soft terrain. My mouth falls open. There is green grass and clear blue skies. How can this be? The heat pierces my skin and I can't help but close my eyes and enjoy the sensation. This simple pleasure, in my now darkened world, brings more joy than I care to admit.

Ragged-clothed children brush past me and tackle Dan to the ground. He laughs with the impact. "Hey, be gentle, guys."

A little boy with black hair and dirt smudges grins down at the former contractor, as the kid sits on his stomach and eagerly asks, "Uncle Dan, is it true that Uncle Jeremy beat you up?"

Dan pushes himself upright, dropping the three children gently on the ground. He cocks a brow at Jeremy and fibs, "Yes, he did. He is a very bad man."

"Was it because you stole his favorite toy?" A blonde girl glares at the black-haired boy.

"No, it wasn't." He pats them on the head. "Now go and play while the sun is still out."

Instead of complying, they turn to Jeremy and plaster on the cheesiest grins. "What?" he barks at them.

They don't even bat a lash at his tone as they hold

111

out their open palms to him. He rolls his eyes. Then he snatches a pack of gum from his beige tactical pants. And hands them each one piece. "If you rat me out again, this will be the *last* piece of candy you'll ever see from me, you little brats."

As they collect their treats, I gasp. Each child has a 'R' embedded on their hand. Upon closer inspection, I notice Jeremy does too.

"Who is *she*, Uncle Jeremy?" one of the boys asks.

"This is a new friend of ours. She will be staying with us for a while. Her name is Ann." When Dan confirms that I'm a friend, they beam up at me and offer their hands in greeting.

"I'm Todd, and this is Tanner and May."

They look at my wrist and squint. "She isn't branded?"

I rub my hand self-consciously. "No, I'm not." I stare at May and blink. "May, was it? You look familiar. Have we met?"

The girl unwraps her gum. "You used to read to me at the library. You helped me with crafts like my Cat-er-pillar." She smacks her gum. "I like your dress."

"Thank you."

This is the same little girl I taught at the library? What the hell happened to her? She couldn't have possibly done anything wrong to warrant that burn. Where are her parents?

Dan elbows me and whispers, "I like what isn't underneath your dress." I stomp on his foot and he limps away.

Jeremy cocks a brow. "I'm curious. What did he say?"

"Curiosity killed the hen. It's none of your business," I spit back, feeling my face turn red.

The kids duck through the same metal door we used to enter. So there's only one way in and out? I rub my chin, trying to determine my odds of escaping. Jeremy leads me a little farther into the field. I breathe in the fresh air, glad to be outside.

Then he pivots to me. "So, what *is* underneath?" I glare at Dan, then Jeremy, and cross my arms over my chest. "Should I guess or would you rather I find out on my own?" Jeremy takes a step towards me. I back up while holding my glare in place. "If you tell me, I will take you somewhere *extra* special."

Dan rolls his eyes. "Jeremy, stop it."

"Well, it is special, for her anyway. What do you say? I mean, what do you have to lose, right?" The rebel throws my own words back at me.

I bite my tongue. If I give him this, he'll show me more of the area, which could be helpful with my escape plans. I step towards Jeremy. He tenses, watching me carefully. I lean in and whisper into his ear, "I have *nothing* on underneath."

He closes his eyes and savors my words. "I had to ask, and now I regret not looking when you were on top of me."

"What! What do you mean? *When* was she on top of you?" Dan stutters.

"When she broke the coffee table with my back—*here we are*." He waves his hand, gesturing to my surprise.

As the blades of lush green grass rub my bare legs, I take in the field's layout. There is at least ten different crops growing. I recognize corn, wheat, green beans, strawberries, collard greens, tomatoes, and squash. And nestled in the corner is a large chicken pen. Who knew murderers could maintain a flock of chickens between killing everybody? I lean down and smile at my feathered

113

friends as they approach me curiously. I go to pet a Rhode Island Red, but she bites me before screeching her annoyance.

"That's strange." I cradle my finger.

"No, that's just Scarlett. She's the mother hen and feisty as hell." He smacks my back. "She's a lot like you."

"Very funny." I suck my finger and dash away as she chases me from her nest. It's odd. The crops and hen house weren't on the map when I looked up the location on my phone earlier. I scan the horizon. Was it because it's so open and hidden from the surrounding hills? Or because the compound is mostly underground?

"It's not much, but it's home. We grow what we need and outsource a few items," Dan announces as he stretches his back.

The grass crunches and we see Dan and Jeremy's mom coming up behind us. "Who the hell authorized this outing?"

Jeremy steps forward. "I did."

"Ann, I hope you're enjoying your little tour." She holds out a hand. "You may call me Sally."

I brush off my own hand and accept her palm. I feel the scar of her brand under my fingertips. "You wouldn't happen to have a hairbrush I could use while you hold me against my will, would you?"

Everyone stares up at my knotted, wind-blown mess. "I think that can be arranged."

"Ann also needs some undergarments, Mom. I really like the commando look, but..." Jeremy adds.

I grit my teeth, regretting having told him the truth.

Sally nods. "Dan gave me a list earlier. I will see to it that we get what she requires." She turns to the son in question. "We need to discuss the situation with Sam."

He frowns. "I was coming to update you. I have to leave for a while to smooth things over with her."

"You realize this will complicate things *here*." Her eyes wander to me, then back to Dan. "Same code names as always?"

"AnnaBelle and Willard?"

My eyes go wide. "You're using my mom's name for your planned bloodbaths?"

They ignore me and Sally continues. "While you are gone, we will proceed as discussed and send trinkets to the King as things progress." Her eyes go to my flat stomach.

Dan salutes. "I will leave right away."

She nods and taps Jeremy's shoulder. "It's good to see you smiling again, son."

He scowls. "I'm not smiling any more than usual. It's just been a long time since I've come across a *challenge*." He tilts his chin towards me.

"Good, because Ann is your responsibility while your brother is gone."

"What? Babysitting duty? I think my skills can be used elsewhere."

"Blame your brother, not me. I have enough on my plate."

I slip away and investigate the garden. I kneel and touch the big green tomato vines before pushing a finger into the dirt. The soil turns to dust as I grind the material between my fingertips. If I'm stuck here, I should consider assisting them in producing better crops. Especially if they are going to be feeding me and my growing child. I stand up and pivot. "I'm sorry. Are we still griping about who's

115

going to be my daddy?" I brush my hands together. "The garden needs fertilizer and more water."

Sally arches a brow. "That's right. She's a farmer just like Jack. There you go, son. Now you have a job for her to earn her keep and stay out of trouble."

At the mention of my dad, everything comes together. "Wait, you said your name is Sally?"

"Yes."

"No," I push out as I take in her appearance. "I thought you were a guy!"

"Excuse me?"

"You're using my mom's name as your code name. My dad helped you during the blizzard…" My head spins. "You're Sal!"

Jeremy crosses his arms over his chest. "What are you blabbering on about? Maybe the sun is too much for you."

"I can't believe you were my mom's best friend." I laugh. "This whole time." I swipe at the corner of my eye. "This is hilarious!"

"Jeremy, you should bring her back inside."

"Seriously, though. Did she know you killed for *fun*? Or were you able to trick her too?"

"You don't know what you're talking about."

"Don't I? Tell me, *Sal*, what would Mom say about you keeping me captive and using me as bait?" I step in her face. "She *loved* you until the day she died. I can't say you have the same loyalty."

"Your mother would do the right thing, no matter the cost."

"Keep telling yourself that," I grind out. "I can't believe I *searched* for you." I step away. "You are just a shell—no, a mere memory—of who my mom thought you were."

Jeremy grabs my elbow. "That's enough." He tugs me back to my room.

When we return, I notice someone replaced the coffee table, added a dresser by the bathroom, shoes by the door, and a bookshelf in the corner. There's some stationary and pens on the counter, more fruit in the fridge, a newspaper on the coffee table, and my vitamin bottles in the bathroom with some light makeup, a hairbrush, and towels. I grab the brush and sigh as I work it through my long, knotted locks.

Jeremy settles on the sofa. "Be careful. With that sort of behavior, you might lose your goodies just as fast as you got them."

"That's rude."

"We have limited resources and we won't waste them."

I twirl the hairbrush. "Those kids were so excited over the gum you gave them." I sit on the couch. "And their clothes were a little…"

"Old? We mostly live off money from generous donors, and those of us who can work do. But for those who have been cursed with *this*…" He shoves his branded hand in the air. "It's a tad tougher."

I gently grab his large wrist and trail a finger over the brand. "Does it hurt?"

He tugs it away. "It did, when it happened." He clears his throat. "I don't know why I'm telling you all this."

"Because you know in your heart that I'm *not* the enemy."

"Stop pretending you know what I'm thinking," he snarls. "Because you are *wrong*."

I can't meet his glare. He's right. I'm beginning to

see that now. I know nothing about the people in my life. Everything I thought I knew… is a lie. I finger my engagement ring before pulling it off and reading the inscription: *to my hen*. The sentiment that Christian put there. Or was it Ryan? Since he helped design it. Has the *real* Christian been destroying families and orphaning children to silence a political group? There's far more questions than answers. The light reflects off the jewelry. This is the last thing I have left of my Palace life. Maybe I can use it to my advantage to gain the trust of the rebels? To get in their good graces and help the children.

I grab Jeremy's wrist and place the piece of jewelry in his palm. I close his fingers around it. "I don't need this anymore. Go ahead and pawn it. Use the money to make sure the kids have what they need."

"I don't want your charity." He passes it back to me.

"*They* need it more than I do."

"This doesn't change *anything*—you know that, right? But I'll make a note of this donation in your folder. Maybe it'll gain some sympathy from those of us who hate you."

"I have a *folder*?"

"Yes. One I have studied thoroughly."

"Any good pictures in there?"

He snorts. "None that come close to the truth." I'm not sure if he thinks I'm uglier or cuter in person; though it's probably the former.

"Oh, and you think *you* are Prince Charming?"

"I do believe that I am."

"Annoying and cocky is more like it, *mama's* boy."

"Look who's talking, Miss *Commando*."

I can't help the smile that tugs at the corners of my mouth. "Now, *that* was accidental."

He walks to the door but pauses. "If anyone comes in here bothering you, the dagger you *failed* to kill me with is on the floor." He nods towards the weapon's location.

"Don't worry. I'll be sure to try harder next time."

"Good luck with that." Then he exits the room, leaving me alone with my thoughts.

New Pal

After Jeremy leaves, I let out a breath. Then I turn off the lights, climb under the cold covers, and stare into the void.

Voices whisper from everywhere, attempting to convince me to pledge my allegiance. My hands fly to my ears. I demand that they stop. But they get louder and louder. Then a monstrously tall Scarlett tries to eat me. She pecks and pecks until her large beak consumes me.

I lurch out of the chicken's gizzard and back into reality. I flip on the lights and sigh into the fridge. "They still don't trust me enough to cook my own food?" I grumble at the premade sandwiches and fruit. I grab what I can, then sit on the couch and flip through the newspaper. There's no mention of the Black Rose or my disappearance.

Still hungry, I peek at the door. Maybe I can find something out there? My mouth waters at the thought of eggs or pancakes. I rest my palm on the handle, say a prayer, and turn. Yes! It's unlocked! I crack the door and poke my head out to scope the area. It's quieter than earlier. I squeeze through and then shut it softly.

"Ann?"

I'm caught! I jump and pivot. I stare at the girl I met earlier. "May, was it?"

"What are you doing up?" She tilts her head as if peering into my soul.

"Sometimes I have bad dreams at night."

She grabs my wrist. "Do you want me to show you where I go when I can't sleep?"

"I don't know if I'm allowed out."

She giggles. "Of course you are."

120

We walk through the compound. People look up from their activities and watch us as we pass, but they quickly ignore our presence. May guides us up the stairs before she huffs as she pushes the heavy door open. A cool breeze caresses my cheeks, and the dazzling stars and bright moon calm me.

"Come on." May tugs.

We approach the quiet pen where all the chickens are presently sleeping. They chirp and peek up at us as we inch closer. May points to a black and white hen. "That one is Spot."

I open the pen and we slowly slip inside. I offer my hand to Spot, and she looks at it curiously. I eye Scarlett snoring in the corner and do my best to avoid the warrior chicken.

May glances around and then puts her hand in her pocket to pull out some crumbs. She brings them to Spot and laughs as the hen pecks the treat out of her palm. "Don't tell Miss Sally. She doesn't like us wasting food."

I offer the girl my pinkie. "I promise."

May uses her own pinkie to grab mine. Then she shakes it. She sits on the ground next to Spot and strokes the chicken softly. "I like you, Ann."

I lower myself beside her and cross my legs. "I like you too, May. Where are your parents?"

She digs her feet into the grass. "Dad was caught helping Miss Sally and they killed him. They branded us, then while Mommy was buying food, a very bad man did awful things to her. Uncle Jeremy found me and brought me here."

"I am so sorry. Do you remember who hurt your family?"

"Men in uniforms." She sniffles as she runs a finger

121

over her scar, and her eyes suddenly glaze over. "They held us down and put this hot metal on our hands. I fell asleep from the pain and when I woke up, my mom was carrying me."

I place a palm on hers. "I'm sorry they hurt you."

She rushes into my open arms. "No one likes to talk about their boo-boos. But I feel like if I don't talk about it, my chest might explode."

I run my fingers down her back. "I understand that feeling."

May traces my smooth hand. "Ann, why are you here?"

I lean against the fence. "I don't really know. I woke up here."

"Did Uncle Jeremy save you too? I saw him carry you in."

I snort at the thought of that beast being any kind of hero. "I don't remember much of that day."

"You sound like you're going to cry. Did I make you sad?"

"I just miss my friends."

"What about your family?"

My lip quivers. "They're all gone."

She wraps her tiny arms around me. "You're in *our* family now. Don't worry, we will watch over you." She stares up at the stars. "Uncle Jeremy said that our dead relatives are watching over us. Up there." She points to the glittering orbs. "His wife is up there too. Aunt Mary. She looked like an angel. She had the prettiest yellow hair."

I cringe at the mention of my adversary. To me, Mary will always be a monster. But it's not my job to crush May's image of Saint Mary of the Rebels. Together, we watch the stars dance in the sky. Eventually we both fall asleep in the comfort of our shared sorrows.

My eyes fly open and I jump as I'm surrounded by a group of hungry hens. May is curled up beside me. I tuck a piece of her golden hair behind her ear and groan as my back spasms. At that tiny noise, The Red Devil herself darts towards us. I gently shake May. She yawns and stretches out, scaring the chickens before she asks, "Did you sleep better?"

"I didn't have any bad dreams." I scurry out of the pen before I'm pecked to death by the protective mother hen.

"See? Our relatives are looking out for us." The attack chicken purrs under May's touch while giving me a side-glance. "Don't be upset about Scarlett; she doesn't like too many people." Of course I'm offended. I've never had a hen dislike me. They're my spirit animals. "Miss Sally doesn't like me sleeping in the pen. Could we keep that a secret too?"

"You're turning me into a criminal, May." I ruffle her hair. "Your secrets are safe with me."

As we descend the stairs, we can sense everyone's eyes on us. And a chill runs up my spine. May stops her descent. "I think they know I slept outside."

The crowd parts as Jeremy stomps through. "Where have you been?"

May jumps against my side. I kneel to her. "He's mad at me, not you. Go before it's too late." The girl looks at Jeremy and then dashes past him. She steals a peek at me over her shoulder, but keeps running. Once she's at a safe distance, I face the brute. "I apologize."

"Do you think that *excuses* your behavior?"

I lift my hands in surrender, not wanting him to direct his beastly attitude towards the little girl. I can handle

King Kong.

"Stay in your room."

I grind my teeth but lift my chin and brush past him. I pause for a brief moment and look him in the eye. "If there is anything I can do to rectify the situation, let me know. But please do not blame May."

I enter my room and dash to the bathroom as my stomach rolls. I fall to my knees and lean my head on the ceramic throne, moaning throughout the process. When I look up, Jeremy's standing there. "You're not very bright, if you thought you could leave without anyone noticing."

I snort. "If I could have escaped, I would have. But that's not what I was doing. I couldn't sleep. Plus, I was starving."

He pinches a blade of grass out of my hair and quirks a brow. "So you thought it was safe to sleep outside?" I stand but my head spins and I sway at the sudden motion. Jeremy catches me before I hit the tile and grinds out, "I will talk to Mom about changing your menu."

I have no choice but to lean into his support. "Being pregnant sucks."

"It won't last forever."

I groan. "I didn't even think about *that*." I hide my face into his chest. "It has to come out somehow."

"You play, you pay."

I cringe and meet his gaze. "Is that your motto?"

He guides me to the couch. "Stay in here."

"Can't you trust me? I didn't try to escape; someone left the door unlocked."

"Not possible. I locked it myself."

"Maybe Tammy was hoping I'd run away and leave

you free to pursue her." I bat my lashes.

The door crashes against the wall and Sally storms in. "*Where* was she?"

"I went outside."

"All night?" she growls.

"I couldn't sleep so I got some air."

She glares at Jeremy. "You didn't lock the door?"

"Don't blame him. I take full responsibility."

May pokes her head in. "Miss Sally?" she squeaks. "It was all my fault." She approaches us with her chin down.

"May, what have I told you about coming in this room?" Sally demands.

"Ann *pinkie* promised not to tell. She thought she wasn't allowed out, but I told her she was," May announces as tears stream over her cheeks.

Sally lets out a breath, then she pivots to me. "You pinkie promised her?"

Jeremy flashes a quick smirk before he turns it into a cough. I lift my hands and shrug. "I can't go back on a pinkie promise." I wink at May. "Especially with friends."

The little girl hugs my legs. "Please don't be mad at Ann. Can she be allowed out? She can help me with the chickens or the plants."

Sally arches a brow. "Ann is grounded. You want to be next?"

May releases me. "No."

"I didn't think so. Now go before I change my mind and lock you up."

The girl pauses by Jeremy as she exits. "I saw Tammy messing with the knob earlier." Then she shuts the door.

125

Jeremy clenches his fists. "Of course she was."

"Another thing you forgot to take care of, son?"

He shakes his head. "I'll talk to her."

"Stay in your room unless told otherwise. If you cooperate, I will consider giving you free time."

I cross my arms over my chest. "I have been cooperating! What more do you want from me!"

"I'll make a list," Sally answers before leaving.

I fall into the couch cushions. "What more can I do? I've already given up my freedom, coffee, and romance books."

"For starters, you can remember to eat and take your pills." He collects the items in question and sets them in my lap.

"How can I remember? I don't even have a clock! How am I supposed to tell day from night?"

He tugs off his watch and snatches my arm. "You're so whiney!" He clasps it on me. "It's a miracle, Miss Timekeeper!"

I grumble as I bite into my sandwich. "Okay, so eat more, take pills, and what else?"

"How do you feel about your hair?"

"I like it."

"How do you feel about *short* hair?"

"Why? What would you do with the leftovers? Make a voodoo doll and poke pins in it?"

"Trust me, I don't need magic to make you suffer." He glares. "We need to remind the Palace of your existence and some of your hair with a little blood should do the trick."

126

I leap to my feet as I choke on my water. He slaps my back. "Are you insane?"

He shrugs. "You *asked* for suggestions."

I take in his stern face, and the color drains from my cheeks. "You aren't joking, are you?"

"No."

This plan could work in my favor too. Maybe the Palace could zero in on my location, or at least realize I've been taken hostage. Oh! Then they could track my car! "I guess it'll grow back." I feign a sigh. "Fine, *if* it'll get me out of this room for a few hours a day, I'll do it."

"I think we could take about this much off." His fingertips tickle my sensitive skin as he lifts my hair up to my shoulders.

"What! That's ten inches! It'll take years to grow back!"

"What? Is it not *long* enough for you?"

I jab him with my elbow. As he bends over and groans, I smirk. "It's longer than *yours*."

When he recovers, he narrows his eyes. "You caught me off guard, again." He twirls me around. "*My* turn."

I don't have time to gain my footing before he lowers his lips to mine. I shove at his chest. "What is your problem? Were you dropped on your head at birth?"

"If you can't pay, don't play." With a wave of his wrist, he leaves.

My fingers travel to my tingly lips. What's wrong with *me*? It must be these stupid pregnancy hormones. I nod with finality, but in my heart, I know those blue eyes will bring me to my knees one day. Whether it's in death or pleasure has yet to be determined.

Intentions

I settle on the floor with the contents of the pitiful bookshelf, a handful of leather-bound novels. It's comforting, doing an activity I enjoy. And one I have some form of control over. When I move past the cover, I'm surprised to see it's somebody's journal. A man named Marcus Sumptor. Even if the name isn't familiar, the wavy penmanship intrigues me.

At first, his narrative is slow-moving as it discusses crop rotation and weather. But, by the middle, I sit forward as it mentions the newly formed monarchy stealing Marcus's land for their *own* purposes, without compensation. He continues to describe how other farmers are losing their livelihood the same way. They hold an emergency town meeting and decide to complain to the new leader. The King refuses to do anything because he sees it as payment for keeping them safe during the war.

I rub the wrinkles from my forehead. What would Dad do if this happened during our time? It'd ruffle my feathers and start a cock fight for sure if someone came after my chickens.

Marcus decides to travel the countryside, leaving his family behind to tell others about these injustices. Soon after, a group of fifty men willing to fight for their farmland marches to the Palace. Instead of listening to them, the King is infuriated and imprisons the protestors. Once their families get wind of his actions, they band together and storm the Palace to stage a demonstration. The ruler then uses a livestock brander to mark those *rebelling* against him with a 'R' and makes it known that anyone associating with the marchers will also wear the mark.

Marcus and his family are shunned in their small

community. They set off for a place they can rally others and speak sense into the next generation. A generation that was willing to fight for freedom and speak out in times of injustice. I scan the last page, then I stare at the ceiling. My frown deepens as I wonder what happened to Marcus and his family… They must have continued if the rebellion is still in progress, right? But maybe it's a separate group, because this one is the Black Rose.

Movement catches my attention. "Hello, Tammy."

"You remember my name." She furrows her brow at my reading material. "Where did you get those?"

"They were on the bookshelf." I clutch the dagger Jeremy left me, tightening my grip on the handle hidden behind my back.

"They really did give you the best room, princess."

"I'd rather have my freedom."

She examines the contents of the fridge. "I tried giving you that opportunity last night. What happened?"

"I don't know if you've noticed, but we are in the middle of nowhere. Where would I go?"

"To your King… or is it your Prince? Which one knocked you up?" She tilts her head, her red locks bouncing with the gesture.

"Why are you here?"

"I belong here! While you're just a thorn in our sides! We have to watch, feed, and give you all of this!" She waves her hands around like a crazy hen. "While we have nothing!"

"How many times do you need me to tell you? I never asked for this! I don't want to be here."

"Well, here's your chance to escape. I'll leave the door unlocked overnight again. Just sneak out the back entrance. Then go to the town a few miles away and call your precious Royals to rescue you. It's easy. Because the alternative is having me breathe down your neck." Her eyes burn into mine.

As she steps into my personal bubble, I shove the knife in her face. "That is far enough, Tammy."

"You really are full of surprises." She snorts. "Watch your back." Then she leaves as quietly as she arrived. I drop to the floor and gulp for air. That girl has issues. Did she lose someone and now she blames me?

Eventually my heart stops hammering, and while I munch, I read through the other books on the shelf. Most of them are about war strategies or government reform. Not really my style.

The door opens and I frown up at Sally. "Were you hoping for my son?" She smirks.

I return my gaze to my reading material. "Which one are you referring to?"

"The one who has your fiancé's eyes."

"But what about the one you planted in the Palace and then at my house?"

"Apparently, you have a thing for blue eyes. Not that I blame you. My husband's were the same color." She walks over to the shelf.

"Or is it because Dan fell for Sam and now he's over me?"

"Yes, Samantha has become an unforeseen issue. But I'm certain Dan can talk her into joining our cause. If not… well, he will have to get over her fast."

"Shouldn't that be Dan's choice?"

Sally clears her throat. "Sometimes children need a little guidance."

I slam the book shut. "What is this? Have you come here to have a heart-to-heart? Because in case you haven't realized, I don't trust you."

"Ask me anything you want." Sally sits on the couch and crosses her legs. "Did you know I was in the delivery room when you were born? Your mom was there for me through both of my births, so I thought it was only fair." She chuckles. "I've never seen her so scared. Not even when she battled cancer in high school."

"She was sick in high school?"

"Yes. I held her hand through chemo and whenever she was hugging the toilet. I even shaved my hair when she lost hers." She swipes at her cheek. "We were the three musketeers, your dad, mom, and me. Us against the world."

"What happened?"

"I went to college and your mom and dad took care of their farm. Then I met..." She takes a breath. "My husband. After I graduated, I moved next door to your mom and started my own family. It was heaven on earth."

"How did you end up here?"

"My husband's sins were kept hidden until enforcers came banging on our door one Christmas morning. After that, everything changed. We had to leave and I was ordered to never talk to your family again."

"Then how did my dad help with the blizzard?"

"After my husband died, I snuck off to visit your house. But when I got there, it was too late. Your mom was gone and Jack informed me that you were getting ready to head to the Palace. I never meant to drag your father into this, but when the blizzard shifted and hit us head-on, some rebels who were living outdoors were buried alive. Jack didn't think twice. He just rescued them. Scar or no scar,

131

it didn't matter. That's when he called Dan to bring his construction equipment. A lot of men died, but the ones we saved were grateful."

"Dad never told me any of this."

"It would have endangered your position at the Palace, Ann. If the Royals found out, they would have imprisoned you, or worse. Plus, Jack didn't want to know all the details, just what he needed in order to do his job. It was a one-time thing."

"Then why did Max shoot him?"

She lets out a forced laugh. "Don't even get me started on *him*."

"You said I could ask anything."

She groans. "It's a long story. Max's parents had deep pockets and assisted with the finances here. Plus, they were close to King Mark and other notable politicians. They purposely got pregnant with Mary so she could be part of the selection when the time came. They molded and pruned her every day of her life. Even forcing her into Christian's path at special dinners and parties. But she met Jeremy and fell in love. When she was eighteen, she left her childhood home and joined our cause. Max stayed with his parents while helping us here and there. When Mary arrived at the Palace, Max demonstrated how his loyalty was to his sister and parents, not to us or the rebellion. Once Mary was married to Christian and crowned Queen, everything went to hell in a handbasket. The two little shits wrote us off, in favor of their own agendas. Even their parents stopped helping the cause. It was a mess. That's when we found out that your father was asked to look into Mary, her family, and their background. Max took it upon himself to follow Jack and..." Her face falls into her hands and her words are muffled. "I loved Jack just as much as I loved AnnaBelle. It broke my heart even more when the King blamed the

Black Rose for everything."

"But what about the rose at my dad's grave? And Suzie's death?"

Her head shoots up. "Suzie got stuck in the crosshairs! Her death was not our fault!"

"Who shot her?"

"The head of the King's guard."

"Vinny? No way. He would have told me."

"Not if he believed she was part of our group and deserved it."

"Was she?"

"Yes, but under the table. She was a sympathizer, who made monetary donations here and there, and we'd gather extra crops if she had some to spare. When you visited Jack's grave, I made the mistake of paying my respects that same day. We just returned to Suzie's house from the cemetery when you pulled up. We didn't think anything of it, until we saw the King walk out."

I cringe. There's a lot of hatred towards Christian because of the rebels' mistreatment. But why didn't he tell me about Suzie's involvement? Maybe he didn't know? Or perhaps he found out after she died?

"Wait, but then why was I shot at? They wounded Sam!"

"We were leaving quietly, but some of Max's buddies slipped under the radar. They were hoping to trade you for Max and Mary's release. Trust me, when they used the herb to kill King Mark, we put our own bounty on their heads. That's why Max hid out in the Palace for so long. Little rat knew we'd come for him."

"So when he abducted me, he wasn't with your group?"

"No."

"And he wasn't really obsessed with me, just playing games?"

"Oh, no. He definitely had a thing for you. You were his prize. The King, the Prince, and even Dan wanted you as their wife. So in his eyes, if he had you, he'd beat them all. He was always a little messed up in the head and very competitive."

I shiver at the memories and carry on with my line of questioning. "You said Max has supporters of his own?"

"Yes. We thought we had flushed them all out, but when we came to retrieve Max and Mary from the Palace, a small bunch only obeyed Max's orders."

"Wait. You snuck into the Palace to grab them? Why not just let them hang for their crimes?"

"Their parents were threatening our existence and the safety of thousands of innocent sympathizers." She sighs. "They said if they were going down, so were we. The only thing that was stopping them was Jeremy's promise to get their kids back."

I vaguely recall Christian saying that Mary's family was conveniently out of the country. And that when they returned, they would be rounded up and questioned regarding their knowledge of their offspring's crimes.

"Where are they now?"

"Jeremy delivered their children as promised."

I swallow hard. Poor Jeremy had to carry his wife's dead body all the way to the Governor's mansion. "Are her parents here? Are they still alive?"

Sally arches her brow, and my lips thin. "Let's just say my son made sure they can't blackmail anyone ever again."

Okay, never mind. Jeremy is still a murderer. "You're sharing a lot of information. Is it because you feel guilty about keeping me hostage? Do you expect me to believe everything you say because of your old friendship with my parents? I'm not that naïve. I require proof."

"You get that from your father. He was very inquisitive. Your mother had more of an innocent-until-proven-guilty way of thinking." Sally tugs at a stack of files. "Do these look familiar?"

I squint and bile begins to rise in my throat. "Those are the folders Max stole from the safe." My fingertip grazes the royal seal stamped on the outside. "He stole them after he tied me up."

"They won't give you all the evidence you're asking for, but it's a start. Even though Max was a piece of shit, he wasn't completely useless." I grab the pile, but she holds my wrist. "I know this means nothing to you. But I do love you and I'm glad that you're here." She pats my arm. "If you have any more questions, just ask."

Once she leaves, I rip through the pages of evidence, begging them to prove her wrong. I read everything twice. I slam the documents on the table. Could someone have forged the seal? I gulp. What about copy Christian's signature to the letter?

The odds aren't looking good, as I begin to question if I've been working on the wrong side this whole time.

Sacrifices

"Dinner." The smell of eggs causes a dangerous amount of spittle to escape my lips. Sally places a plate in front of me and smirks but doesn't say anything as she passes me a rag.

"Thank you." I respond between bites. "These are so good."

"May picked them for you and insisted on cooking them for her new friend."

My molars creak and pause. Was that a piece of shell? I roll it around with my tongue before swallowing it. Yup, it sure was. I chug my water. "That was very kind of her."

Sally nods. "She's a troublemaker, but we love her anyway."

It's amazing having a full belly of warm food again. I'm feeling generous so I decide to warn Sally. "So, apparently I'm escaping tonight."

"Really?"

"Tammy came in and let me know she was leaving my door unlocked, what door to go through, and how to make it to the nearest town."

"Interesting."

I shrug. "My guess is *she* is the one who's really into blue eyes." I return her words.

Sally clears her throat and tugs at her boot laces. "They are good friends, but I think it's more than that."

"Are they sleeping together?"

"Jeremy is a grown man. What he does is his business."

"You mean who he does." I bite my lip.

She gives me her best *mom* look. "No."

"So, what did you mean by *more than that*?"

"Tammy lost her mother early in life. And a few years after my husband died, I started seeing Tammy's father. I raised that little girl alongside my boys, so she may be feeling jealous of the attention we're all giving you."

"Where is her father?"

Sally's jaw ticks. "He died in the Palace during the extraction."

"I'm sorry."

"We didn't realize Max's gang had brought explosives." She swallows a lump. "He was trapped under the rubble. Then, when they cleared it, he was interrogated."

Oh no. I know how Christian treats the rebels he catches. "Maybe he's still there?"

"I don't need false hope and neither does Tammy. I told her that her dad died and that's the truth."

"Maybe we can ask Dan or Sam to look into it?"

"No. We need to focus on the mission at hand. That's what he would want, and that's what I want." She straightens her back and pulls a pair of scissors out of her pocket. "Jeremy said you were willing to help?"

"If it means I gain some trust so I can have some more freedoms."

"I will exchange some hair and blood for a newspaper a day."

"That's it? I give you two items and you give me one. That's not fair."

"Ann, work with me here."

"It has to be a new daily newspaper with no cuttings or blurred-out crap. Not even a coffee stain!"

She extends her hand, and I feel the rough 'R' as we shake. "I know you think my decisions are peculiar, but there is a method to my madness."

"The insane rarely know they are insane."

"That's true." She laughs. "Are you enjoying the journals?" She motions to the bookshelf by the couch.

"They're educational."

"So they aren't the normal stuff you are used to?"

"Not really."

"Well, Dan has another book coming."

"I love his books."

"Me too. His work is strategic, filled with mystery and suspense. Although, to be honest, I wasn't very happy he left us to do construction and write. But I'm proud he went out on his own and made a name for himself."

"And he speaks very highly of you."

"I'm glad. As a mother, you never know if you're doing the right thing for your children. You question everything."

"I think you raised him right. Jeremy, on the other hand…"

The man in question strides in, flipping through a newspaper. "I still can't find it."

"Right there."

He squints. "Congratulations?"

She laughs. "You sound so happy for him."

I arch a brow. "What is it?"

Sally passes me the newspaper. "Look on page twelve."

"You could have given *me* the page number." Jeremy

frowns.

"Dan and Sam are engaged?" I question. "That was fast." I tilt my head. "What will their kids call you? Granny?"

Jeremy snorts, then quickly clears his throat as Sally glares at him. "I do not expect grandkids anytime soon."

I rub my belly. "You never know, Gammy."

She rolls her eyes and wrinkles the paper. "Enough, you two." Jeremy and I share a grin, enjoying our game of poke the rooster. "You may have your first newspaper after I get what I came for."

My hands trail over my long locks. "Fine. Cut away."

Sally pulls out gloves, a baggy, and a pair of scissors. The cold blade rests on the back of my head and I squeeze my eyes shut. Once she is done, I feel lighter. My lip trembles as a breeze tickles my neck and my hand pinches my short hair.

"Does it feel better short?" Jeremy asks.

"Not really," I push out, holding my tears at bay.

"Remember, it'll grow back in no time. Besides, the spawn of Satan will probably pull on your hair anyway. So this is a good thing. Less to tug on."

"Not helping, Jeremy." Sally elbows her son. Then she grabs a vial with a tiny funnel before handing both items to him. "Do it over the kitchen sink."

"Don't you want to do it, Mom?"

"I did the hair. Plus, with my arthritis, I don't trust these shaky limbs."

Jeremy grumbles under his breath and it sounds something like, "You're too soft. You wouldn't want to hurt your godchild."

I hold my arm over the sink. "Hurry it up. Before I change my mind." Jeremy joins me and I tug his knife out. "Here, take it... Jeremy?" His eyes are glazed over; he's off in his head. Maybe PTSD? I suck in a breath, then cut into my palm. Blood trickles as I bite my lip to hold back a squeal. Jeremy starts at the sound and takes over as he gently maneuvers the funnel with the vial under my dripping palm.

Once the container is full, he corks it and wraps a rag around my hand and squeezes. "Stop being a baby. Just hold your hand above your head for a minute."

Sally nods as she grabs her goodies. "Thank you. We'll get these to the Palace as soon as possible. Hopefully they'll contact us on our dummy phone in the next few days." She walks past us. Then stops short. "Ann, good luck escaping tonight." She smirks in my direction before exiting.

"You know, if you wanted to escape, you probably shouldn't have told us." Jeremy grabs some munchies, then helps me sit on the couch.

"Tammy came by today."

"She doesn't know when to quit." He glances at my arm. "You can bring it down now."

"She really wants me gone. I'd be surprised if she doesn't kill me in my sleep." I tap my shoulder on his. "Unless you beat her to it. It'd be easy, considering all the time you spend in here."

He unwraps my hand to peek at the cut. "To be honest, I came in here the other day mad as hell and itching for revenge. Then you started apologizing to me. Not something I expected. Then you attacked me. Again, I never anticipated a little woman being able to take *me* down. And when you were given the opportunity to kill me, you didn't." He meets my gaze. "I'm sorry Tammy is

140

giving you a hard time."

I tug my wrist away from my almost murderer. "I can handle her," I whisper, mostly to myself.

"I know you can, but you shouldn't have to. You have enough going on right now." His eyes travel to my stomach.

Is he actually showing concern for me and my... what did he call it? Oh, that's right! My *spawn of Satan*. I could shove it aside and ignore him. But I decide to keep the honest train chugging. "This pregnancy doesn't even feel real. Well, unless I'm throwing up. Then it's very real."

"Well, at least you have something to look forward to." He nods. "I hear Dan should be back in a few days."

I arch a brow at his sudden change in subject. Didn't he bring it up? Why is he shying away now? "I'm sure when Dan returns, he will have a lot to share with your family. I mean, he has a wedding to plan."

"You're right. Dan always has a lot to say during his short trips back here. And normally it's all about you, or the chickens, or his construction jobs."

"So he was spying on me this whole time and reporting it to Sally?"

Jeremy thins his lips. "Dan was watching over you."

His mouth catches my attention and I remember the quick kiss we shared. My heart races, then I look away. "Listen, it's been a long day. I think I'm going to shower and go to bed early."

"Of course." He tugs a worn novel from his pocket. "This might be more of your reading style. Just hide it from my mom, and if she finds it, don't tell her I gave it to you."

The pages are yellowed and dog-eared from overuse, but what really catches my attention is the cover

141

advertising the man-on-man romance. Wow. So, Jeremy isn't into girls? Did Mary steer him to the other side? Not that I blame him. And I certainly don't judge his choice in lifestyle. So that kiss was just his way of getting back at me for catching him off guard?

As he approaches the exit, my mouth opens. "Jeremy?"

"Yes?"

"Have a good night and thanks for this." I wave the naughty novel in farewell.

Long Live the King

The romance novel keeps me warm for a few hours. The escape is much needed, but when it ends, so do my hopes for a happily ever after. When night falls, I drink the sleep aid concoction from Sally. But nothing works. I toss and turn all evening. I go to the bathroom and groan at my reflection. My newly short hair is sticking out like a chicken going through a molt. I shove the unruly strands down and attempt to brush them into submission. How do people live with this length?

I trudge to my usual spot on the couch, wondering what I could give up for some coffee. Maybe a kidney? It's worth it at this point. I'm going through horrible withdrawals. A new spine catches my eye and I grab it off the shelf. Oh, it's a pregnancy book. Yes, finally I can do some research for this whole process. I'd rather be overprepared than under. I devour all the information, but after a few hours, I slam the cover shut.

"What did I get myself into?" I groan.

Jeremy strides in, waving my newspaper around triumphantly. When our eyes meet, his brow furrows. "Why the queasy face?"

"Have you ever heard of a mucous plug?"

"Um, no?"

I slap my palms over my face. "Why do people have sex?"

"I'm sure there are a few reasons." He hands me the paper and pivots like he wants to make a clean getaway.

"Name one?" I demand. I love watching Mr. Macho squirm.

"Uh… well." He looks up at the ceiling. "The *closeness* you develop with someone else as you share an unforgettable bond while becoming one person, in perfect harmony."

"Well, look who's a bit of a romantic."

"Plus, it feels good."

"Not worth it."

"Then you aren't doing it right."

"Tell me that *after* you push a baby out of your body."

My heart stops as I scan the paper. The front page has a portrait of Christian's handsome face, but the bold headline informs us that he passed away last night. No… This can't be happening. I run to the bathroom and heave. I gulp for air as my broken heart throbs in my ears.

Jeremy hands me water. "I didn't know you could run that fast."

"You could have warned me!" is all I can push out.

He crumbles the newspaper and tosses it aside. "That was *not* intentional. I didn't even glance at it before I delivered it to you."

I muster all of my strength and peel myself off the floor and onto the bed. "Whatever. Just go away."

He sits on the edge of the mattress. "Do you… uh… want to talk about it?"

"Sure, let me just sit here with my fiancé's murderer and *talk* about it." I shove a pillow over my head. "I hate you. I hate this place. Just leave me alone."

"It's not all my fault. What I did to Christian during the raid was in exchange for what happened to my wife. The woman I swore to protect. The act was rage-driven. And it wasn't our mission to kill anyone at the Palace, just to extract the two idiots. Then Max's goons turned the tables, looking to scare Christian into signing a treaty. *Everything* went horribly wrong. Especially when Max got his hands on you and that guard shot Mary in the head."

His arguments fall on deaf ears as my tears flow silently and images of Christian flash behind my eyes. We were happy. Then one day had to *end* it all. He may have had his secrets, but he didn't deserve what happened to him. And now Ryan will officially be King. Which means the child I am carrying will be next in line to the throne. I bury my face deeper into my pillow and scream as I choke on my sobs.

Despair rips my soul until darkness comforts me. But something tugs me back. Warm hands lift and cradle me in the corner of the bed. "Just let it out," he whispers.

I also hate how weak I am in this moment. Letting a rebel soothe me. I bury my head into his chest. We sit together, mourning our losses, bonded by our pain and suffering. After a few hours, my body is depleted of tears. I breathe in his earthy smell and my lids flutter. Then his embrace shelters me with strength and empathy as I drift off to sleep. My dreams allow me to relive memories. They let me touch the people I love the most. People who have left me too soon.

Christian sits next to me as we talk about work as if no time has passed. He brushes my long hair out of my face and leans in to kiss me. But when he pulls back, I scream. His body is in a casket. Pale and unmoving. Next to him lies my dad. A flurry of black feathers cascade around them. The bodies are lined up with the caskets left open. I brush my fingertips against the cold, glossy wood until I reach the smallest one. I see a tiny lifeless child until suddenly the baby's eyes shoot open.

I look around, desperate to get my bearings. Jeremy's gaze anchors me. "I'm…"

"You are mourning the loss of someone you love."

I curl up against his chest, listening to the thrum of his heart. "I should have expected this. I should have been

145

better prepared."

"Nothing can ever prepare you for something like this. But now that you're up, you need to move your fat ass. My legs fell asleep an hour ago and my muscles are tingling." He gets up and groans as he rubs at his cargo pants. Once he stretches, he glances back in my direction. "I don't need you doing anything ridiculous in your anguish. Let me get some blood flow back in my legs, then I'll return to babysit you."

"You mean like shooting an innocent man?" I scoff. "No. Go. I need to toughen up anyway."

"For what?"

"For childbirth." My lips twitch at his reaction.

"That one you can do *solo*."

"Aw, you don't want to hold me through it?"

His chuckle warms the air. "I will check on you later."

I drift in and out for the rest of the day. Going from crying to feeling numb. By dinnertime, I look up and smile as Dan hurries inside. He scoops me into a hug. "I came as soon as I could. I'm sorry about King Christian." I squeeze him tight and nod as I pull away. "Are you eating?"

"Yes, Dad."

"How often?"

"Often enough. Now can we discuss *anything* else? Like how your engagement is going?"

"I'm really surprised Sam said yes."

"I'm happy for you guys." I suppress the question gnawing at the back of my mind. *If he told Sam the truth about everything.* Because I don't want to spoil the mood and I know I'll get to hear his story eventually.

"Thank you. How are things here?"

"About the same."

"I didn't realize you were authorized to return yet," Jeremy grunts as he enters.

"Well, it's nice to see you too, brother."

"We don't need any unwanted attention from the Palace." He offers me a white pill.

I pull my hand from Dan's and take the capsule. "What's this?"

"It's a safe pain reliever. You must be feeling hungover after all this."

I swallow the medication, then return my focus to Dan. "How are Karen, Vinny, and the babies? Oh, and Snowball and Elizabeth?"

"They miss you, of course, but they are staying strong. Olivia is teething and making everyone miserable." He laughs before checking his watch. "I need to give Mom my report. Then I have a gift for you. I'll be back soon."

"Well, he diverted the second half of my question gracefully." I pout at the closed exit. "Why are you scowling?"

"No reason." Jeremy stomps to the fridge.

I lean against the wall, watching him. "Jeremy?"

He passes me food. "Eat."

I sit on the couch and grumble under my breath as I do exactly what he asked of me.

"Dan comes back and all of a sudden *you're fine*?" he blurts.

"Haven't you been babysitting me for hours? Watching me *cry*? I'm anything *but* fine."

"Exactly! *I've* been here with you. Then Dan arrives and you… well… you're smiling!"

I stare at the two-headed man in front of me, trying to understand where this is coming from. "Are you jealous of your brother's friendship with me?"

"That's cute. Me, jealous of him? No."

I pop a strawberry into my mouth. "Okay," I draw out.

"Ann, I am *not* jealous."

"Then why are you getting all defensive?" I toss a piece of fruit at his face. "Just let it go, you big baby."

He catches the berry. "I was just curious as to what caused the sudden change in emotions—that's all."

"Well, it's called being pregnant. And, for your information, nothing has ever happened between Dan and me." I flick a grape past my lips.

"I never asked. Never cared." He rolls the strawberry around in his hands, avoiding my gaze.

Oh, there he goes, squirming again. Time to have some fun. "Okay, good. Because I lied."

The strawberry tumbles to the floor and he scrambles to pick it up. "Well, that's your business."

"So, me spending the night with your little brother doesn't bother you?"

"I need to go check on something." He tosses the strawberry at my face before rushing out the door.

Sucker.

I return my attention to the obituary and burst into tears as it mentions Christian leaving behind his fiancée. *Me.* Great. I'm stuck here and can't even mourn his loss and return for his funeral. As I get to Ryan's title, I growl. And he's just ignoring the fact that I'm here! Not even attempting to rescue me or even mentioning in the article that I'm *missing*.

I slam my fists on the coffee table. No matter what I do, I can't get a break. Loss and devastation follow me everywhere I go. I cringe as pain sears across my palm. I tug out a few splinters stuck in my skin, further proving my point. My tears sprinkle on the wound and blood follows suit. I curl up into a ball on the couch, staring unblinkingly at the wall. Life is cruel.

"You never slept with Dan!" Jeremy proclaims as he stomps in. "Ann?" He tugs at my chin, forcing me to meet his gaze.

"What?"

He grabs my bleeding wrist and lets out a sigh. "I thought..." He swallows and shakes his head.

"You thought *what*?"

"I saw blood and your eyes... Don't scare me like that."

"Jeremy, I'm not suicidal."

"Someone could have slipped in here and hurt you."

I smirk. "Well, then, you wouldn't have to watch over me anymore."

"Trust me. This is the *only* job I look forward to. You're easy."

My lips twitch. "I'm easy? Really?"

"I've got news!" Sally bursts through the door and slams a stack of papers on the counter. "The Palace has received the ring."

"I thought you pawned it?"

"We did. But of course the Palace found out about it, and now they have it in their possession. No doubt trying to find something on it. This proves they are searching for answers regarding your disappearance."

I scratch my chin. "Is it weird that they haven't printed missing posters or even asked for information about me in the news?"

"It seems they want to keep the incident under wraps." She bites her lip. "But why?" she asks herself.

"My guess is the Royals don't want people to suspect they are losing control. So they are providing false stability, especially after the King's recent death," Jeremy suggests.

"If the Palace won't publish anything, maybe we can bring something to the media's attention ourselves," I chirp in.

"But what?" Sally questions.

"What about a photo? We could tie Ann up or something?"

"Jeremy!" I slap his arm.

"What? It would be a *fun* photo shoot. We could even add duct tape to your mouth." He smirks. "It'd be quiet and peaceful around here again."

"Let's think of another idea, please," Sally interjects.

My brain goes a mile a minute. This could be a great opportunity to sneak home. "It's been a while since anyone has snapped a picture of me. I mean, I could just stroll around the city and be *seen*. Let people start asking questions. Who knows? Maybe the Palace will have some questions of their own."

"This could backfire." Jeremy shakes his head. "They may question if you're with *us*."

"They'll get the blood and hair soon, right? Which means there won't be any doubt in their minds."

"If they see you with us, they'll question if you're with

the Black Rose willingly," Jeremy counters.

"What if the citizens assume she's still with the Palace? We have a few uniforms from the raid. We could dress someone up in one and send Ann out with them."

"But where? It can't be too far or too close. Plus, it'd have to be a quick outing, otherwise the enforcers will be on us," Jeremy adds.

"I could go to a bank and withdraw some money for the cause." I shrug. "It'd kill two birds with one stone. You guys get some cash, and the bank cameras will witness the exchange."

"How much money are we talking about?"

"Mom! You are not seriously considering this? If she gets caught, it could ruin the whole plan. It's not worth it."

"*Or* it could get you some money for the compound while also allowing me to be spotted out in public. You know, raise some antennas but not too many." I watch Jeremy's face redden at my suggestion.

"No. It's too risky." He turns to his mom.

She pauses but finally agrees with my plan. "After the Governor pulled his financial contributions, we've been struggling to get what we need. I don't necessarily *like* the idea, but I think it's the best we have so far. But go in and do a wire transfer. That way, it isn't suspicious. Say it's for a summer expansion to your property or whatever. Just get in and out quickly. They have to be monitoring your accounts, so once the money is withdrawn, I guarantee the Palace will see it as a red flag and check it out."

"I'll do whatever is needed, especially if it gets me out of this room for a few hours."

"Mom, please think this through for a moment."

"Son, our plan will never work if no one cares that

Ann is gone. The Palace all but ignoring her absence is disappointing. Who's to say if they will even acknowledge the baby? No. We need to remind them that she's here."

Jeremy watches as Sally leaves. Then pivots his icy glare towards me. "I don't like this one bit." I swallow hard, worried he can read the escape plan written all over my face. He huffs, "You are making a big mistake."

Disarming

The compromise between Jeremy and Sally is that if we haven't heard anything from the Palace in the next few weeks, we will go through with our plan. Originally, I thought they trusted me, but I question that when I'm only given the information I absolutely need for the trip. The weeks pass quickly as we train for this short mission. And all the preparation keeps my mind off Christian's death and Ryan's coronation.

"Come on, Dan."

"I'm not hitting a pregnant woman."

"It's just for practice. I need this!"

"No, Jeremy is going to keep a close watch over you, so nothing is going to happen." He resumes making a diagram of the bank.

"Come on!" I punch his arm.

"Ouch!" He grabs a couch cushion and tosses it towards me. "That's all you're getting from me. If I leave a bruise on you, my brother will have my head."

I duck the projectile and smirk. "You don't need it. You don't think much anyway."

"Why don't you finish editing that manuscript I brought you?" Dan raises his palm. "I know I said romance wasn't my genre, but I really enjoyed writing this story. Plus, Sam is a superb research assistant." He waggles his eyebrows.

I hear the knob rattle and I meet Jeremy as he struts through the door. I leap on his back and wrap my arms around his neck.

"Ann!"

"Come on! Dan sucks."

153

"And you're just learning this now?" He lowers himself onto the couch and peels me off him. "You don't know who you're messing with, little girl. Trust me, you don't want to fight me. I always win."

"Promise?"

"Are all pregnant women this spunky and full of energy?"

"Only the ones caged in their rooms," I grumble as I rub my back. "You didn't have to be so rough," I tease, attempting to get a rise out of him.

His brows shoot up. "Hey, you asked for it when you attacked me. You're lucky I didn't drive a stake into your heart."

"That's a vampire."

"No, that's *you* draining the life out of me."

I throw the cushion at his head. "Jerk."

Jeremy catches the pillow as the door opens again. "Careful, there is a prowler in here."

I narrow my eyes at him. Then smile as Tammy walks in. She glances over her papers. "Did you say a prowler?"

"Tammy, can I punch you?"

"Only if I can hit you back?"

I lift my fists. Cabin fever has finally made me crazy.

"Stop!" Jeremy commands.

We glance his way and I whisper to Tammy. "We should probably take this outside anyway."

Jeremy grabs me around the waist, sets me in his lap, and holds my hands behind my back. "You are worse than a child!" he snarls. "Tammy, is that the safety routes?" She passes the documents over. I crane my neck to take a peek but Jeremy pulls the papers out of my view. "They're not for you to see."

"What if you can't keep me safe and I need one?"

"I have never failed a mission and I don't plan to start now. Plus, we can't let you know who our contacts are. You might blab when you get back." He scans the paperwork and returns it to Tammy. "Redirect route A to go around the lake."

"Like this?"

"Perfect."

She beams and then exits.

"I think that was code for *I'll meet you later under the moonlight*." I lean against Jeremy's chest and bat my lashes.

"Dan, I think she's reading too much of your latest nonsense."

"Hey, it's a great novel." Dan points a pen at him.

"It's a great love story. It gave me chills," I praise.

Dan grins. "Any other symptoms?"

"Well, actually, last night…"

"Hey! Focus here!" Jeremy blares.

"Sam helped with the whole sound effects and touching stuff," Dan says, ignoring his brother.

"Oh, really?"

"Yes, she does this one thing where she grabs…"

"Dan," Jeremy warns.

Dan returns to his diagram. "Man, someone needs to get some."

"Jeremy would love your novel." I grin.

The man in question pulls my face to his. "You're

wearing down my patience."

"Enough to punch me?"

His tough guy exterior falters and his lip twitches. "You are relentless."

"Only when it comes to you." I wink. "My arms are going numb. Do you think you could release them?"

"Keep up this nonsense and I'll handcuff you to the bed." He drops his hold, then gets up to stretch. Dan meets my gaze with a smirk. And Jeremy clarifies, "That *wasn't* a dirty promise; it was a punishment."

My fingers shake as I pull the zipper up on my dress. "I'm too fat."

Jeremy strides over in his guard uniform. "Just suck in." I inhale and he tugs it up. "See?"

My hand travels over the silk dress, then my small baby bump. "Is this too much?" I twirl.

"You look like a Palace girl."

"I can't stay long. I just wanted to say goodbye," Dan interrupts. "Ann, you clean up nice."

Jeremy clears his throat. "Dan, focus on the mission."

"Okay, Mr. Bossy. Here is the earpiece. Xander rewired it to communicate with us." Then his hand goes to my baby bump. "Man, this thing is wasting no time growing! How far along are you?" He rubs my stomach.

"Honestly, I don't know. Maybe close to two months?"

I glance at Jeremy to see if he can guess.

And his blue eyes burn as he scowls at his brother. "What did I just say, Dan?"

"He is grumpy."

I nod. "He has performance anxiety."

Jeremy rolls his eyes. "Okay, goodbye, Dan."

"I almost forgot." Dan grabs something out of his pocket. "When I moved your car back to your house, I found this." He drapes the necklace my dad gave me around my neck. "It'll bring you good luck."

"Thank you." I hug him close. "It means a lot to me."

"Good luck, guys." He nods, waving as he exits the room.

I glare at Jeremy. "Why are you so mean to your brother?"

"Him touching you irritates me."

"Well, stop."

He tugs on his guard jacket. "I hate wearing suits."

His biceps make the uniform look tiny, the seams straining against his size. I brush off the collar and adjust his sleeves to cover his scarred hand. "It'll have to do." I meet his searching gaze. "What?" I swipe at my face. "Do I have something hanging out of my nose again?"

"Even though you're a *royal* pain in my ass, I'm glad I'm the one escorting you today." He kneels and kisses my hand. "My lady," he taunts.

"Stand up, you big idiot. You're going to bust out of that jacket." I shove him off. "Now, let's hope people assume I ate one too many cream puffs." I tap my belly as Jeremy clasps on my footwear. "And that I don't injure my other ankle wearing these heels."

His snort grates on my nerves. "Are you serious? You hurt your ankle wearing heels? How is that even possible? I thought they trained you girls to do all that regal junk."

"Regal junk?" I huff. "You should wear them sometime and give me your *official* assessment." I salute Mr. High-and-Mighty. "And it was only one injury." I blink back the memory of Christian carrying me. "I'm sure I can manage better. Now quit yapping and let's get moving."

"As you wish." He bows, and I resist the urge to meet his face with my knee.

"Do I have to?" I groan at the piece of fabric dangling from Jeremy's fingertips.

"We have to keep some secrets." He smirks. "Now be a good girl and turn around."

"You seriously don't trust me?" I feign a pout. "I thought we were beyond this."

He spins his finger around in a circle. "Do I need to spice things up and add a gag and wrist restraints too?"

"You're a sicko," I grumble as I do as instructed.

He ties the blindfold over my eyes. "Don't pretend to be innocent. Dan's new book contained a lot of explicit content."

"I didn't think *those* types of books were your thing?" I goad him. He tugs on the ends, tightening the cloth too much. "Ow!" I swat at him but hit air.

"The blindfold is secure and tested," he shouts by my

ear to the other rebels. They laugh as I wave like an idiot to get him away from me.

We start our journey in a car, then another, and *another*. We switch vehicles so often I'm soon leaning my head between my legs, car sickness taking hold of my gut.

"Ann, do you want to pull back on the mission?"

"No, I want this stupid blindfold off," I grumble. "Does anyone have a bag they aren't fond of?" I hear rustling and people talking. Eventually, a container materializes in my hand. I wipe the sweat off my forehead. By the time we switch vehicles again, Jeremy is holding my short hair back while I throw up, still blindfolded. "Are we there yet?"

Jeremy puts a napkin in my palm. "Yes, we're almost there. Do you remember what you need to say and the account numbers?"

"Stop fussing over me. I have *three* lines to recite. Then back to the car with the three stooges: you, Jared, and Tammy."

He tugs the blindfold down. "You overlooked Xander."

I'm blinded by the sudden light. "Sorry, Xander."

He nods from behind the wheel.

"How did you do that?" Tammy pouts. "We never said a word."

"Well, you always smell like popcorn, Tammy. And Jared is a heavy breather when he gets anxious."

"I don't smell like popcorn," she grumbles.

"Now, remember: in and out, and if somethings off…" Jeremy instructs for the hundredth time.

"The gang will abandon us to our fate. I got it."

"Ann, you need to take this seriously. It's not just your

life on the line. It's all of ours."

"I know the risks, Jeremy. We have been training for this." I turn to look out the window.

"Ann…"

My neck snaps in his direction. "What?" I snarl, done with his mother hen attitude. I know this is important, and I feel guilty for what I really want to do. *Run like hell when no one is watching.*

He squeezes my hand. "You look beautiful." He attempts to disarm my foul mood.

"Puke and all?" I smirk.

He releases my palm. "Gross."

We pull up to a tall building in an unknown city. Jeremy gets into character and opens the door for me. "Thank you, *servant.*"

"Ann…"

"Tsk-tsk. It's *Lady Ann* to you, peasant." This is fun!

The bank isn't busy, but I feel all eyes on me as we stride in to one of the offices. Jeremy taps his earpiece. "We are in."

A plump lady with bright-red lipstick smacks her gum before waving us over. "How can I help you?"

Showtime. "I would like to wire money from my account to a contractor to make some improvements on my farmhouse." I give her the account numbers as rehearsed.

"Of course, Lady Ann." As she types, she side-glances me. "So, we're all wondering if the rumors are true." I frown as she continues. "You know, about you and King Ryan? I mean, I have always wanted you two together!"

My confidence falters. "I am sorry. That is private

information. I'm sure you understand."

Her eyebrows wiggle. "Gotcha. So does that mean the selection is really happening?"

"What?" I squeak past my shock. Jeremy's hand dances on the small of my back. I swallow and nod. "Again. I cannot comment on the comings and goings of our King."

She pouts but prints out my receipt. "Here you go. Have a great day. And good luck!"

Jeremy guides me out. My feet follow as my mind reels. Would the Royals really continue with Ryan's selection, knowing I'm missing and pregnant with his child? Wouldn't they focus on getting me back *first*? Leave it to them to ignore the situation and act like everything is okay. When is his twenty-first birthday? What's today? I scramble to check the paper the teller gave me, but Jeremy tenses and the atmosphere changes.

"Wait." He tugs on my elbow. A man examines our car, then starts yelling incoherently. Our getaway vehicle peels away, and Jeremy gracefully pivots us before walking in the opposite direction. The bank alarm sounds, and we start running. "Now the fun really begins."

I groan as I kick off my shoes to run faster. "You're just bad luck!" I hiss at my partner in crime. "This was supposed to be easy."

"Hey, you did say you were bored. You jinxed us." Jeremy skids around a corner and down a dark alley and starts pulling off his uniform, revealing black clothes underneath.

"You were so confident we'd be caught you wore back-up clothes?" I rub my sore feet. "Not fair! You should have brought some for me too." I glance around, trying to find my own escape route, but nothing is familiar.

He trashes the uniform in a dumpster. "Stop whining!

This was *your* idea, remember?" He taps his earpiece. "We have been compromised. Taking route A." He grabs my wrist. "Stay close," he demands. "And no funny business, or else." We stride through the alley, trying not to draw attention to ourselves. A cool breeze tosses my hair, and I shiver in the thin fabric of my dress. "Man up." He wraps an arm around my neck. "What do you think of your first outing? Was it worth it?"

"Well, if I die, at least you guys have my money to remember me by."

"That's the spirit." Jeremy taps his earpiece and scowls. "Got it." A string of curses spews from his lips. He drags me into another back street. "The local enforcers have been alerted and are on their way. I didn't expect them to react this fast. We need to get to a safe house until the heat dies down."

"Do you think the teller was stalling with her small talk?"

"Maybe. Either way, if they get their hands on us, they'll be no small talk. They'll shoot first, then ask questions."

I swallow my thoughts of escape. Would they really do that? Wouldn't they recognize me? Or would they only see who Jeremy was? He bangs on a metal door of a large warehouse three times. I step closer to his body as the wind picks up again. The aroma of rain thickens the air. And the sky confirms it, as dark clouds loom over the city.

The entrance is cracked open and the shadow of a man glares back at us. "What?"

I lean into Jeremy's chest at the stench of the stranger's breath. Then I whisper, "He's your doppelganger."

Jeremy offers his marked hand and we're waved through. He taps his earpiece again. "We made it."

Boxes are stacked in every possible corner, with aisles only big enough for a forklift. The onlooker's eyes sweep over my curves. "Who's the girl?" He all but drools.

Jeremy tucks me behind him. "She's none of your concern."

"I did not sign up for this."

"Don't make me remind you of what we've done for you, Gary. You *owe* us."

Gary spits at our feet. "This way." He leads us to a crowded office and gestures to some chairs. "One hour. Then out you go." He disappears.

"Nice guy." I throw a thumb back.

"Yeah. I saved his son's life a few years ago." Jeremy settles into a squeaky chair and I question if it'll hold his large frame.

"I didn't know I was in the presence of a genuine *hero*." I bat my lashes.

"Does that mean you're finally impressed by someone other than yourself?"

"Keep dreaming, big boy."

He laces his hands behind his head. "Dream killer."

"You'd think he'd be cleaner." I scoot a roach off the cluttered desk. "Snowball would love it here. Bugs galore."

"Maybe we can ask Dan to bring her to you."

"I love her too much to subject her to *this*. She lives a pampered and lavish life for a lady of her species." I smirk. "Let her enjoy herself." I continue to indulge my curiosity, when a paper catches my attention. My fingers still over the Monarchy's seal. "Jeremy..." I whine as I shove the folder in his lap. "Is it normal for a sympathizer to also work with the Palace?"

163

Jeremy shuffles through the evidence. "Sometimes, but not Gary." He brings a hand to his earpiece while grabbing my wrist and tugging me out. "We're not safe. Moving on to route B." He uses the boxes for cover as we weave through the warehouse. "We're almost there. Get ready to run when I say."

As we turn the corner, I'm slammed into a chest. The stench tells me it belongs to Gary. I scream and kick, desperate to put distance between our bodies.

Jeremy draws his sidearm. "Let her go! Don't make me shoot you."

"Sorry, no can do. Do you know how much ransom I'll get for her?"

Jeremy meets my gaze and gives a slight nod. I jab my elbow as hard as I can into Gary's beer belly, then up to his nose in one quick motion. He releases me as he recovers. Jeremy kicks Gary backwards. Once my would-be kidnapper tumbles to the ground, Jeremy orders me to run. As we near our exit, Gary snarls and shoots above our heads. I screech, but the pressure of Jeremy's hand on my back calms my uncertainty.

The fresh air fills my lungs, but we don't stop until we're out of breath and far away from our crazed attacker. We huddle behind a white business van to make sure we aren't being followed. Jeremy slides down the side and onto the ground. He releases my hand and we both watch as crimson pools on his shirt.

"Jeremy?"

"I'm fine," he grunts out. "It's just a flesh wound."

I've seen enough bloodshed to know better. It needs to be cleaned and stitched up. I rip off a piece of my dress and apply pressure. "Damn you for getting in that bullet's way!"

He pinches his eyes closed. "Go."

"What?" The blood soaks through the thin fabric and wets my fingertips.

"You can finally be free." He cringes as I push another strip over the wound. "Just leave me and return to the Palace. I know that's the real reason you came today. So now you get your wish. I won't stop you."

I take in my surroundings. I could leave him. It would be easy, and that's what I do best when things get tough, right? I run. But do I really want to return to the Palace after everything I've learned? I shake my head. *Think, Ann.* What do *you* want to do? Abandon Jeremy and gain your freedom? Or help him and continue being a captive? I don't like my odds with either.

"Can you walk?"

He hands me the earpiece. "Go to the next safe house and they will guide you from there."

"What?"

"You heard me." He pushes me away. "Stubborn little brat."

I offer a hand. "Jeremy, get off your lazy butt and let's go!"

He slaps my wrist. "Ann, go! That's an order." I sit beside him and look around. "You're being stupid."

"And your vocabulary sucks." I kick his foot. Once I catch my breath, I stand and tug him upright. "You need a diet."

He bites his lip as he helps me lift him. "Look who's talking."

"Where is the safe house?"

He points to a mechanic shop a few blocks away. "The guy's name is Wayne. Code name is Kerry," he says slowly as he concentrates on moving forward.

I tap the earpiece. "We're almost to the safe house."

I knock on the shop office door and a young man opens it. "Can I help you?" He arches a brow at our disheveled appearance.

"We're looking for Wayne. Code name Kerry," I wheeze out.

He wraps his arm around Jeremy's waist and helps him to the back of the garage. He sets Jeremy down. "He doesn't look too good."

"Do you have a first aid kit, a sewing kit, and some clean towels?" Once he dashes off, I report, "We made it to the safe house."

"We're sending a transport now, but it will be some time," the voice reports.

"Okay." I rub my face, trying to arrange my thoughts. The man returns with the supplies. "Thank you, Wayne. My name is…"

"Lady Ann." He nods. "I recognized you," he adds coldly.

"Listen, a lot has changed since my Palace days. Please. I just need to fix up my friend here, and we'll be on our way."

"Under one condition."

"What?"

"Could you sign something for me? My wife is a huge fan."

"I will sign a hundred things if you want."

Jeremy's shirt is caked against his skin, but we cut it off carefully to get a better look at the damage. He swats our hands away, sweat beading on his forehead. "Ann, you need to go. We can't stay in one place too long. It isn't safe."

I throw a cotton ball and it bounces off his thick head. "Quiet, you." I clean around the afflicted area, but heave at the oozing hole. The projectile passed through but the wound's bleeding a lot. Jeremy clenches his fists. My hands shake as I approach the sterilized opening with a needle and thread. "You are going to hate me forever."

"Nothing new. Wife-killer."

"I can't do this. I can't cause you *more* pain."

"Just get on with it, ya' big baby." He leans back and grits his teeth.

I turn to my new friend. "I need you to hold him down."

"Why me?"

I wipe my forehead with the back of my hand. "I hardly weigh enough."

The mechanic shakes his head. "It won't be pretty, but I'll sew him up. You straddle him and hold his hands down so he can't hit me."

I meet Wayne's gaze. Thank goodness he's taking over, because this blood is making me lightheaded and nauseated. I sigh and look at Jeremy. "*Don't* bite me. I'd hate to become a grumpy werewolf like you." Then I straddle him and clutch his wrists above his head. My short hair tickles his cheek. "Sorry."

He opens his lids. "If I don't make it, I want you to know..."

"No. Stop. We're going to make it out. Both of us. And you can tell me *I told you so* for the rest of your life."

"Deal. No matter how short it may be."

I hold him tight. "We're ready, Wayne."

The mechanic nods and takes a breath. I feel Jeremy tense and moan as he tries to squirm. "Just a little longer," I whisper into his ear. "Tell me. Why do you fight alongside the rebels?"

"My dog," he grunts.

"Your what?"

"The enforcers killed my dog, took my parents, and destroyed my life. Pay back is a bitch. I defend the weak and help the poor."

"Like Robin Hood." I smirk.

"I don't want to hurt you, Ann, but I don't know how much more I can take."

"Stop acting like a two-year-old. There's not much left. What more can I do to help?"

"Anything. Just take my mind off *this*."

My brain is foggy with exhaustion. "Do you want to hear how I lost my virginity?" He coughs a laugh and I take that as a yes. I whisper the juicy details into his ear, careful not to let Wayne hear the specifics of who and where.

The mechanic rises with bloodied fingers. "I can't do anything more. I'm going to wash up."

I go to stand, but Jeremy grabs my hips. "Thank you for not leaving me behind. I misjudged you."

"It was my fault you were here to begin with. It was a stupid idea. I'm so sorry I put you in danger."

His calloused thumb rubs a tear off my cheek. "Stop. I will be fine."

We touch foreheads and our breaths mingle. Even though I hate this jerk, I can't see a life without him constantly around. "You better be." My body aches as I finally push to my feet. I'm getting too old for this. I press the earpiece. "The wound is cleaned and dressed."

"Await transport," Tammy informs us.

I settle on a fold-up chair and stare at my dirty feet.

"That was intense." Wayne sighs, leaning on the wall.

"Let's hope it never happens again. I've had my fair share of excitement, enough to last a lifetime. Thank you for your help. What did you want me to sign?" I follow him into his office and sign a few trinkets for his wife. Then my stomach's growl bounces off the walls.

"The misses is out shopping, but I might have some frozen pizzas I can make?"

"Wayne, you're my *new* favorite person."

"Hey, traitor," Jeremy groans.

Wayne pats my shoulder and climbs the stairs.

I smirk at Jeremy's shirtless form. "Don't worry, I'll be dreaming of those abs for the rest of my life."

My jab hits its target and his lips twitch. "You're too much."

I sit next to him and offer him some water. He guzzles it, then leans back. I wind my fingers through his dirty-blonde locks. "Are you getting sleepy?"

He peeks through his lashes. "No. Why? Are you?"

I laugh and shake my head, knowing he's about to drift off. The mechanic returns with the pizzas, and I eat my fill. A comforting silence blankets us as we watch Jeremy's steady breathing.

"Why aren't you at the Palace?"

"It's a long story, but they need me more than the Palace does right now." I nod towards the rebel on the floor. "Can I trust you to keep my... *appearance* a secret?"

Wayne watches me for a long minute before he nods. "Of course."

"Thank you."

There are three knocks on the closed shop door and Wayne checks it out. Then he jogs back with Jared and Xander. I help them lift and place Jeremy in the back of the SUV. Then I climb in and lie next to him. They cover us with a big blanket to conceal our presence. And we start our long drive back. I snuggle as close as I can to Jeremy. As the vehicle moves, I trail my fingertips down his abs, letting the warmth soak into my cold hands.

He shivers and snatches my wrist. "Stop drooling."

"I think I've earned it," I tease.

He releases my hand and grumbles, "I'll never hear the end of this, will I?"

I continue to peruse his chest, and soon his breathing is even and slow. I lean my head by his face. "Are you sleeping?"

When he doesn't answer, I close my eyes. I'm glad he's able to rest, and I'm relieved when we don't switch vehicles during the return trip. Once we arrive at the rebel compound, I watch helplessly as they carry Jeremy away. I rub my arms, then slowly drag my feet to my room.

"Ann?" Sally waves me over from the medical bay. When I meet her, she frowns and I see her eyes glistening. She wraps me in a tight hug. "Thank you for saving my son." She sobs into my shoulder. "I don't know what I'd do without him."

As the team tends to his wound, I can't help but question, "Is he going to be okay?"

"Yes." She wipes her eyes. My head spins and I grab her arms to steady myself. "Ann, why don't you shower, throw on some clean clothes, and get some sleep."

My palm rests on my belly. "I think that's a good idea."

"Ann?" Jeremy rasps.

"Looks like you'll survive this after all, you big baby."

"No thanks to you." He returns my smirk.

I swat him and whisper in his ear, "I'm going to go take a long, hot shower."

He groans. "Just go already. I can smell you a mile away."

"I'm going to forget to put underwear on too."

"Go, *dirty* girl."

I pivot to return to my room but stop as I notice everyone watching me. I blush. And quickly brush past them. I let out a breath as I enter my prison. And Sally comes in after me. "Ann."

"Can this wait until morning? I'm exhausted and sore."

"I wanted to inform you that you may roam the compound as you wish. You are no longer confined to this area."

I tug the earpiece out and hand it to her. "Why the sudden change of heart?"

"Because you sacrificed a lot for us when you didn't *have* to. You could have run, but you saved one of our own. I believe that warrants certain privileges, don't you?"

I shrug her off before walking towards the bathroom. Then I pause, not able to meet her gaze. "Thank you."

She nods and pivots back through the door. And I do as I promised. I take my time showering, scrubbing away all the memories of Jeremy being shot. But no matter how hard I try to forget, I can't. I slide to the tiled floor and cry into my knees. Once the water turns cold, I peel my body off the ground, square my shoulders, and remind myself to be strong.

Even though a lot has happened, tomorrow begins my new routine. It's another opportunity to thrive and grow. I'm a free woman. Or *freer*. I set my necklace on the bathroom counter before running the brush through my hair. I think my parents would be proud of the choices I made today when I put Jeremy's well-being ahead of my own. I drag on my pajamas, minus the underwear, and head to bed.

Loyalties

I sleep until midday, only rousing when something thumps on my bed. I rub my eyes. "Good morning, May."

"You mean afternoon." She watches me get up. "Jeremy has been asking for you."

"Here's a little secret: always keep them *wanting* you." I stretch my bruised limbs before I snack so I can take my pills. "Does Sally know where you are?"

"She's waiting for you too. She wants to talk to you about what happened yesterday. What did happen?"

"Top secret. Now, let's go."

"But you didn't change." She wrinkles her nose at my pajamas. We hold hands and stride to the medical bay. The atmosphere has shifted now that I can roam freely. I'm excited to explore what the compound has to offer.

Jeremy tilts his head at me. "Why are you still in your pajamas?"

"I asked the same thing." May climbs on the bed with him.

"Aren't you supposed to be doing chores?" He ruffles her hair.

"Even injured, you are bossing everyone around," I add.

May watches me approach Jeremy. "Are you two getting married?"

"No, May." I shut down her fantasy real fast.

"I just assumed since you're pregnant Jeremy would *have* to marry you."

My jaw falls to the floor and I narrow my gaze at my newly designated husband, who is equally as shocked. He pokes May's nose. "How do *you* know Ann's pregnant?"

"It's obvious." She waves to my growing abdomen. "I'm not stupid. I'm almost eight." I rest my cold hands on my cheek and sit on the corner of the bed. May puts her little hands on my stomach. "It's like a tiny pumpkin!"

I pull her into a hug. "Go do your chores before Sally has a fit." She laughs and runs off. I sigh at her carefree attitude.

"Ann?"

I pivot to Jeremy. "No, I won't marry you just because I'm pregnant."

"That's not what I was going to say."

"And, no. I'm *not* wearing underwear."

His gaze travels downward, then he shakes his head. "Stop. Listen…"

"There you are!" Sally comes around the corner. "We need to talk about yesterday." She turns to her son. "Can you stand?"

We help him to his feet. Then we all meet in the dining room at a long table. Once everyone is settled, we explain what happened.

"Ann, you went against a direct order," a bald man accuses.

"With all due respect, I've never pledged myself to you or the Black Rose. I was going by instinct. Saving a fallen comrade."

His plump face turns red. "Listen here, young lady…"

Sally holds up a hand. "Ann doesn't plan on doing any more field work. This was a one-time situation. And we all appreciate her courage, dedication, and sacrifices." Everyone nods. "Good, now I'm calling this meeting over."

I offer support as Jeremy stands. "Where is your

room?"

"Sorry, but I'm not that kind of guy."

I roll my eyes. "Who are you trying to kid?"

"Ann, wait," Sally interrupts. "I was wondering if you wouldn't mind helping outside with the chickens and the garden. Plus maybe teaching a children's self-defense class?"

My heart soars at the opportunity to put my skills to use. "Of course."

"Good. You start tomorrow."

I arch a brow at her departing figure. "Your mom can be pretty intense."

"You have no idea."

Jeremy guides me to his room and I help him to his bed. I glance around the grey-colored interior and stop as my eyes fall on his nightstand. Resting on top is a single picture frame. I run my thumb across the glass. There, smiling back at me, is Mary and Jeremy holding hands, surrounded by their families. "You guys look happy."

"That was a long time ago. People and situations change." He grabs the picture and sets it face-down on his nightstand. Then he opens his arms. I lay my head on his chest. "What I was trying to say back there—but you kept running your mouth—is thank you for saving my life."

"Well, your memory must be slipping, old man, because you already told me that."

He brushes my hair aside. "But I never showed you my gratitude." Then he slowly eases his lips to mine. This feels so right, lying here in his arms. I moan softly. His touch calms every nerve ending in my body. It's magic. But I've been here before, too many times. My hand goes to his lips.

"I thought you were into men?" I blurt out.

"When did I ever say that?"

"I just assumed, because of the book you gave me."

"That novel belonged to my dad." His fingertips trace my jawline.

Goosebumps take over my arms. "Wait. So the book was your dad's? Was this a guilty pleasure of his?" I smirk. "Because I devour all kinds of genres and tropes, no matter what genders are involved. Love is love."

"My father wasn't the nicest guy. His loyalty was always to the cause, and he ran it with an iron fist. When King Mark married Elizabeth, my dad decided to find a woman who could bare him children for the selection. But, when he married my mother, he forgot to mention that he enjoyed having physical relations with men."

"How did she find out?"

"She caught him with his lover. She was going to let it go, because she loved him. But in the end, my dad chose Derek and divorced her."

Poor Sally. She fell in love with a man who only married her so she could incubate his spawn. Then, when she didn't have any females for the selection, he dumped her for...

"Wait. Derek? You don't mean..."

"Yes, the same Derek who was King Mark's henchmen."

A shiver runs up my spine, and Jeremy takes it as a cue to continue his heavy petting. "Jeremy, we can't," I stutter. "You... I..." Why isn't my mouth working properly? I leap from his embrace so I can clear my thoughts. "I'm cursed, and you'll just end up getting hurt. Or worse."

"Wow, I've never heard *that* line before."

"I have no idea where I'll be in a few months. Plus, I'm carrying another man's child."

Jeremy stands and places his palm on my only form of exit. Even in his injured state, he towers over me. "Listen, I wish I could be logical about this, but I can't. I almost didn't get another day and I'll be damned if I waste any more without you." He tugs my face close to his. "The ignorant Princes discarded you when things got tough, but I'm *still* here. And knowing all the obstacles that are coming our way, I choose to continue to stand by your side. They acted as if you were *beneath* them, but to me, you are my equal in every way."

I attempt to retreat, but the doorknob digs into my back. "You aren't thinking clearly. You're going to get what you want and then hate me." Tears spring from my eyes as I look away from his piercing blue gaze.

He pulls me to his chest and kisses my head. "You are mistaking me for that douchebag Ryan. He had *no* right to promise you things he never intended to do." He lifts my chin up. "I will be here for you, always and forever."

"What if I'm *forced* to marry Ryan because of the baby? What if you have to kill me to prove your point? I'm just a pawn. Nothing more."

"Ann, look around you. You're part of us now. There's no turning back. I will always protect you."

"And what about the baby?" I recall his snippy *spawn of Satan* reference.

"I have no loyalties to *it*."

My heart splinters. He is exactly like those people he says he hates. "How can you say that?"

"It has royal blood coursing through its veins, and you *know* what they're capable of."

"It also has my blood too."

"The sooner that *thing* is out of you and your life, the better."

"How dare you!" My lip trembles.

"You actually want it?"

"It's a baby! It has no concept of right or wrong." He settles on the edge of his bed and glares at me. "All that talk meant nothing to you," I seethe. "You are *exactly* like the Royals! The only difference is I stopped before anything got too physical with us."

I suck in a breath and hold back a sob as I run from his room to mine. How could he devote himself to me but not my child? It makes no sense. Something doesn't add up, and if he can't be mature enough to spell it out for me, then I'm not going to dwell on it.

I'm glad this was shut down so fast! I never wanted to be in a relationship with him anyway. As much as I repeat this over and over in my head, my heart still aches for the loyalty and devotion his words promised. Because I ignorantly believed he could actually follow through.

In the coming months, I do my best to avoid Jeremy as I keep myself busy with training, chickens, and the garden. I enjoy the laborious activities; they keep my mind too busy to second-guess myself. The children are fun and energetic. Soon they can best me in a boxing match, especially as my belly gets bigger and my coordination worsens.

"Okay, Tanner. Watch my glove." I jab right past his face. Then he retaliates, hitting my knee. I stumble and fall on my butt with a thud. They laugh as I wipe at my face. "Good job, guys. Class is over. Go clean up and get something to eat."

They dash for the exit, leaving me stranded in the grass. A cold breeze tickles my neck and reminds me fall is in full swing. The sun is blocked out by a figure towering over me.

"Hello, stranger." I smile at Dan. "You are a sight for sore eyes and, in my case, a sore butt."

He offers a hand. "You are too big to be letting these kids beat you up."

"Today is my last day. From now on, it's just the chickens and veggies."

"Good."

"How is married life treating you?"

"Busy. We're trying to put together a late honeymoon." He sighs as we descend the stairs. "And apparently, I'm getting lazy because Jeremy beat me during our sparring match shortly after I arrived."

"He has been in a mood lately. Ignore him. That's what I do. Where does Sam think you are?"

"She thinks I'm at a construction job." He arches a brow. "Why is my brother in a mood?"

"Beats me."

He laughs. "Oh, I bet it has *everything* to do with you."

We reach the ground floor, and I jump as a loud bang comes from the training area. Once the arena is in full view, I see Jeremy has Henry pinned. Our eyes meet but I look away. I know he's mad at me and taking it out on everyone else. I hate witnessing him overexerting himself every day. So I do my best to brush past them without irritating him further. Once we get to my room, I change quickly. And as I step back out, I see that Dan and Sally are flipping through his book I edited.

"This looks good, Ann," Dan comments.

I wave a hand over my shoulder. "I know, I know. I'm the best."

Jeremy enters, stomps by me, then stalks to Sally. "You called me?"

She pats the couch. "Your brother is home for a few days. Come and look at his new book with us." She passes it to him.

And he refuses to take it. "No thank you."

She hands the book back to Dan. "Well, I loved it. It's wonderfully written. Great job."

"Thank you, Mom." Dan pushes to his feet with an outstretched hand directed towards my belly. "Ann is getting huge! What happened to that petite little woman?"

Sally laughs. "There's more of her to love, I guess."

"May I?" He kneels and looks up at me. When I nod, he places his palm on my baby bump. "It's so weird." Then he jumps back. "It moved!" He puts his ear to my stomach. "You can hear it moving around."

"It's probably just my lunch."

"Ann, this is amazing!"

"It's just the circle of life, Dan. I'm sure you and Sam will have one of your own soon."

"Baby, this is your Uncle Dan." He rubs my belly. "Kick once if you recognize me." He pouts. "Guess I need to spend more time with it."

"Get off the floor," Jeremy barks.

Dan stands and rubs his hands together. "Are you ready for my present?"

My eyes beam. "For me?"

"Well, for everyone really. But, yes, mostly for you." He tugs my hand to the hospital bay. "You too, grumpy butt," he calls over his shoulder to his brother.

There, in one of the bays, is an ultrasound machine. I stop short and drop Dan's hand. Jeremy plows into my back with an *oof*. He frowns down at my pale face. "Are you scared of a tiny machine?"

I plead into his icy-blue eyes. "I can't."

Dan frowns. "You can't what?"

"I can't see it." Because if I do, it'll be real. Too real.

"You don't even want to see it?" Jeremy rolls his eyes. "Make up your mind. You want it. You don't want it."

I poke a finger into his chest. "Don't mock me, you little hypocrite!"

"Me?" he snarls.

"Woah! You two need to calm down." Sally tugs on my elbow. "Listen, Ann. We would like to check on the baby and make sure everything looks good. Is that okay?"

"I don't have a choice." I frown at Dan. "Do I?"

"I thought you would be excited for this. I mean, we can finally tell the gender and stop calling the baby an *it*."

"Is it really necessary?"

"We need to send the King a picture of the baby to remind him you're still here and the child is well," Sally soothes.

The technician strides in. "Is everyone ready?"

"I'll wait out here," Jeremy grumbles.

"Why?"

"To guard the place."

"Please stay." As much as our relationship is strained, I can't imagine anyone else I'd want by my side right now. His presence is calming to me, and I need that.

He folds his arms across his broad chest. "Hurry up then. I don't have all day."

I lean back on the chair as the technician lifts my shirt and applies a cold liquid. I hiss at the unexpected temperature, and Jeremy stomps over, ready to backhand the woman. I snatch his wrist. "It's just cold."

He averts his eyes towards the screen. The image is blurred as the technician moves the wand around. Then, on the screen, there's a little peanut shape. My hand flings out and clutches Jeremy's. He squeezes it softly in return. We all witness the baby kick and move away from the technician. "He is very active. That's a good sign," the woman says.

I suck in a breath. "He?"

She nods. "He." Then points to the screen. "These are his boy parts." She collects a few measurements as everyone else is tearing up. Even Jeremy. Each of us lost in our own thoughts and memories. "Well, he is healthy and tracking perfectly. Congratulations." She nods before passing over a few pictures.

Dan gently wipes off my belly. "He is a handsome one."

Sally rubs my arm. "We are excited to welcome him into the world." She sniffles. "I'm sure your parents are smiling down right now, enjoying this moment also."

They all file out, one by one, leaving me alone with Jeremy—who is still holding my hand. I meet his gaze but frown at his far-off stare. "Are you okay?"

"I need some air," he huffs and marches out the closest exit.

I return to my room and sit on the couch. Moments later, Dan knocks and walks in. "Ann, I'm sorry. I really thought you would like this."

"Dan, are you and Sam happy?"

"Yes, we are."

"Do you think she will accept you once she finds out about your involvement with the Black Rose?"

"I wouldn't have married her otherwise." He sits. "Why do you ask?"

"When the Monarchy finds out what I've done… I'm not sure they'll be so forgiving."

"Are *you* doing what you feel is right?"

"Yes."

"Then that's all that matters." He rests his hand on mine. "One day, we will all be held accountable for our actions. And you need to be proud of what you have accomplished."

"But it's not that *easy*."

"No, it's not. But remember: whatever you do now is for our future and theirs." He places a hand on my belly. "Our children." He grabs sandwiches, fruit, and water from the fridge.

"Do you think Jeremy will come around?"

"My brother is complicated. I know he cares about you. But you are also competing with his past life with Mary. Just as he is competing with the memory of Christian and the possibility of you going back to Ryan." He shakes his head. "You want my opinion as a friend? Don't get attached to Jeremy." He shrugs. "But as a brother, I want nothing more than to see him happy with someone as amazing as you."

"I'm trying to ignore him, but it's hard. I've never felt

this way before. It's like he understands and accepts me for who I am. It's an amazing feeling, as if I can conquer the world, if only he's by my side." I stare at my feet.

When I look back up, I'm surprised to see Jeremy leaning on the doorframe. Dan pats my knee. "We'll talk again soon. Good night, you two." Then he walks out.

"How much did you hear?"

"Enough to know I should walk away before we both get hurt again."

"Oh." It's pitiful, but that's all I can say. He's abandoning me like everyone else in my life. I just wish it didn't hurt so much.

"But I've *tried* staying away, and I'm finding it hard to breathe without you. For the life of me, I can't remember how I lived before you came into my world."

"You could just continue to beat the crap out of people. It seems to be working for you."

"And you can continue to work yourself to exhaustion every day."

"At least until I return to the Palace." I frown at my belly.

"Are you having second thoughts about the mission?"

"I know what needs to be done, Jeremy," I grind out. "I just... I can't..." Tears slip past my barriers. "I don't want to leave you." There... I said it. My heart feels lighter now. But my future is still uncertain. "You are my *strength*. The glue holding me together."

He lowers himself next to me, his elbows on his knees and his face resting in his hands. "Shit. We are one hell of a mess." He tugs at his hair. "But I'm willing to wait and see what happens." He warms my hand with his. "Every day I look forward to bickering with you, laughing at you, and even bleeding underneath you."

184

I rest my head on his shoulder. "Just hold me and lie. Tell me everything will be okay. That everyone will get a happily ever after. Because I'm *beyond* scared." I bury my face into his neck and breathe deeply, wishing the world could pause in this moment. The instant when two imperfect people refuse to give up on each other, no matter what.

"There's nowhere else I'd rather have you than in the safety of my arms, shielded from anyone who'd dare to harm you. I'd happily die if I only knew you were safe and taken care of." He kisses my head.

Before I can formulate a response, I cover my ears as an alarm blares. We separate and dash into the common area. Chaos has erupted as everyone is running around like chickens with their heads cut off. "What the hell is going on?" I yell.

"The compound's perimeter has been breached and we're going under lockdown. Don't worry. The doors will seal us inside until the threat is gone. Go back to your room," Jeremy demands as he runs towards his mom.

My mouth falls open as my eyes scan the room in search of the children. I see all but one huddled in the dining room. "Where is May?"

"We last saw her outside." They point to the upper level. I take the stairs two at a time, praying I'm not too late.

"Ann!" Jeremy growls. "Stop! You can't go outside! The doors are set to automatically lock! You won't make..." His warning is severed as the door closes behind me. True to his word, they trap me outside. I spot May trembling beneath the nesting boxes, and I dive under them and hug her. Thank goodness she's safe.

She whimpers into my chest. "I couldn't sleep. I'm so sorry."

I hear a familiar screech before there's a painful peck on my ankle.

"Scarlett." I shoo her with my foot. "This is no time to get territorial, you little horror."

Scarlett puffs her red feathers and barrels towards me, her wings raised at half-staff. What's wrong with her? I've never had a chicken live up to its common nickname, Little Raptor, until now. Her screeches rebound off the hen house, and a cold sweat forms on my forehead as I hear shouts and footsteps.

I clamp a hand over May's mouth, to keep her from screaming, and squeeze our bodies under the nesting boxes. I practice slow-breathing to hopefully silence my heart, which is currently hammering in my ears and muffling everything around me. The footsteps stop outside the pen, then stride towards the compound door. The tall figure tugs on the handle and curses when it won't budge. Then stalks off.

I slowly drop my hand and whisper in May's ear, "They're outside. We need to be extra quiet."

She snuggles into my chest as I stroke her hair and hold her tight, while I continue to defend myself from the crazy creature pecking my foot. I hear a loud thump and men shouting. My heart soars. We're saved! The rebels have come to rescue us. I chuckle inwardly. I never thought I would ever see *them* as my saviors. But a lot has happened over these last few months and they've proven time and time again that the world has misjudged them. Well, the world and me.

"You said they were *here!*"

"I swear they are! I followed them, then reported it to you. Please let my son go. I did what was asked."

I know that voice. I bite my lip to keep from screaming. It's that traitor from the warehouse—the one who shot

Jeremy.

"Your son is a rebel supporter!" A deafening click sounds on the other side of the wall. "And he will perish, just like his father." Then a single gunshot rings out in the darkness, illuminating three male figures in a split-second, before an unearthly silence blankets us.

I don't have a second to blink as May releases a bloodcurdling scream. Scarlett takes off and I muffle the girl's mouth with my hand. I listen for movement, my heart fluttering in my chest. I hear Scarlett's warning just as my scalp burns and I'm tugged backwards.

"Well, damn. Maybe the old man was right. Pity he'll never get his reward."

The other intruder takes hold of May. He throws her over his shoulder like she weighs nothing. "Shut up, kid! Or your little friend gets it."

He cocks his gun back and she suppresses her trembles to the best of her ability, as a blinding light focuses on me. "Please, let us go."

"Well, well. What do we have here? The spawn of a rebel?" The flashlight illuminates my belly.

"No! You don't understand…" My cheek burns as he hits me and I fall to the ground.

"No one asked you to speak, rebel scum."

I shield myself as he moves his leg back to begin his assault. "I'm Lady Ann!" I announce. The boot pauses inches from my stomach and then I see his face.

"You're full of shit."

"It's true," May stutters out.

The other man drops the small girl next to me and our would-be attackers stare intently. Then turn towards each other. Their pause gives me a moment to assess the situation. They're dressed in enforcer uniforms, with the Palace crest shining back at us. I steal a quick glance at the body lying a few feet to our left and gag. He was shot right between the eyes. All because he was trying to protect his son and follow the order of the law.

"Call in the location to the station and ask for a description of Lady Ann," the taller man says.

"Roger." The shorter man pushes his ear and speaks, but then pauses midway. "The comms are dead."

"You incompetent prick." The enforcer slams his finger on his comm and makes the same face. My blood runs cold as they both turn their glares on May and me. I collect her in my arms before they can blink. "Fine, throw them into the trunk. We'll go back and report it ourselves."

The smaller man tears May from my grasp, and when I attempt to pull her free, he backhands me across the face. "Boss, we only need to bring one in." He trails a finger over May's trembling lip. "Why don't we lock that one in the trunk and have some fun with the little girl?"

"No! Please!"

His counterpart rubs his chin. "Maybe it will lure the other rebel punks out from their hiding place." He clasps a large hand over May's wrist and twists it into the flashlight's beam. "She's already dead with that brand anyway. At least that one doesn't have anything—yet."

I sob as I try to crawl to May. But the guard snatches my elbow and tugs me up. "Shut up!" He blares in my ear before he handcuffs my arms behind my back. "Let's go, your ladyship." He shoves me forward and glares back at the other officer. "Make it loud. Let's see how much they *really* care about their own."

May screams and kicks. "Ann! Help me! Don't let him hurt me!"

My heart breaks. Her screams urge me forward and I jam my head into my captor's nose. Then I kick my knee into his lowered face. We tumble until he is straddling my thighs.

"So, you want some attention too?" He heaves, his breaths coming out in heavy pants.

I spit blood in his face as I glare at him. Before he can retaliate, I see a red blur running in our direction. I turn my face as Scarlett starts her assault on us for being too close to her nest.

"What the hell!" the officer screams, stunned by the feathered renegade. With those few precious seconds, I'm able to crawl away from his grasp. "Shoot the bird!" he yelps as he protects his eyes.

When I see the gun raise, I kick as hard as I can, moving the officer into the line of fire instead of the hen. After the slide has snapped back before slamming forward again and releasing its projectile, I stare at the blood coating my upper body. Then I let out a breath as I watch Scarlett scurry away. Unharmed.

"Ow! You little shit!"

I turn to see May biting and clawing the remaining enforcer in an anger-fueled frenzy. I slam my shoulder into his chest and he flies backwards. A large pine tree cushions his fall, but his head thumps against the trunk, unmoving.

"Ann, is he…" May whispers as she clutches my arm.

"No, of course not, honey," I lie. I pull myself together and instruct her to grab his keys, in order to find the one that unlocks my cuffs. Then I handcuff the enforcer to the tree.

"See? When the doors unlock, they can take care of him. Okay?" I run a palm over her cold face. "Now, let's go into the chicken pen until we can get back inside." I cover her eyes as we pass the other lifeless guard. And once again, we settle ourselves under the nesting boxes.

The morning light breaks through the velvety darkness, the compound door slams open, and a group of rebels rushes outside. I stir when I notice Tammy's red hair. I squeeze out of our hiding place, holding May in my arms, and groan as my sore and tired body cradles hers.

At the sound of my approaching footsteps, Tammy pivots, her gun raised. Her eyes scan our bloody mess. "Over here! I found them."

We're finally safe. Exhaustion takes the place of my adrenaline and my head spins. I falter just before I pass the small girl over to the red-headed rebel. Once the heavy burden is lifted from my arms, my brain shuts down and I flutter to the floor in slow motion.

"May!" I scream.

"Ann, she is safe. You protected her," Dan soothes.

"What about Gary and the enforcers?"

"You and May are safe and that's all that matters."

"And the chickens?"

He chuckles. "Yes, they're fine too. Not a feather out of place."

I'm safe in my room, I repeat over and over until my heart slows to a normal pace. Jeremy and Sally storm in, and I groan at the heat radiating off their tense bodies. "Oh, yay. Another family reunion."

"What the hell was that? I told you to stop!" Jeremy booms.

"Jeremy, take a breath," Dan suggests. "We're all just a little upset right now."

"*May* was out there!" I sit up too fast and my vision blurs.

"Just relax, Ann. Your blood pressure is a tad high." Dan attempts to calm me again.

"You ran outside *unprepared*! You had no weapons. No backup." Jeremy slams his fist on the counter. "Nobody even *knew* May was in the garden. I would have gone outside *with* you, if you took a second to say something." He squeezes my hand. "Whether you like it or not, you're not alone anymore. We're your family. And family looks out for each other." He kisses my palm.

It's been so long since I've heard those words. Can I believe them?

The three rebels embrace me and shove down my insecurities. I return the hugs and let the tears of joy fall between us.

Out of the Ashes

The next few weeks are as close to heaven as I can get. After the scare with the enforcers, the kids are on their best behavior and the other members aren't sending dirty looks my way. Even Jeremy's icy exterior seems to be thawing. It's not perfect, but it's nice being together when he isn't off saving the world. I'm glad Sally trusts me and doesn't ask him to babysit anymore, but that means he's away from the compound more than he's here. Usually helping others find their way to safety, collecting supplies, or checking in with rebels who refuse to leave their homes behind.

One morning as I eat my breakfast, I snatch a discarded newspaper from across the table. I scan the front page and choke on my eggs. In black and white is a picture of Ryan surrounded by ten beautiful women. The heading reads: *New Selection Begins*. I could claw out Ryan's smug face. He's not even going to acknowledge that I'm missing. Let alone try to search for his son?

I crumble the article between my fist and make my way to blow off some steam. I bang on the office door before pushing my way into the private meeting. I slap the paper down and glare. "Why didn't anyone tell me?"

They don't even need to look at what I'm referring to. Jeremy clears his throat. "We didn't want to upset you."

"If I had some form of warning, I may have been better prepared. Do you realize how painful it was to read? To see that Ryan has completely overlooked his son!" I spit.

"Let's give them a minute." Sally gathers her things and guides her friends towards the exit. She pauses and squeezes my hand. "I'm sorry you found out like this." Then the door closes us in.

"I do know how it feels. Remember, I had to watch my

wife get married. Then attempt to start a new family with Christian." He snarls the name. "I know the suffocating pain of self-doubt. We'll get through this and make them realize everything they're missing." He rests his forehead on mine. "Together we will break through the agony of everything we lost, standing tall amongst the ashes of our pasts. We will seize control of our future. Keep that chin up." He tips my head. "You're a fucking queen; it's time to step out of the shadows and claim your crown."

"I don't want a crown."

"How about a feathered tiara?"

"Does it come with a feather boa?"

"Whatever you want, my feathered dream."

"That's corny."

"Are you okay?" He points to the paper.

"I will be. It just brought up a lot of painful memories... feelings of abandonment. Oh, he must enjoy my suffering." I run my fingers over my son's aerobatics. "Are you ever going to tell me why you hate babies?"

"I don't hate them."

"Just this one?"

He clenches his jaw. "Some memories can be more haunting than the actual event," he whispers. "Do you know what I mean?"

"You know I do, Jeremy. But you know you can tell me anything. I'm here for you."

"What I'm about to tell you stays between us."

"You can trust me."

"Before the rebels knew the selection was official for Prince Christian, Mary and I were a normal newlywed couple. We lived happily at the compound, working towards a better future for our friends and families." He swallows. "The week of the official announcement, Mary found out she was pregnant."

My heart splinters. I wait for more, but nothing comes. "What did she do?"

He stares at the wall. "She decided the *mission* was more important. More essential than our child's life."

"I don't know what to say."

He flicks his palm over his cheek. "When I said I *couldn't* protect your child, it was because I couldn't even protect my own kid. Not because I don't love children."

I kiss his lips softly, trying to absorb his pain so it's less of a burden. "Thank you for telling me." I wipe away my own tears and try to change the mood. "Do you have any good baby boy names?"

"How about *baby*?"

My eyes fall on the leather-bound journals that are back in the office where they belong. "What about Marcus?"

"My ancestor?"

"He was a member of your family?"

"Why do you think we have his journals." He laughs.

"Well, I like the name. It's strong. What do you think it means?"

"Ann, don't you think you and Ryan should discuss this. At a later date?"

"Just because the baby has Ryan's DNA, doesn't mean he has the right to name him. Plus, if I discuss it with you first, I can consider talking him into the name later," I tease.

"Why are *women* so manipulative?"

"What? That's not true! Men are equally manipulative,

if not worse." Our comforting embrace reminds me of more pressing matters. "You know, Jeremy, this will never work."

"What won't work?"

"Us. It's too complicated."

"Isn't that part of the fun?" He tilts his head at my frown. "Ann, it won't be easy. I know we both have our missions to complete. But I want you to know I'm devoted to you. And if we can share a future together, then I'll be the happiest man on earth. But, for now, I'll settle for an intimate friendship with you." His lips twitch into a grin that makes his eyes twinkle.

I quirk a brow. "What? An intimate friendship." I laugh. "Why does that sound dirty?"

"Because of your dirty mind. Man, I'm trying to be romantic here." He presses his body against mine until my back taps the wall. I close the distance and devour his mouth. He groans before pulling away. "That child is kicking me." He rubs his side.

"Get used to it, my intimate *friend*."

"I'm never going to live this down, am I?"

"Nope. Always and forever."

Jeremy lifts me into his arms. I squeal at the sudden movement and snake my wrists around his neck. My doe-like eyes meet his. "Let's get you off your feet, your feathered highness." He maneuvers until he lays me on my bed.

I wiggle my toes. "The first order of business is to massage my aching feet."

"As you wish." He puts his strong, calloused hands to good use as he kneads my arches and I melt into the covers.

A girl could get used to this.

Circle Beard

As we lie in bed, looking through the pregnancy book, Dan and Sally join us. "Feeling better?" Dan asks.

"I owe everyone an apology. The newspaper caught me by surprise, and I lost it. But it won't happen again. I'm committed to going through this." I peer up at them and let out a breath.

Sally sits on the edge of the mattress. "We all have our weaknesses, dear. None of us have come to this point without our own suffering." She pats my leg. "But I can honestly say you've brought us all hope. Thank you for that. It's been a long time coming." She fiddles with a worn scrap of paper. "I thought you may like to see this."

I run my finger over the photo. "Is this who I think it is?"

"That's your family and ours when your mom brought you home from the hospital." She clears her throat. "I snuck that picture into the compound in my bra." She lets out a strained laugh. "I know I shouldn't have risked it, but I couldn't go all that time without a reminder of what I was fighting for." She chokes on a sob. "You're all I have left of my best friends."

I hug her as she lets her memories flow down her cheeks. "Thank you."

"I wish I had more to offer you."

I close her hand over the photo. "You should keep this. And when you're in the neighborhood again, I'll give you more pictures. I even have one with Dad picking a wedgie."

She laughs. "You've always loved photography."

"Yes, but living at the Palace meant I never had time to take any pictures."

197

"Well, make sure you take tons of this little one. They grow up fast." She grabs her sons' hands and squeezes. "And treat them right and they'll make you proud."

Dan smiles. "It's about that time, Mom. I should get back to Sam." He hugs her, then turns to me. "The next time I see you, you'll be a mother." He brushes my hair aside. "I look forward to meeting him soon." He places a soft kiss on my belly.

"I'll walk you out, honey."

Once they leave, Jeremy grumbles, "Are you sure you and Dan were never a couple?"

"We were never in a relationship like that."

"Sometimes the way he interacts with you makes me want to punch him in the face." Jeremy clenches his fists.

"Aw, brotherly love." I smirk at him.

"Come on." He smacks my butt. "We have work to do." He rolls out of bed with me trailing behind.

I glare at the newspaper and run my finger over Ryan's face. Jeremy's chest warms me from behind. I meet his searching gaze. "I'm okay. It's just... so much has changed. After Christian abandoned me during the raid and Ryan rescued me, I hoped we would be together forever. I never imagined..." I let the words fall between us. I squint at the image and giggle. "Although, I do find that mustache and goatee combo kind of hot."

He leans in closer. "I think they're called circle beards." He stands straight with an arched brow. "Wait... you said it's *hot*?"

"I mean, all these other chicks seem to like it."

"So, you're going with the crowd, huh? You like your men hairy?" I wrap my arms around his neck while he entangles his around my waist. "Because I'm telling you now I will *not* accommodate that ridiculous fantasy." I nibble his ear before planting kisses over his neck. He sways. "Mmm… I'll meet you halfway, with a mustache."

"You are perfect exactly the way you are. Just don't lose those abs—*that* is a deal breaker for me."

He runs a hand through my hair. "Deal." Then he kisses me tenderly.

We pull apart so I can change. I scowl up at Jeremy as he removes some fruit and water from the fridge. "My pants don't fit."

"I don't see the problem. Just walk around half-dressed."

"I'm serious!"

He attempts to corner me. "Me too."

I shove a hand between us. "If we keep latching on to one another, we'll never get out there."

He wraps his arms around me again. "Sounds good to me." His lips trail over my shoulder. His body is magnetic, tugging me to it.

"These pregnancy hormones are going to kill me."

"Or help me get lucky."

"Oh, no. You seem to forget… *that* is what got me into this mess." I pat my stomach. "A dress will have to do, for now." I pick a blue sundress with a sigh.

We head out into the compound. I smile as May runs over. "Ann!" She hugs me tight.

Jeremy gives me a quick kiss on the cheek before meeting his comrades in the training arena. "Cheapo," I call over my shoulder as May and I move to the stairs.

The men and women waiting for Jeremy in the arena laugh at my comment and make kissy faces at him. I notice him pinken before he barks, "Enough! Back to training!"

"So, is Jeremy the daddy?"

"You ask a lot of questions."

"I'm a kid. That's what we do."

"The subject is top secret. Sorry."

As we stride into the sunlight, I slip off my shoes and walk barefoot. It feels amazing on my sore feet. I've never been so fat in my life. May runs after the other kids and then we pick weeds in the garden and clean the chicken pen. May taps my arm and points at Scarlett. The red hen pecks the ground and chirps to six little fluff balls hopping alongside her. It's been a long time since I've had the chance to hatch any babies. It's nice to see chicks again. I rub my bruised ankle. Plus, now that Scarlett's nest is clear, her attitude should mellow out. Once we wrap up our chores, I wipe my forehead and lean on the fence as I enjoy the cool breeze.

"Ann?" May smiles up at me.

I pluck a black feather from her hair. "Yes?"

"Tammy told me not to get used to having you around. She said you'll be leaving soon."

"May, I hope I can return one day. But she's right. I'll have to leave soon."

She nods and hugs me tight. "I'll miss you."

The other kids join in. "I'll miss you all too."

After we finish and eat dinner in the dining hall, I slump back to my room. I cringe at the unwanted houseguest. "Tammy, I'm hot, exhausted, and not in the mood."

"I was just coming to check up on you and make sure you didn't have any more stupid ideas."

"Good night, Tammy."

"I heard you and Jeremy are together."

"Well, then your source leads a very boring life if all they have to talk about is me." I push past her and into my room.

"You know he's just doing his job, right? Keeping you happy and in line until the baby comes," she purrs from behind me.

"Tammy. Have you ever heard the saying: If you have nothing nice to say, don't say anything at all?"

"How about... the truth hurts." Then she turns to leave.

By the time I settle under the covers to read for the night, Jeremy comes in. "Is it just me or was this the longest day ever?" He plops face-first on the bed. "By the way, the guys were giving me crap all day about that kiss... You're quiet. No snarky remarks or chicken jokes?"

I ignore him and read my book. "I'm not in the mood."

He looks at the cover. "Dan's book, again?"

"It's the most romance I'll be experiencing for a while."

"I'm willing to change that." He rests his hand on my thigh.

I cross my arms over my chest. "Do you know who greeted me at my door?"

"I would say Santa Claus, but I'm guessing that isn't it."

"Tammy."

He groans. "We've been over this. Just ignore her."

"I've been trying. But she shows up everywhere."

"I'll talk to her."

"Is it true your mom made it your mission to date me?"

"No."

"So her mission was for you to pretend you like me then?"

"No."

"Tammy said it was for you to keep me happy until the baby arrives."

"Ann, come on. We are two very strong-willed individuals. Do you really think my mommy could force me into a relationship? The connection we share is as real as it gets." He crawls over me and grabs my chin. "Don't let Tammy get under your skin."

I lean my forehead on his. "What will I do without you?"

"Let's not waste time thinking about that." He massages my sore shoulders.

"You're going to have to do better than that."

"I'm exhausted."

I pick up my book again. "Guess your brother can keep me company then."

"That's not playing fair," he growls, snatching it by the cover and tossing it aside. Our mouths meet in an intense kiss. He pulls away and starts kissing my neck, trailing caresses and nibbles as he goes.

"Jeremy, I don't want things to go too far," I say, running my hand over his stubble.

He kisses my wrist. "I understand."

As he grabs us a drink, I bite my lip. "Jeremy?"

"Yes?"

"When you walk back, could you possibly lose your shirt along the way?" I bat my lashes.

"That's an awkward request, considering you made me pause some of my best moves a minute ago."

"You see, my logic is that your abs really aren't as amazing as I originally thought. Could you help me decide?"

"I don't think that's a safe idea. It might give you the wrong impression of my intentions." He shuts the fridge. "I'll make you a deal."

"I'm listening."

He leans against the counter. "If you lose your shirt, I'll lose mine."

"I don't know."

He shrugs. "Take it or leave it."

"What if I promise to leave Dan's book on the floor for the night?"

His jaw ticks at the discarded romance novel. Then he tugs his shirt off. "What's the verdict?" He holds his arms out.

"That I was giving you way too much credit." My lip twitches.

He rolls his eyes and pulls his shirt back on just as his mom walks in. "Jeremy?" She quirks a brow.

I bite my lip, holding in my giggle. Jeremy nods at her. "Mom."

She walks past him and sits down on the edge of the bed. "Ann, how are you feeling?"

"Fine."

"Good." She wrings her hands together. "I wanted to run something by you. I was thinking it might be a good idea to move Jeremy into your room. To keep him nearby in case you need assistance. He can sleep on the couch or a mat on the floor."

"What kind of assistance are you expecting I might need?"

"Well, this is your first child, so maybe preterm labor. Or reaching for something high up. Maybe opening a pickle jar." She tilts her head. "What do you think?"

"How could I ever live without a pickle jar opener?" I elbow Jeremy. "What do *you* think? Do you want to open my pickles for me?"

"I know how you can't live without your pickles."

Sally arches a brow. "Has this turned into a dirty joke?"

"Mom. Not that I don't want to be Ann's official pickle man, but what's the real reason for moving me in here?"

"We just caught wind of a group heading this way through the tunnels. They'll be here by nightfall."

"How many are we talking?"

"The last report claimed that fifty people were on their way."

"Can we even support that many?"

"We'll have to do our best. They're compound was compromised and now they're homeless."

"There are more rebel compounds?" I ask.

"Yes, but we have the largest," Jeremy answers. He narrows his eyes. "No more dirty jokes." My lips thin to keep them contained.

"You both can say no, and I'll figure out another solution. I've already bunked as many people together as I can, but it's still not enough."

"If Ann is comfortable with it, so am I."

"Sure, let Jeremy sleep on the floor."

"Thank you both."

"I'll collect my things." Jeremy nods.

"After that, meet us in the tunnels with medical supplies and water for our new arrivals."

"Us?" My ears perk up. "Am I invited?"

Sally pats my hand. "Only if you're feeling up to it. I don't want you to overexert yourself."

"Let's go." I leap up and follow her out to the office.

"We have a situation," Tammy reports upon our arrival; she purses her lips at me.

"Ann is helping, Tammy. You can say whatever it is you were going to say."

My heart soars as Tammy narrows her eyes but continues. "The enforcers who attacked… their vehicle may have had an additional tracker."

"Impossible," Xander argues. I've learned he is the main tech guy around here. There's nothing he can't do with a computer. "I removed it myself."

Tammy shoves papers in Sally's hands. Sally frowns at them. "They've doubled their numbers and patrols."

"And they're constantly in our area," Tammy adds as she points to the map.

"The base could be compromised." Sally falls into a chair. "And we have a group arriving tonight."

"Is there any way we can turn them around, or have them halt at their position until we know it's safe?" Tammy asks.

"No. It's too late to turn them around now."

"Maybe we could move them to another location— temporarily? I'd be willing to open my home up to them, if that'd help," I offer.

205

"You may as well put a bullet in their heads now," Tammy snaps.

"Tammy!" Sally warns.

"No! I'm done with everyone treating her like she's one of us! You're the reason we're being hunted with such force! After that damn speech you made about reporting rebels, they've doubled their enforcers and deaths have skyrocketed. Yet, here you are." She steps closer to me.

"I'm trying to help."

"Well, stop it."

"Girls!" Sally breaks us up before a cock fight erupts. "We're all on the same side and running out of time." She narrows her eyes at Tammy, then she pats my shoulders. "I appreciate the offer, but the Palace sends patrols to your home on a weekly basis so that location is off-limits."

"My things are in Ann's room. Are we ready to move out?" Jeremy interjects. He frowns at our sour expressions. "What'd I miss?"

"I'll tell you on the way." Sally passes the papers to Tammy. "Keep eyes on them. If there's any sign of attack, sound the alarm so we have time to evacuate." She shoos everyone out of the office. "We're running late. Let's move."

True Love

We move between the shadows, weaving around the trees and shrubs. The flashlights illuminate a path only the others can see. I look over my shoulder and cringe. If I get left behind, there's no way I'll be able to find my way back.

"Ouch!" I yelp as something scrapes across my leg.

"Hold still." Jeremy kneels and pulls a thorny bush away from my footpath.

When the beam of light hits the plant, I gasp. "Black roses." I rub my wound. "Where did they come from?"

"They were here when the rebels bought the compound. Rumor is the occupants before us were grafting roses, and these were the product."

"Are they everywhere in the woods?"

"Only in certain areas. They light the path for the lost rebels so they can find their way to safety." Jeremy runs a finger over the leaves, then guides me away.

"It amazes me that the enforcers haven't noticed them yet."

"They aren't the only black roses in the country."

"So how did these become your calling card?"

"Black roses are a dark beauty. They're a powerful symbol of mortality, while signifying the death of an old order in hopes of a brighter era of peace and prosperity."

"You know, some people would say they're just a flower." I tap my shoulder to his.

He snorts. Even in the dark, I know he's rolling his eyes. "And what do you think, my feathered princess?"

I trip over a hidden root, but Jeremy keeps me steady.

207

"Whenever I hit my lowest, I always reach out to chickens and gardens. Because when life's falling apart, they remind me that the world isn't such a harsh place after all. I don't know why, but they always brighten my day. So I do believe they're more than just animals and plants."

"So that's your secret."

"My secret?"

"I've monitored you over the years and even read through your profile, and no matter what pain or mistreatment comes your way, you still have a smile on your face and an attitude to match. It takes an extraordinary individual to go through dark trials without blood coating their hands."

Even in the pitch black, I know he's referring to his own actions.

"The only *secret* I've learned, through all of this mess, is that revenge breeds nothing but destruction. The only way to end the cycle is to be the better person and spread love instead of hatred."

"Hippie," he retorts.

"Call me what you want, but if we're going to change the world, you have to start somewhere, right? And war hasn't worked thus far."

Jeremy's fingers graze mine and we clasp hands. No words are needed. I know Mr. Alpha agrees with me, even if pride keeps him from outwardly admitting it.

"Hold." Sally's voice rings out and we all crouch and freeze. A bird call echoes through the night sky. "Move out," she declares. Suddenly a massive group of people approach us. They look tired and travel-worn. Some of their clothes are ripped so thoroughly they're basically walking around naked. Once they're close enough, the two groups converge and embrace each other like old friends. "All right, everyone, let's get you home. We have clean beds, warm food, and plenty of time to hear your heroic tales."

We stay up late before collapsing in bed. All too soon, an alarm blares in my dream. I swat, attempting to murder the irritating sound. Instead, I slap a body and squeal. What the…? Jeremy grabs me before I can scurry off. The heat from his bare chest rests on my back.

"Jeremy?"

He breathes in my scent. "This is how we'll sleep from now on."

My eyes flutter to the small couch. I can't expect him to sleep on that tiny thing. And a floor mat would destroy my back. I don't want to subject him to that either. I guess we can just be adults. Adults with boundaries.

"Wear a shirt next time."

"Why?"

"Because it's too much of a temptation," I grumble.

"You're stronger than that."

"Do you think I also have the *patience* to not throw your alarm clock across the room?"

"Point taken."

"Why are you getting up so early anyway?"

"These abs don't just appear on their own." He winks.

I rub my eyes. "What I wouldn't give for a cup of

coffee."

"Caffeine isn't good for the baby."

"You know what *is* good for the baby?" I walk my fingers over his bicep.

"Pickles?"

"Sleep." I slam his pillow into his face.

"You're not a morning person. I'll add that to your file."

"You'll do no such thing! I'm part of the team now, remember? No need to keep tabs on me."

He smacks my butt. "I'll put all the tabs on you I want," he growls before leaving the bed.

As much as I don't want to get up, I'm too wound up to sleep. I stretch before starting the day. As I turn the corner, Jeremy is beating a punching dummy, sweat glistening along his contoured body. I step forward but falter as Tammy tosses him a towel. They exchange words, then she whispers in his ear. Flashbacks of Ryan and Mary hit me hard in the gut. Am I missing something again?

"Ann, you're up early." I meet Sally's searching gaze. "Is everything okay?"

"Your son's alarm clock woke me up."

"My apologies. I'll make sure to talk to him about that."

I swallow the bile pooling in my mouth. "We've already talked. You don't have to worry about it. I should start on chores."

I take the steps two at a time, eagerly putting distance between Jeremy's abs and my spinning self-doubt. The door shuts and I lean against it. The warmth of the early morning sun glitters across my skin as my mind wanders to another time. When I had everything I needed. I didn't have to worry about what would happen tomorrow. Movement catches my attention.

"Are you sleeping with the chickens again?"

May pivots. "Ann, I woke up early and came out here to check on the chicks with my new friend."

A hunched figure extends a hand. "My name's Betty. Pleasure to meet you." I shake her thin palm. How old is she? She could easily pass for one hundred. Thunder rolls through the sky and forces a breeze to stir the dry ground. "My bones are aching—rain's finally coming."

"I should grab their breakfast," May announces before she runs off. As the door closes, the clouds shudder and let go of their bounty.

Betty rubs her hands together, cleaning the soil from under her fingernails. "We were beginning to lose hope. We thought the clouds were going to abandon us. But here they are." She upturns her exhausted face and rain kisses her cheeks. "We're at the mercy of mother nature, yet she always provides. No matter what, we get what we need. But in her time, not our own."

Her words settle deeper than the chill of the atmosphere. Thunder vibrates my toes. It's a reminder that no matter where I've been in life, the universe has never abandoned me. I swipe at my lashes, tears mingling with the cold droplets. I won't lose hope, because when the storm clouds roll away and the sun warms the grass, I'll be waiting for my happily ever after.

Betty cackles and spins in the sudden downpour. I can't help but smile. She may be my elder, but her outlook on life is something to aspire to. I squeak as my wrists are tugged and she encourages me to join her. We flop in the mud until the storms move on.

"Thank you, Betty." I turn to face her but pause. The older woman is sound asleep beneath the clearing skies. I hear crunching grass as Jeremy approaches. I grind my jaw, remembering his interaction with Tammy.

211

"Mom told me to turn off my alarm for a while." He leans on the fence of the chicken pen.

"And I told her you weren't sleeping with me anymore," I lie.

"I never knew you hated alarms that much."

"Why was Tammy whispering in your ear this morning?"

"Ann…"

"Don't *Ann* me! She's been nothing but mean and manipulative to me. And then I come out to find her flirting with you, and you not doing *anything* to fend off her advances!" I poke him in the chest.

"Woah, you went from zero to murderous in two seconds. Calm down. Tammy is just a friend."

"So, now she's a friend? Before she was nothing." I step away and he grabs my arm.

"*Don't* do this," he snarls.

I tug my wrist back. "Do what, exactly?"

"Pull away from me."

"Then be honest with me."

"Tammy and I go way back. We were *raised* together. Then, when Mary died, she thought I would turn to her for more intimate company. But I didn't. Although she keeps asking me, I still tell her no."

"What's she telling you about me?" I know it isn't as simple as he says it is; Tammy is way too controlling.

"She's trying to fill my head with lies, saying you're using me as a shield until we bring you back to the Palace, then you'll turn on me. On all of us."

"Why does she think pitting us against each other will get her what she wants?"

"Is her plan working?" When I don't answer, he continues. "You can't keep doing this. You're acting like a roller coaster of emotions with all these ups and downs. Why can't you just learn to *trust* somebody other than yourself?" He tugs on my wet hair. "What can I do to prove myself a trustworthy gentleman?"

"It's not that easy. I've been hurt too many times. It needs to build gradually, through actions not just honey-laced words."

"Challenge accepted." He grins. "Can I still sleep in your room and help you with your pickle jars?"

I shove his cocky smirk aside. "Stop. I'm being serious."

"How about some breakfast? Or do you need time for that too? Maybe you want to wait until the hen craps out the butt nugget? So you can collect it fresh yourself." He doesn't let me answer as he pulls me back inside.

We settle with our *butt nuggets* in the dining hall. It's packed since the others came in last night. The noise is deafening compared to the normal chirping.

"I heard May was sleeping outside again." Sally squeezes in next to me. "Any suggestions on a disciplinary action?"

"What about meditation? I can switch our defensive training to meditation and breathing exercises. That way she can learn to relax her mind and hopefully sleep better."

"Great idea." She stabs at her lettuce.

"Is something wrong?" I question.

Sally glances around before leaning towards me. "Winter is fast-approaching, and the crops and eggs were estimated for less people. If I can't figure out how to get more supplies, we're looking at possible starvation."

"Have we talked to our sympathizers?" Jeremy asks.

She nods. "The enforcers are cracking down on them, especially after our little bank trip. They're scared and we're running out of time."

"We can access our emergency supplies of MREs and ration servings. That'll buy us a few months." He squeezes his mom's hand. "We've survived through worse—don't worry. Plus, Dan can bring some items to us too."

"Sally, they're asking for you in the office," a woman announces.

"Thank you. I'll check in with you both later."

When she leaves, I pivot to Jeremy. "What are we going to do?"

"I'm late for training, but we can talk more about this tonight."

I groan. "I have to wait all day?"

"Hey, you can meditate and do your *breathing* exercises to help relax you." He walks towards the training area, laughing and shaking his head along the way.

Maybe Jeremy was right to poke fun at my suggestion. It's very hard to get children to calm their minds. I have to take multiple breaks to let them run out their abundance of energy. By the end of the day, I'm ready to crash.

When I get out of the shower and wrap a towel around me, I groan. I forgot to *bring* my clothes into the bathroom. Having a boy in the room complicates things. I peek out, and not seeing Jeremy, I tiptoe to the dresser. As I pivot to return to the bathroom, he enters, blood dripping from his nose.

I rush over with a tissue. "What happened?"

His throat rumbles as I put pressure on his wound. "Stop coddling me. It's just a bloody nose. Back off. I'm not one of your pupils. I'm a grown-ass man."

I whip my hand away. "Okay."

"Sorry. It's been a long day," he grunts. I bite my tongue and turn towards the bathroom. He catches my wrist and pulls me to him. "I think out of *all* your outfits, this one is my favorite." His eyes darken before he wraps his arms around me. His lips tease my neck.

My body melts into his. "Jeremy," I whisper softly. He redirects my hands from holding the towel to intertwining around his neck. The towel slips and I squeal before I shove him and collect the discarded fabric. "What has gotten into you?"

His lips twitch. "I needed to see that smile. It's all I've been able to think about."

"You're a caveman."

"No, I'm a man hungry with desire." He runs his tongue over my collarbone. "So hurry up and change before I release the beast and throw you under the covers like you deserve."

I do exactly what he suggests. When I return, Jeremy and his mother are engrossed in an intense conversation.

"Did the new newspaper arrive?" I point to the paper. Jeremy's face says it all. I'm *not* going to like what's being reported. He hands it to me, but before he releases his grasp, our eyes meet. He doesn't speak, but I know he's asking a silent question. A guarantee that I won't lose my shit when I uncover the source of his anxiety. I lift my chin in agreement and he relents.

There, on the front page, is Ryan and two beautiful women, announcing the elimination of the other eight prospects. Jeremy's chest warms my back as I read through it. The heat sends a comforting tremor through my cold skin.

Sally pats my hand. "King Ryan is expediting the process."

"How are we countering this?" Jeremy clenches his fists.

Sally doesn't answer immediately; instead, she rubs my arm. "What are you thinking about?"

My fingertip glides over Ryan's smile. "He isn't the same guy I fell for. Do you know what he told me about love? He said I would know I was in love when that person was somebody I could spend the rest of my life with. Someone I could tell anything to and do anything with. And when I saw them, I'd smile from ear to ear while looking forward to seeing them again when they're away. I've been away. For months," I push out the last two sentences.

Jeremy twirls me around. "Forget that prick," he spits. "He doesn't know what the hell he's talking about. Love isn't a *feeling*; it's an action-oriented *commitment*. It's a choice to never give up on each other. To give your best to someone, even when they're at their worst. And above all, it means helping someone even when they're in no position to repay you." He's doing it again, communicating with his stare. Demanding that I understand *our* relationship is based on love, much more than what Ryan and I—or even Christian and I—ever had. Only time will tell how accurate that is.

Vote for Peace

I crush Jeremy's screeching alarm clock. "Jeremy!"

He tugs me against him. "Five more minutes." He snuggles into my neck.

"*This* is going to be across the room in five minutes." I gesture towards the bane of my existence.

"But I was having an incredible dream." He grins at me. "Never mind, I wasn't dreaming."

"That was cheesy. You need some new lines, old man." As much as I want to spend all day in this warm bed, my muscles are screaming at me to move.

"You're such a tease." He tries to pull me back but fails.

I get dressed and do my morning routine. As I'm brushing my hair, Jeremy climbs out of bed and collects his tactical pants. When he passes the door, he reaches in and hits my butt. "Hurry up."

My mouth falls open and I glare at the back of his head. "*I'm* ready."

The dining hall is too full so we grab our food and eat in the office. As suggested, everyone is offered portioned meals.

"You know how I feel about you eating in here." Sally sweeps up crumbs and throws them away. "I don't want bugs."

"Why are you so tense?" Jeremy pokes a fork at her.

My gaze follows his utensil. She's shaking like a leaf. "Sally?"

Her eyes meet ours. "We're running out of time. The enforcers are planning something big. If the Palace doesn't act soon, I'm afraid we'll have to move, or risk being destroyed."

217

Jeremy hugs her. "Don't lose hope."

"Maybe I don't have what it takes to protect our people anymore." She swipes at her eyes. "I'm failing them."

"No, you're not."

My brain goes a mile a minute. I don't want any more bloodshed. We have to do something. "I have an idea." All eyes land on me. "We do a video chat and let the Palace see me with my belly in all its glory." I lay my hand on my abdomen. "Then we set up a meeting between all parties, in public or at the Palace, so we can talk about a compromise. It could even buy us time and distract the enforcers so we can sneak people to a safer location."

"What do we have to lose?" Sally sighs. "I'll talk to everybody and put it to a vote."

"Hey, Ann?" Tammy pops her head in. "Can I speak to you for a minute?"

Jeremy narrows his eyes, but I rub his shoulder. "It's okay." I brush past Tammy. "I need to take my vitamins. Why don't we go to my room."

Once the door closes, she begins. "I don't hate you."

"Well, you show love in the oddest ways."

"I never said I loved you. I just don't hate you."

"Then what do you call it?"

"Listen, Jeremy is my best friend. We grew up together." She shrugs. "I don't want him getting hurt again. It was extremely hard to watch him lose Mary." She sits on the edge of the bed. "He loved her."

"I know."

"But… I see he also loves you." She sighs.

"Why are you telling me this?"

"Because I think you need to know."

218

I arch a brow at Miss Fluctuating Emotions. "Thank you?"

"Ann, I did some mean things to you... out of spite. But after you rescued Jeremy and then May, it made it really hard to want to plot your demise." She smirks.

I cross my arms over my chest. "I never intended to be anyone's hero. I'm just doing what's right."

"I know you are. Everyone does."

I take in her words, and I can't help how high my heart soars to know they have faith in me. My new family. The baby kicks and I rub him gently.

"May I?" Tammy waves a hand.

"Sure."

She warms my stomach with her open palm. "Does it feel weird? When *it* moves?"

"He."

She frowns. "Sorry... when *he* moves?"

"I feel like an alien is expanding inside me, and at any minute, it's going to burst out."

She laughs, then leaps up. "He moved!" She looks down with a grin.

"He's probably reminding me to take my pills."

"Oh, okay. I'll just let you do what you have to do."

My teeth dig into my cheek. She's trying to make amends. "Do you have any dirt on Mr. Perfect?"

Her eyes glitter and I know we're on our way to becoming friends. "How much time do you have?"

Tammy is a lot like me, and it brightens my day when she talks about her and Jeremy growing up together. They didn't have much, so the little things they did have were meaningful. And they were always getting into trouble, which led them to being good at their jobs now.

"What is it you do exactly?"

"I help strategize and bring down an iron fist when necessary."

"What did your father do?"

Her eyes flutter. "He was a nurse, so he took care of most of the medical stuff."

I can tell it's a tough subject for her, so I move on. "What about Jeremy's dad?"

Her jaw ticks. "He was a lying, cheating dictator who got *exactly* what he deserved."

I flinch. "What happened to him?"

"Sally shot him."

"What?"

"It's her story to tell. But trust me, she had no choice but to put him down."

I swallow and stash this information away, so I can ask Sally or Jeremy about it at a later date. Because it doesn't make sense to me. Sally is one of the gentlest people I know.

"Why do you think the Royals won't publicly acknowledge that I'm missing?"

"By Royals, you mean King Ryan, right? Well, I suspect he's being pushed to continue to exhibit strength and unity. Especially after the King's death." She shrugs. "Plus, I bet he's suffering from depression. I mean, think about it. He lost his father, his brother, and the woman he loved was abducted." She taps her head. "That shit messes with your mind."

I rub my arms. She isn't lying. It does. Maybe I've been

too tough on Ryan.

"Hey." She snaps her fingers in my face. "Stop that. He doesn't deserve your pity."

"But you just said…"

"You asked me why I thought he wasn't coming for you. But he has access to the best therapists and treatment the world has to offer. He only needs to reach out and take it," she spits. "If *we* can go through this turmoil and survive with compassion and love, so can he. It's not that hard to be a good person."

We turn and notice Sally snuck into the room while we were chatting. "We're going to move forward with your suggestions. So, get ready, Ann. It looks like you'll get to see your Palace family soon."

Brittany Putzer

The Black Rose Beginnings

A look inside Sally, Jeremy, and Mary. And how
their journey with the Black Rose began.

Sally  Age 35

Laughter fills the air as everyone gathers around the Christmas tree. It's twinkling lights reflect brightly in the children's eyes as they gawk at the colorful packages nestled underneath its branches. Their squeals of delight ring throughout the house as they rip through their gifts, producing a rainbow of colors as strips of paper flutter to the floor.

When my husband Willard sits next to me, I place my hand on his leg and his twinkling blue eyes meet mine. Then he returns my smile before he focuses on our two young sons as they continue their assault on the unsuspecting boxes.

He runs his hand through his blonde hair and leans into the couch cushions. "You really spoiled them this year, Sally."

"I wish it could be more. They're great kids."

"If you gave them any more, they would be spoiled rotten. Besides, love can't be bought, my dear."

The two boys start assembling their action figures and pretend to zoom 15,000 feet in the air, circling the world in their combat flyers. They chuckle when one of the black wings falls off and bounces on the dog sleeping at my feet. The fur baby yelps and takes off as fast as he can into the kitchen, causing him to slide on the tile and slam headfirst into the back door. I roll my eyes as the boys grab their stomachs and roll on the ground with tears of amusement.

I push off the couch to check on the poor pup. "Oh, Ruffy, are the boys being mean to you again? Come here, sweetie, I promise I won't hurt you."

The greying mutt places his head in my hands and nudges my palms. I stroke his dulling fur and kiss the top of his head. This sweet thing was brought home with Jeremy on his first day of kindergarten and now those two are inseparable. I never liked dogs. They were smelly, unclean, and got into too much trouble. But this one's the exception. He always seems to sense when I need him the most and never misses the chance to snuggle into my lap while I grade papers late into the night. Ruffy lifts his head, and his ears prick up. I frown as he takes off to the front door and barks before the doorbell rings.

"Sally, bring the boys out back," Willard whispers as he looks out the peephole.

His tone sends chills up my spine. What's going on? I won't leave my husband's side. "Jeremy, grab your brother and go to the shed until I come and get you. Go now."

Jeremy does as he's told and tugs Dan along with him without a backwards glance. I bite my lip as they silently close the back door behind them. I nod towards Willard, who's assessing the stranger currently standing in front of our house. "Hello, can I help you?"

"Willard Sumptor?"

"Yes, that's my name, officer. What can I do for you?"

"By order of King Mark, you are to be branded for your involvement with the Black Rose terrorist group."

"I'm sorry, officer, but you must be mistaken. I'm not involved with any terrorist group."

The front door splinters as it's kicked open, and my husband is thrown to the floor while handcuffs are slapped around his wrists. I clasp a hand over my mouth as the chaos unfolds. Ruffy senses my panic and jumps at the officer's leg. There is a short struggle before the dog is kicked across the room with a yelp and a deafening crunch. I dash to Ruffy's limp body, but the officer pulls me back before securing me in my own set of cuffs.

"By order of the King, all family members are to be branded along with the accused." The officer tugs us outside and throws us into the car.

They rough us up, in an attempt to extract information, while further threatening our lives. We disappoint them with our lack of cooperation, so they resort to torture. They hold our wrists and jam a scalding metal 'R' on the sensitive skin of our hands. The stench of burnt flesh stings my nose before the mind-numbing pain scorches my body. I promised myself I wouldn't cry in front of these monsters, but I fail as I crumble at their feet in agony. I curse the rebels I've met prior because they lied to me. They said when they were branded, they passed out and woke up in an unknown street or an empty grassy field.

Neither of these happened to me.

When I don't succumb to the pain, they continue to question me to the point that I'm struggling to breathe and blood is dripping from the corners of my mouth. I spit in their face as I attempt to hold on to my inherited stubbornness. The enforcer wipes the saliva from his cheek and laughs. He snatches my hair until my neck stretches and burns. "You will regret that, you little wench!"

They take turns using my body as they see fit. I pinch my eyes closed, wait for my inevitable end, and thank the higher powers that my husband's passed out so he doesn't have to witness this brutality.

"Sally? Can you walk?"

I'm in an open field. Is this heaven? I turn and cough violently. I clutch my side as I watch blood dribble to the ground.

Willard wraps an arm around my waist and lifts me up. "We must move quickly before someone sees us."

I place one foot in front of the other. The only thing keeping me from collapsing is knowing that my children need me. It's hours before we finally reach any recognizable landmark. I gaze at the white church steeple a moment before spitting on the ground. As we limp past the building's exterior, I fight the urge to fling up my middle finger.

"Just a few more hours and you may lie down in your own bed and rest."

"We can't lead them back to the boys, Willard, or they will suffer the same fate as us. AnnaBelle and Jack can look after them until it's safe."

"It's already too late for them. If we don't make it home before school starts, the officers will find the boys and brand them there."

The sun is just peaking up over the horizon when we finally make it to our front door.

"Jeremy? Dan?" Willard yells into the dark house.

"Where could they be?"

"Don't panic. You know they wouldn't have gone far. Why don't you go check with AnnaBelle, while I start packing the essentials and burn any evidence of our friends and family so they can't be tracked." Willard gently kisses the top of my head, anchoring me to the present and easing some of the dread. "We need to hurry. We don't have much time. They will come to raid the house soon."

My legs automatically hobble to our nearest neighbor's

227

farm. When the door opens, AnnaBelle's hazel eyes widen to the size of saucers. She helps me to the couch and grabs me a cup of water. "Sally, what happened to you?"

"Did the boys come by here?"

"They're outside with Jack, gathering eggs for breakfast." I stand but fall back on the cushions. "Take it easy. I told Jack the boys came over to wish Ann a Merry Christmas." She gives me a pointed stare. "I thought you and Willard were being careful helping the... *them*?"

We have no secrets between us. We've been friends for far too long for that. I shake my head as tears burn my eyes. "Of course we've been careful. Do you think I'd risk my children's lives? I'm not sure what happened."

"Will you be safe where you're going?" she gasps. "Will I ever see you again?"

"We'll be safe." That's all I can promise her. And even that's not a guarantee. I watch the soft-spoken woman sitting to my left. She's like a sister to me. We even vowed that our oldest children would marry one day and unite us legally, since our kids are so close in age. "Oh, Anna. You know we need to go into hiding now. It's no longer safe for us. But maybe one day our children will find each other." I don't add in: if they *survive* and don't get branded themselves. AnnaBelle swipes at her eyes as she tends to my wounds. I notice her lids have dark circles under them. "Are you sick?"

"The doctors found more cancer. I was going to tell you after your birthday celebration this weekend." She pats my leg. "Don't fret about me. You know I'll fight this just as strongly as I did the last time. Remember?"

"I've tried to forget those days. You were throwing up while you were trying to finish your midterms. It was hard seeing you go through all those treatments."

"But I made it through, didn't I? I'm a force to be

reckoned with. By this time next year, we will be together and celebrating another victory."

I know she's hiding something else from me, but I let it go. "You know what to do, right? Burn everything that could tie you to us. *Immediately.* Don't say our names to anyone, not even Ann. Let her forget she ever knew us."

We share a look. Unspoken memories of our childhood drift between us. We know this will be the last time we see each other. Rebels never last long once they're branded. If anyone knows we're friends, AnnaBelle and her family will face the consequences of my actions. And I could never let that happen.

I lift my chin and swear on my children's lives that I'll be stronger. Smarter. That I'll survive this ordeal at all costs.

Jeremy  Age 12

The darkness weighs heavy on our hearts, as we listen for our parents. Mom told us to go to the old potting shed in our backyard, but that was hours ago. Dan grips my elbow. "Jeremy, how long are we going to stay out here?"

"Mom told us to stay put until they come for us."

"What if they killed them and they never return?"

My hand flies across what I assume is his face. The sudden contact followed by his grunts tells me I hit my target. "Don't *ever* say that again, especially in front of me," I seethe. My parents wouldn't approve of me hitting my younger brother, but it's the only way to snap him out of his negative thinking and get him to focus on what's important. We continue our wait but now he's standing as far away from me as he can. He shuffles towards the shed door, and I grab a limb to stop him.

"Let go of me. Mom can't expect us to sit here forever. I need to use the bathroom."

A pungent smell has me wrinkling my nose. This *cannot* be happening right now. I fumble around to find a bucket or shovel, but darkness has taken over everything. I curse as my hand runs over a sharpened blade on one of the shelves. "You're not five years old. You can hold it in. Just squeeze your cheeks together."

"I am going to crap on you if you don't open this door right now."

As if on cue, that rancid stench assaults my nose again, and I gag. What the hell did he eat? I grumble as I open the door. A bird flutters past at the motion and into a tree, landing on a branch and chirping at us. The sky is cloudless, and the cool breeze helps to fan out Dan's odor. However, once the wind kicks up and the breeze carries the ungodly smell, even the bird flutters far away.

Dan pushes past me and runs forward, his legs pressed together as he enters the house. I race in front of him to check the interior. The Christmas tree is still twinkling with wrapping paper littered all around it. So much has changed. I pick up the toy plane that landed on Ruffy.

"Get out of my way, you big idiot." Dan shoves me and I can see that he will need to change his pajama bottoms when he's done. He slams the bathroom door and explosions commence.

"Ruffy, come here, boy. The bad guys are gone." Normally, my best friend would have padded over by now, his tail going a mile a minute. "Dan, did Ruffy follow us outside?"

"You mean when you forced me into the shed? I don't know. I wasn't paying attention."

He's no help at all. I place the toy on the counter and push open Mom's bedroom door. Ruffy likes to hide under her bed during lightning storms. Maybe he's there. "Ruffy? What are you doing under there? Come here." He's scared stiff. I don't blame him. I belly crawl closer. A lump forms in the back of my throat and suffocates me. "Hey. Wake up," I squeak, and my eyes well as I rub his hard stomach. I wait for his chest to rise with a breath. When it doesn't, my tears plop onto his fur. "Ruffy, what happened to you? Who could do something like this?"

Dan comes around the corner and falls to his knees. "Ruffy, are you okay?" I shake my head in response, handing the limp pup to my brother. He cradles our best friend in his arms and rocks back and forth with tears wetting his own cheeks. "Why would they kill him, Jeremy? He wasn't a threat. He wouldn't even hurt a fly."

"Because they are fucking monsters, Dan. They don't care who they hurt to get what they want." I swipe at my face and see his wide eyes watching me. "Why do you think Mom told us to hide in the shed? These people will

231

kill children at the drop of a hat. I'm going to get a shovel. Meet me outside in ten minutes." On my way out, I grab Dad's gun and pocket it. He hid it in a keypad lockbox, but I've seen him open it enough times to know the code.

"Do you even know how to shoot that?" Dan follows me outside with Ruffy resting on his chest.

"Dad has been teaching me since I was your age."

"Why hasn't he taught me?"

"Do you have any interest in *shooting*? Even for your own protection."

"I'm sure I could talk to them and explain why killing isn't necessary."

"Yes, you do that. Talk your way out of a life-threatening situation. Idiot."

"It could work. Words are powerful. Especially if you use them correctly."

"Oh, yes. Paper cuts are super dangerous." The shovel vibrates my arms as it hits solid ground. I work on making a grave for Ruffy behind the shed. Memories push past my eyes and down my face.

"Jeremy, you need to stop. You're bleeding."

I stare at my blistered hand. The pain feels good. It's better than the numbness in my heart. "Throw him in." Dan kisses Ruffy's head, then passes him to me. My lip trembles. I kneel and place our dog inside the shallow grave. "I promise your death will not go unavenged. I will find out who did this to you and put a bullet through their chest."

"Jeremy, you don't mean that. They were just doing what the King told them to do."

I clutch Dan's shirt and pull him upright. "Then I will put a bullet in the King." I spit on the ground. "That damn coward. Hiding behind his goons, while he sits safely on his blood-covered throne. He is a pathetic lifeform that needs to be destroyed." Dan grabs the shovel and lifts soil over Ruffy. When the tool becomes too heavy for him, he starts kicking at the dirt. I place my hand on his shoulder and squeeze, and he buries his face in my chest. I pat his back until his body stops trembling. "We need to get away from the house, in case the officers come back looking for us."

"Do you think Mom and Dad told them we were here?"

"If they did, it was because they were tortured first. They would never willingly give up our location."

"Do you really think they were tortured?" Dan's green eyes burn into my icy ones, pleading for me to lie to him. Just one simple lie. I mean, I am his big brother, and I should protect him.

"There you two are."

I grab the gun and aim, but quickly lower it as I blink up at Mom's friend, AnnaBelle.

"Ann helped me make some fresh cinnamon rolls. Why don't you come with me until your parents return?" She takes the weapon from my hands. Then she wraps her arms around us and squeezes. We walk the back way to her house, avoiding the main road. Our feet thump over the tall grass.

"Did she put extra icing on some for me, Ms. AnnaBelle?"

She smiles at Dan. "Yes, of course she did. She always looks forward to seeing you guys."

"Did Mom contact you?"

"I'm sorry, Jeremy, but no. I saw the officers pull up from our window—they took your parents with them. I tried waiting as long as I could before interfering.

But when they didn't return, and I saw you two in the house… well, I figured you might need something to put in your bellies." She rubs my arm.

"Can we play with the chickens while we wait for Mom and Dad?"

"Absolutely, Dan. I'm sure your parents will be over any minute now."

I hear her voice crack before a tear falls down her cheek. She's Mom's oldest and dearest friend, and it's going to be hard for them to say goodbye and erase each other from their lives, now that my parents have been branded. Dad told me stories of other rebels and how they had to leave everything and everyone behind in order to keep their friends and families safe. AnnaBelle and Mom will have to burn photos, letters, and anything else that could link them together. If not, AnnaBelle's family will be branded, or worse. I rub my smooth wrist. We are lucky the officers didn't know about us. But that won't last. Eventually, we'll be tracked down and branded just for being the children of suspected criminals.

"Jack. Ann. Look who I found outside playing. I lured them over with promises of cinnamon rolls."

Ann walks over with a baby chicken in her arms. She nods at us and then smiles at AnnaBelle. "Mom, Dad needs your help outside. One of the hens got stuck in your lilac bush again."

"Can't you climb in there and grab her, Ann?"

"I would, but then I might touch a spider again." Ann cringes.

"Boys, you may help yourself to the cinnamon rolls on the counter. Don't be shy. I'll be right back."

"Why are you holding a chicken?" I arch a brow at Ann.

"Why don't you mind your own business." She sticks her tongue out and turns towards the kitchen.

"Wait. Ann. What is the chicken's name?" Dan ambles over to her. I roll my eyes as they talk and pet the baby chick. Stupid girls. Who needs them? I grab a cinnamon roll and bite into it, thinking about Ruffy and my parents. I vow to one day bring down the Monarchy—single-handedly if need be. Then all this pain and suffering will cease to exist.

Hope never tasted so sweet.

Mary  Age 12

The ruler slaps across my knuckles and I bite back a yelp. "Mary, you better start paying attention or you will be sent to your room without dinner."

I blink the tears away before they can fall and my mom can chastise me further. I nod because I know it is better not to provoke her nasty temper by speaking out. My mother smiles as she places the ruler on the corner of my desk. Both a threat and a reminder.

"Now, let's try this again, please. Name the states, in alphabetical order."

I swallow the lump in my throat and do my best to list them, but I miss one.

"Honestly, Mary! Don't you want to marry Prince Christian and become Queen?"

"Yes, mother."

"Then stop acting like an uneducated moron and pay attention to what I am attempting to teach you. Or you will fail, like everything else you do around here. Now, hold out your hand." My mother grabs her favorite weapon and swings.

"Mom. Dad wants us in the dining room."

"Max, what have I told you about interrupting me while I am teaching your sister?"

My brother holds out his palms with a grin. Max is younger than me and a complete oddball. He enjoys our mother's barbaric teaching methods.

"Come along, Mary. You can just skip dinner tonight while you study your states. It wouldn't kill you to lose a few pounds anyway."

I glare at my mom's departing figure. "You're welcome

for rescuing you," Max whispers.

"Thanks, Max. Now I don't get dinner."

"Don't worry, sis, I will sneak you some table scraps." He pats my head like a pet and I narrow my eyes. Sensing my foul mood, he runs off towards my mother. And I shake my head as I follow close behind like the loyal dog they've groomed me to be.

"We've received word that a group of enforcers picked up the Sumptor family at their residence yesterday morning." My dad's secondhand man and Palace insider, Derek, stops and turns to us as we enter. "My-my, look at my little niece and nephew. You grow every time I see you." Although we are not family, he still insists on addressing us as such. I think it's so we feel comfortable around him, but that won't be happening. Derek ruffles Max's hair and hugs me, holding on too long and smelling my hair before releasing the embrace. "How is your training coming along, Mary?"

"It would go better if I could remember the states in alphabetical order, Uncle Derek."

He chuckles and turns to my mom as she rolls her eyes. "Maybe you need a different teacher? I'm willing to give it a shot."

"Derek, it's not her teacher that is the problem," Mother spits.

"Derek. Focus. Where are the Sumptors now?" My dad interrupts.

"The King was informed that they were left for dead in the valley, north of their home. The report said they were beaten to near death before they were released."

I swallow back my bile. King Mark is ruthless with his treatment of the rebels. Although Father is highly regarded amongst his supporters, and has many people inside the Palace keeping their ears to the wall, it is increasingly obvious that the King is smarter than he originally anticipated.

My dad scratches his cheek as he glances at me and Max on the couch. "Willard Sumptor is a strong soldier and I have no doubt that *he* is alive and well, but I don't know much about his wife or children. It is a real tragedy."

"Should I dispatch a recovery team to pick them up?"

"Unfortunately, it is too dangerous, especially if King Mark is tracking their whereabouts. Willard will make it to the compound in his own time."

"Won't it be difficult to travel with an injured wife and children?" I frown at my dad.

They all turn towards me as if they just noticed I'm sitting here. Derek squeezes my thigh. "Only the strong will survive, Mary, and *that* is what the Black Rose needs: strong and capable individuals."

I take in Max's innocent face, then my dad's stoicism. "Please send out a recovery team, Father. I implore you. The children were beaten by no fault of their own and deserve some protection from a sympathetic leader. Maybe if you show sympathy in their time of need, they will reward you with loyalty and devotion in yours."

A slow smile spreads over my father's face. "Spoken like a true politician, my dear. Derek, send a group and assist them to the compound for medical treatment."

Derek nods and walks out without a backwards glance. And I shiver. That man gives me the creeps. I stand but a hand flashes across my face and I fall to my knees, cradling my cheek.

"You insolent girl. Don't ever question your father in front of a subordinate. It makes him seem weak and incompetent."

My father places a hand on Mother's shoulder. "That is enough, Nicole. Mary knew what she was doing. She was only reminding Derek of her compassion and leadership skills. Now he will return to the King and speak highly of our future Queen." He winks at me. "And Prince Christian will have no doubt in his mind when he picks our sweet Mary as his wife when the time comes."

True to Mother's word, I'm sent to my room to study instead of sitting with my family at the dinner table. There is a knock, and Max pops his head inside and tosses me two rolls. I drop my history book and catch them. "Thank you."

"Luke called and told Dad that the recovery was a success."

"Did he say if the children made it?"

"I only caught half of the conversation before Mom spotted me eavesdropping." He holds up a bandaged hand. "She got so mad she forked me."

I bite into my roll. My mother is getting more dangerous every day. It's one thing to hit me, but my brother is only eight years old. "Max, you shouldn't listen in on adult conversations; it's rude."

"You sound exactly like Mom. If I'm meant to be trained as a spy, I should start acting like one."

I ruffle his hair. "Try not to grow up too fast. You are young and have your whole life ahead of you. Now go and get ready for bed before she comes in here and finds out you snuck me food."

"You are young too, Mary."

239

"Yes, but what does Mother say? I was bred for a single purpose. My life is already laid out before me, but *you* have options."

"You can run away and start your own life. We could run away together."

"I love your enthusiasm. But I need to do this for the thousands of rebels who've lost their families, friends, and freedom. That's why I'm here. To become Queen and slowly free the rebels from the inside. Create sympathy, where currently there is none."

Max wrinkles his nose. "You sound like Dad. Do you practice that in front of the mirror every day?"

I shove him out. "Good night."

When the door clicks closed, I suck in a breath. Max is right. I do repeat that in front of my mirror. Because if I don't, I will fall into despair.

Before the sun rises over the horizon, I'm dressed and at the breakfast table. The butler smiles as he sets down biscuits, gravy, bacon, and sausage with a side of orange juice.

"Thank you, James, everything smells delicious."

"You are most welcome." He looks around. "We hate it when your mother withholds food from you. You're a growing young lady."

I do my best to pace myself. If I eat too much, too fast, I will be throwing up—in a very unladylike fashion.

"Good morning, Mary."

"Good morning, Father."

I arch a brow at my father's casual attire. He normally

wears business suits. He sips his coffee, looking over his rim. "I'm traveling to the compound today to question the Sumptors. If you are up for the challenge, you should join me."

"You mean I can actually go with you?"

"Mary, your mother is doing a wonderful job of teaching you the basic knowledge needed to be Queen, but you are in desperate need of a more hands-on experience. Plus, how can you continue to train so hard without knowing who or what you are fighting for? It's high time you meet our people and interact with them regularly. Not only for your sake but theirs too. Because you, my dear, are going to bring them hope and strength when they need it most."

"Why do I need to be more hands-on, Father? What would a queen need with that sort of skill set?"

"When you are Queen, you will have an army of men and women at your beck and call, and I expect you to fight side by side with them, as all leaders should. Now, finish up your breakfast. We have a long drive ahead of us."

With a newfound eagerness, I devour my food. I was bred for *more*. To not only be Queen but a military leader as well.

Sally  Age 35

My dreams are on repeat. And time and time again, my corpse is taken and beaten. I scream out to anyone listening, begging them to end my life. End the nightmare.

"Sally?" The soft whisper causes my eyes to flutter. I groan as I hold my bandaged side. "Take it easy. You are safe. You are in the medical bay at the Black Rose compound." Why did Willard bring me *here*? I would have been better off dead in the valley. "Do you want some water?" I knock the glass to the floor. "Why don't you rest while I go update your husband and boys?" The man offers me a smile that would be kind if I weren't so irritated.

Then it hits me, square in the chest. My family's here. "Where're Jeremy and Dan?" My brain revs up, knowing my children need me. I force my eyes to take in my current situation and focus on the man in the tiny makeshift hospital room, small strips of fabric the only thing separating me from the other patients.

"Everyone made it here in one piece. They are safe with your husband."

"No one is safe with *him*," I grind out as I place blame on the one person I can. "I want to see my kids. *Now*."

"I can bring them to you if you *calm* down and lie back," he demands just as sternly. "You have been through a lot and your body needs time to rest."

"Don't pretend to know what I've been through."

His green eyes mist and he offers a hand. "You are wrong. You were lucky enough to escape with your family. Whereas I buried my wife and son shortly after my own arrival to the compound."

Do I trust his words? No. I'm done trusting men. But

242

the way he speaks and his body language both tell me he's been through one hell of an ordeal. "I'm sorry for your loss."

He rubs his scar. "My daughter survived, and for that, I'm thankful."

I lie back in the bed and stare at the ceiling. I'll do what he wants, if it means I can get what I need.

"I'm going to bring your family to you." His footsteps grow softer, as I yawn and my eyelids become heavy.

"Mommy!"

"Daniel. How are you doing?" I wrap my boy in a tight hug.

"My feet are sore, but I'm fine. How are you feeling?"

My sweet baby. He hides his emotions well and cares so much for others. I wipe his wet cheek. "I'm feeling a lot better now that I know you guys are safe."

Dan steps aside and Jeremy watches me. My oldest. He reminds me a lot of his father. Assessing every situation and planning what he will do next. I open my arms and he hugs me too. "You were out for almost a week, Mom. Are you sure you're okay?"

I pat his back before he pulls away. "Yes, of course. I just needed to catch up on all that sleep I lost with you two." I swipe the corners of my eyes.

"Why don't you boys follow Tammy to your next lesson?" My husband instructs.

Once they're out of earshot, I glare at Willard as he stands next to the stranger among us. "Why did you bring us here?"

"Sally, my father helped build this compound, shaping it into what it is today—a safe haven for anyone who needs it."

A dark-suited man walks in and nods towards Willard. "Governor Patrick is here to debrief you, Commander."

What? Commander? I pinch my cheeks. Have I entered a multiverse? My husband's a traveling salesman. Not a rebel leader.

"We will talk soon, my dear. Get some rest." He pats my leg and leaves.

"Here's some water in case you get thirsty, Sally," my would-be caretaker announces.

I fist his shirt and tug him towards me. "Why did that man call my husband *Commander*?"

"Did you not know that he's the Commander of the Black Rose?"

I release the fabric and fall against my pillow. "Apparently, I know nothing of the man I married. Other than he has ruined my children's chances of ever having a real future."

"Commander Willard is a great leader. I know he never intentionally meant for you to get hurt. He is always extremely careful with his missions."

"Yes, so *careful*," I spit. "Just get out." I squeeze my eyes shut. I don't want anyone to see how weak I am. A chair scrapes to the edge of my bed, and I glare at my unwelcomed visitor. "Are you deaf or just *dumb*? I told you to leave."

"Neither." The cocky tilt of his head unnerves me.

"Why am I here?"

"Would you rather we left you to die? Or let you get picked up and questioned *again*?"

Silence blankets the small room. Of course, I didn't want that. But I also want the best life possible for my kids and this isn't it. I worked too damn hard to lose it all now.

"Daddy?" A small squeak vibrates around us. My eyes flit to the doorway and to the small redheaded girl about the same age as Jeremy. She's frowning at my self-appointed friend as she holds up her arm and blood drips from a gash.

"Tammy, what happened this time?"

She squeezes her eyes shut as the wound is cleaned and dressed with skilled fingertips. When she doesn't answer, the man lifts a brow in warning. "Well, I might have run into barbed wire."

"How do you *run* into barbed wire?"

"Fine. I was trying to get past the fence and got snagged."

"Tammy, what have I told you about trying to leave?"

"That it isn't safe, and I need to stay close. But, Dad..."

"No *buts*. Do *not* make me repeat myself. Go to your lessons with Jeremy and Dan. Now."

The redhead stomps out, grumbling under her breath.

"She's spunky." I can't help the twitch in my lip.

He tosses out his latex gloves, never meeting my gaze. "Her mother was always pushing my buttons too." He sighs. "Tammy wants to be out in the world. It's hard for her to understand why we are such a hated group in our own country."

"So, you understand *why* I'm mad. My boys were safe. We were happy. Until my husband got wrapped up in all this."

"Just because you felt a *false* sense of security and happiness doesn't mean it was real. You can't simply turn a blind eye to those suffering around you, Sally." He stomps out, shaking his head. I bite my lip and close my eyes. Is he right? Am I being naïve? Allowing others to suffer just to protect my own?

"I'm sorry I had to leave you earlier. The Governor is crucial to our mission, and I needed to update him on what has been going on." I watch as Willard sits next to my bed. He grabs my hand and brings it to his lips. "Luke tells me you are upset about being here."

I pull my arm out of his grasp. "How long have you been lying to me? How long have you been undercover?"

"You knew that I helped the rebels."

"I knew that *we* helped branded orphans and families when we could, but that was it. Or so I thought. Answer my question."

Willard rubs the back of his neck. I feel an uneasy tension building around us as he hesitates. "I have been part of the rebellion my entire life. I was born and raised here."

"But we met at the university in the city."

"I was on a mission when I met you."

"Do you even *love* me? Or was I simply part of your agenda?"

"That is why I married you. Why I've kept my missions *separate* from our family. I was trying to protect you and the boys." He's holding something back. I can feel it. The tension and pressure.

"All this time, I thought you were traveling for work."

"I *was* traveling for work."

"You told me you were in *sales*. Not a commander."

Willard stands, his eyes darkening. "We are now rebels on the run. This is the safest place for us right now. You would be wise to accept that fact and embrace who you are."

"Get away from me, you *liar!*" My lips tremble as my life crumbles around me.

"The sooner you come to terms with our living arrangements, the better." He exits with his head held high. Not a care in the world, or regret for his actions. People flock to him and shake his hand with adoration in their eyes. He is an important person amongst the rebels—that much is evident. I just wish he could have entrusted me with *who* he really is. I deserved the chance to choose my future.

I could have handled it. I am stronger than I look. I will prove to him how capable I am. Then no one can hurt me or my family. Because I won't let it happen. *Not again*, I vow.

Jeremy  Age 12

Luke's fist flies past my cheek. I slam into his chest, and we fall to the ground. After rolling around for a few moments, I hear a satisfying tap near my ear. I stand and offer a hand to the old man.

"You are your father's son." Luke pats his face with a towel and tosses me a bottle of water.

I chug it and blink as a golden goddess walks past our sparring match. "Who is *that*?"

Luke waves at the girl in question. "That's Governor Patrick's daughter, Mary." He arches a brow at my expression. "Jeremy, don't even *think* about it. Mary is a mission in itself. Stay away from her."

"How can she be a mission? That makes no sense."

"Mary will be Queen one day. And you would be smart to stay out of her way."

I finish my drink, although my mouth still feels dry as I watch Mary climb the stairs that lead outside. A towel slams into the side of my face.

"What? Can't a guy *look*?"

Luke chuckles. "That was not just looking, Jeremy. Stop it. I mean it."

Mary's curves float across my mind and I grin. "Queen, you say?"

"Yes, she will be drawn as one of Prince Christian's potential wives when the time comes. Mary is here to train and get to know the rest of the group. Just wait and see. One day she will free us from this shit hole."

"Dad. I thought you were giving up curse words?" Tammy rolls her eyes as she inserts herself in our conversation. She hands him a piece of paper.

"I am a grown-ass man. I can say what I want when I want." He scans the document. "The Commander needs me for a task." He ruffles Tammy's hair, then he jogs off to my dad's office. "Behave," he shouts over his shoulder, and I can't be sure whether he means Tammy or me. Probably both, because we're always getting into trouble.

"Want to spar, Jeremy?"

"And get yelled at for beating up a girl? No way."

"I won't get beat up. You'll be the one crying like a little baby."

"Tammy, stick to what you're best at. Tech crap. Leave the fighting to us men." I push my chest out like a proud rooster. Tammy takes this moment of confidence to slam me to the ground. I groan as I stare up into her wild eyes.

"Women can fight just as hard, if not harder, than men."

I brush my fingertips over her cheek. She blushes, and I take the moment of vulnerability to roll on top of her. I pin her quickly and have a knife to her neck. "Women are weak. Especially when they let their emotions get the best of them."

She squirms. "You think we are weak because of our emotions? Well, men are weak because they are too self-confident." Tammy brings up a knee but I roll away from her.

"Cheap shot, Tam. Even for you."

"Jeremy, come here, son," Father demands.

He's standing next to the Governor and Mary. I pat my face with a towel and strut over. "What's up?"

The girl's gaze sweeps my taller frame, and I know I have her attention.

"I would like to introduce you to Governor Patrick and

his daughter, Mary."

I extend my hand and shake theirs. "Nice to meet you both."

"Would you have some time to show Mary the basics of self-defense?"

Now it's my turn to undress the goddess with my eyes. "I don't think I'm qualified for that. I might hurt the little princess."

She thins her lips as my dad nods. "It's just self-defense, Jeremy, not rocket science. And I trust you can teach the girl without harming her."

"I can teach her, sir," Tammy pipes up as she stands next to me. "We are the same age and I have studied her assessment. I know her strengths and weaknesses."

No way is she stealing the princess from me. I ruffle Tammy's hair. "He wants someone with skill, Tam."

The defiant redhead swats my hand away and glares.

"Jeremy." My dad commands my attention.

"If you want me to teach the princess self-defense, Father, I will."

"Great. You start now. Governor, why don't we meet Luke in my office and go over our strategy for the next mission."

They walk off, leaving me with the two girls. I fold my arms across my chest. "So, princess, what do you know about defending yourself?"

"Stop calling me *princess* and I will answer your question."

"All right, Goldilocks." Mary narrows her eyes, and I know I've hit a nerve. I sweep my hand over the mat and bow. "After you, my lady."

"I am supposed to be meeting your mom for math tutoring. I'll see you later, Jeremy."

I wave Tammy off not even meeting her gaze.

Like two predators watching their prey, we dance around each other. Each of us ready to pounce or block as needed. The first swing connects with Mary's shoulder. She doesn't even flinch. She's tough. That's when I notice bruising in the shape of fingers on her upper arm. Who the hell would put their hands on a kid like that? As I begin to ponder that very question, she kicks my feet out from under me. And like a wild animal, she pounces and pins me to the floor.

"And you say women are weak because of *our* emotions," she purrs.

"Are you using my words against me, princess?"

"Stop calling me that." This time, it's more of a hiss.

"It's true, isn't it? I mean, you are going to be a princess one day. And then Queen after that. The holy one who sets her people free from persecution."

"I am more than that." Her claws come out. I run my palm over her face. But this trick doesn't work on her. My eyes grow wide as she leans forward and moans. "Don't think for a minute that I will lie down easily for you. I'm in it to win it."

"I'm looking forward to it."

Several hours later, her dad collects her to return home. I lift my hand as she waves to me.

"I told you to leave her alone." Luke smirks.

"Hey, Dad asked me to train her. What was I supposed to say? Sorry, Commander. *Luke* told me no."

He chuckles. "Well, I'm second in command. I have some pull when it comes to what goes on here."

"Does Mary's dad hit her?"

"Why do you ask?"

"She has bruising under her sleeves and on her hands."

"It's not her father. Mary's mother has a ruthless mean streak."

"Her mother?"

"Listen, I don't agree with the way she treats her, but that is *not* my place. And it's not yours either."

"Is it true that her parents only had her so that she could be placed in the Palace when the time was right?"

"Again. Not our business. Drop it and do your job. Keep your emotions and *hormones* in check."

I won't ignore the fact that Mary is being physically abused by her mother. Or the fact that no one sees her for who she really is: kind, intelligent, and one hell of a woman with a wicked left hook.

Mary  Age 14

"There is only seven years left until you leave for the Palace. So sit up straight and pay attention."

"Yes, Mother." But my gaze shifts out the window again, as my mom drones on about Palace procedures. The sun is glimmering off the pond and a blue bird flies to a tall oak tree. Dad's car slithers into the driveway. I jump up and go to greet them at the front door. "Dad and Max are back."

Mom hollers after me, but I ignore her as I leap into my dad's arms.

"Mary, shouldn't you be studying, honey?"

"A whole day has been wasted because she refuses to focus. It's all *your* fault. Ever since you brought her to the compound, that is all she cares about. I think she shouldn't be allowed to go this week."

"Mom. Please. Don't take this away from me." I shouldn't have made demands, but I couldn't help it. This is the only time I have away from her. Tears spring to my eyes as her open palm reddens my cheek.

"You are not Queen yet, little girl. Go to your room immediately."

I flop on my bed, hugging my pillow. Dad only brings me to the compound once a week to spar with Jeremy, learn about warfare technology with Tammy, and meet other rebels to discuss odds and ends. It is the only reprieve I get from my mother. And instead of my trips lifting her mood, they have made it worse. Now her hits are more intense. I fear jealousy may have slipped in. Or maybe it is the knowledge that one day I will rule over her, and her life will be in my hands. The thought makes me giddy. All these years of abuse will come back to haunt her.

253

I escape inside my mind. This is the only way I remain sane. Losing myself in my daydreams. When my eyes close, I replay my last sparring match with Jeremy. The way his muscles rippled when he swung. The sweat inching past his icy eyes. The grin spreading across his lips as he pinned me to the ground, breathing hard. A shiver racks my body. I flop to my stomach.

Jeremy looks like Prince Christian, and if I entertain the idea long enough, I can almost pretend that the two are interchangeable. I groan and throw a hand over my face. The two are nothing alike. The Prince is an obnoxious know-it-all. The two times Dad brought me to the Palace, all the Prince talked about was himself and what he was accomplishing in his studies, or he droned on about foreign politics. Even his brother is more interesting.

Images of Prince Ryan reading in the garden float in my mind. I shake my head. Ryan is too big of a nerd and has no spine. He is easily manipulated and not my target. I feel my stomach clench as I see Jeremy's face again. He's stubborn and can talk about any topic without hesitation. A grin stretches my cheeks. We even talk about wedding night activities. That conversation was very educational. I place my finger to my lips. What I wouldn't give to… *spar* with Jeremy in those areas.

"Catch."

I instinctively turn and grab a scone before it hits me in the face. "Max, that was a little too close."

"A simple thank you would suffice." Max plops down on my computer chair and twirls as he munches.

"It's a bummer Mom is making you skip your trip this week."

"That is an understatement, little brother."

"It's a good thing Dad was never planning on bringing you to the compound today anyway."

My head shoots up. "Are you playing another mind trick on me? I told you to stop it."

"Nope. I'm being serious. Dad thinks it's too dangerous for us to travel back and forth to the compound every week."

"What? He can't do this to me!" Panic is sewn into my voice as I jump off the bed. I pace, as horrible thoughts race through my mind. Thoughts of never seeing Jeremy again. I shake my head and take a steadying breath. "If that's what Father thinks is best, then of course I will accept it." I smooth the wrinkles out of my dress as I lower myself onto my sofa. I side-glance Max and am rewarded with his grin of mischief. I almost release a sigh of relief. But think better of it as I lean back against the plush cushion. "Oh well. I guess that opens my schedule a bit, leaving me more time to play makeup with my little brother. I really have been meaning to test out a new color palette. Do you think Prince Christian likes pink or red better?" I stroll to my lighted vanity.

"You are *not* putting makeup on me again!" Max squeaks.

"But what will I do with all this extra time?"

"You won't have extra time anymore because Dad brought Jeremy and Trevor here to train us."

My heart stops. Is this a dream? "Jeremy is here?" Max tilts his head, assessing my reaction again. I compose my face and toughen my voice. "Well, that is absurd. How is it any safer for us to have them in our home?"

Max arches a brow and shrugs. "They aren't marked so it will be hard for any onlookers to know their true identity. Plus, they are staying in the basement, not the main house."

I shove pieces of my scone into my dry mouth. Jeremy is *here*? Under the same roof? I feel my body warm and my face flush. It makes me ask the question: *How badly do I want to be Queen again?*

Sally  Age 37

"Tammy, you need to focus please. I will explain the process one more time."

"I'm trying, Sally, honest." Tammy scribbles on her paper but gets her algebra problem wrong for the fourth time.

I rub her back and lean down to her level. "Sweetheart, is something bothering you?"

She tosses the pencil across the room. "I'm never going to be able to use this shit anyway! Why are you pushing me so hard to get it right? We are all going to rot in this godforsaken place." She throws back her chair and storms out.

I pick up her scattered materials. Tammy isn't the only one who's felt this way. I pray, with the Prince's semi-arranged marriage, new optimism will sprout as they watch Mary climb the ranks and win his heart. I smile at the thought. Mary's a force to be reckoned with. A laugh escapes my lips. Especially when she can take Jeremy down in combat, and me intellectually. And she's only a teenager.

"What are you laughing about?"

My hand goes to my chest. "Luke. What have I told you about sneaking up on me like that?"

"I can't seem to remember."

"Like father, like daughter." I shuffle papers over my tiny desk. Luke has quickly become my only friend here. Everyone else finds me prickly and unapproachable, whereas Luke is dead set on breaking through my ice barrier. I'm not sure if it's because it's his job to keep tabs on the commander's wife, as my husband's right-hand man, or simply because he pities me. Either way, I will never admit how grateful I am to have him around.

257

"Has Tammy been neglecting her studies again? Should I talk to her about it?" He leans against the wall and crosses his arms over his chest.

"Please do us all a favor and save your breath. Your daughter doesn't listen to you any more than my offspring listen to me at this point." I plop in my chair and start grading essays on democracies versus monarchies. His eyes burn into my forehead. I toss the pen aside and lean back. "Is there something else you wish to discuss with me? Are the chickens not laying enough eggs for us? Should I chat with them next? Because you and I both know they are more likely to listen to me than our children ever will."

"I was going to give you a surprise. But I can see you are busy." He pivots, and I glare at the back of his head. "And don't give me that look," he calls over his shoulder.

"You are so conceited, Luke. No one is bothering to look at you." I shake my head, and he turns on his heel and waves a small plastic package in my direct view. "Where did you get that?"

"Oh. You wouldn't be interested in this." He returns the package to his tactical pants.

"I'll play you for it."

"I thought you weren't interested?"

"You play dirty, Luke." I lay the worn game board on the table and place the chipped pieces on top.

"How are you doing with Jeremy being away from the compound?"

"Shut up and play."

"It must be hard, not having him in your sights while he's at the Governor's home with that abusive woman." He moves his red piece forward, refusing to meet my gaze.

I send a laser beam through his forehead, using the heat of my gaze. "You know I didn't have a say in this situation. And unless you want these pieces shoved down your throat, you will heed my warning. Let it go."

His lip quirks as he jumps one of my pieces and removes it from the board. "I'm just expressing my empathy. That's all."

I toss a jumped piece at his nose. "Empathy. Really? Where were you when I was begging Willard to keep Jeremy at the compound?"

"I honestly tried, but both of our hands were tied. The Governor demanded it. And you know as well as I do that we need the Governor on our side."

"He knows too much. He should have been eliminated a long time ago."

Luke goes wide-eyed as he scans our surroundings. "Shhh. He has spies everywhere. Plus, without his money and protection, we wouldn't last long." We play for a few more minutes before Luke leans in and confiscates another piece of mine. "Jeremy will be fine. He can take care of himself. Besides, he volunteered for the mission. No one forced him to do it. He will have food, clothes, and a mansion to explore in his spare time. That sounds more like a vacation than a mission to me."

My face reddens as I flip the board and send the rest of the pieces flying. "Jeremy is fourteen years old. He should be going to the movies and hanging out with his friends. Not risking his life with military missions. If it was such a damn vacation, why didn't you send Tammy? Leave me alone and concern yourself with your own child." I stomp towards Willard's and my bedroom. My hand pauses on the doorknob and I freeze. I hear grunting from inside.

Luke slides in front of me. "Why don't we talk about it some more."

259

"Who is inside that room with *my* husband, Luke?"
I step towards him, my face inches from his. I watch as
sweat starts to form on his brow. "This is your one and
only warning. Get. Out. Of. My. Way."

"I can't do that. I'm sorry. I have my orders."

"Your orders? From my lying, cheating husband? Fine.
I'll just discuss this with him later." I pretend to turn and
leave. Once Luke relaxes, I bring my knee to his groin
and my hands to his shoulders. I throw him to the floor
as he cradles his pride. "You were once a married man.
You should be ashamed of yourself for covering this up!"
I throw open the door and stare, wide-mouthed, at the
occupants on the other side.

"Shut the door, Sally," Willard has the balls to demand.

I blink, unable to process the scene in front of me.
Willard and Derek are naked and lying side by side in *our*
marital bed. Their hair is tousled, their faces red, and their
bodies drenched in sweat.

I hear the door close behind me. "Sorry, sir." Luke
coughs and looks at his feet.

Derek stands and stretches out. "Well, we seem to have
the start of a threesome here." He runs a hand over my
cheek. "What do you think, Sally? Want to join in on our
fun?" His fingertips graze my chest. I leap to attack him
but Luke holds me back. And Derek pouts. "Maybe next
time then?" He smacks Willard's thigh. "How does that
sound, Will?"

"I can't believe you," I spit. "Let me go, you ass-
kisser." I stomp on Luke's foot and elbow him hard in the
stomach. When he loosens his grip, I charge Derek.

And the jerk never loses his grin. In one quick
movement, he slams me to the floor and pins his body on
top of mine. "I have always admired your feistiness." His
tongue drags across my neck. "I would love to beat you

into submission."

"Enough, Derek. You may return to the Palace," Willard instructs.

Derek smirks and stands with an exaggerated bow to my husband. "I eagerly await our next *meeting*, Commander. Until next time."

Once the door is closed, Luke offers me a hand up. "If there is nothing else you need from me, Commander, I will take my leave." His jaw ticks. I'm not sure if he is mad at me or Willard.

"Luke, I need you to help Sally grab her things and move into the guest suite, until I can arrange better accommodations."

"Are you sure that is necessary?" Luke looks between us.

"I don't wish to keep my wife unhappy any longer." Willard steps towards the door.

I place my hand on his chest. "You owe me an explanation. Is this why you haven't touched me in two years? Why you are always so distant?" I feel my eyes burn as I pound his chest with my fists. "Did you ever love me?"

"Sally, I am sorry you had to find out this way."

"But we are married and have two boys. How could you do this to us?"

"They are old enough to know the truth."

"And what is the truth?"

"That I married you out of convenience. So we could have children to place into the Palace when the time came. But we failed to produce a female. Now our marriage is no longer necessary."

"What? But you love the boys."

261

"Yes, I do love them. They are both great assets to this organization now."

My knees weaken as the realization hits me. He used me for his own cruel agenda. And now I'm nothing to him. Although I've lost *everything* because of him.

"Take care of her, Luke." Willard watches me, his eyes full of pity. Then he walks out of the room without a backwards glance.

Luke hands me the gift he brought me earlier. I stare down at the coveted chocolate bar and cry into my hands. Everything was so much simpler when all I thought I was missing in my life was this damn candy.

Jeremy 🌹 Age 14

It's been a few weeks since Dad sent me to the Governor's mansion. It's comforting, knowing there's always three meals a day and a hot shower after a long day of training. A luxury I'm trying not to get used to. I know my mission is not a permanent one, and I will be returning when my job is done. Although my dad told me it would be challenging, I have yet to discover what he meant. We spar together as a group when Mary and Max finish their studies. Then, once we eat dinner, we go our separate ways. Mary and I work on self-defense and stealth, while Max and Trevor work on spy and mind manipulation techniques.

One night, after our usual session, the Governor calls us into his study. "Please have a seat, you two."

Mary glances at me, and I shrug as I sit across from her parents. "Is there something wrong, sir?"

"Not at all, my boy. You are doing a great job with Mary's training. May I speak bluntly to you both?" Her dad watches us. "And as adults?"

"Yes, sir."

"While the competition is mostly intellectual and playing dress-up, there are other aspects that we need to address before Mary is ready to leave." The Governor watches us expectantly.

I side-glance Mary's arched brow. "I'm sorry, sir, but I don't follow your train of thought. What more would you like me to teach Mary?"

He leans back and turns to his wife. She nods and takes over. "Prince Christian will no doubt be immensely impressed with Mary and her knowledge, but he is just a man after all. And what catches a man's attention first,

Jeremy?"

My face flushes. "Beauty, ma'am?"

A grin spreads across her face as she nods. "Smart boy."

I'm very uncomfortable as everyone watches me. When the silence becomes too much, I swallow and clear my throat. "Mary is already beautiful. What exactly do you need me for?"

"That is true. So, once the Prince realizes that she has beauty and brains, what do you think he will look for next?"

"I'm not sure what you mean, ma'am."

"He will inevitably crave a *physical* relationship and an intimate connection between himself and his future partner."

I let her words roll over me. *Is she trying to pimp out her own daughter?* I steal a glance at Mary's deep-red face as she stares down at her feet. *Shit. Maybe she is.* I look towards her parents and blink. They are mentally disturbed. How could they possibly do this to their daughter? She isn't a pet that can be trained and molded to what they want. She's a living, breathing human with feelings and needs too.

"I may be out of line, ma'am, but isn't it against the contest rules to have a sexual relationship before the competition?"

They both laugh. "We are not asking you to take it that far, dear. Just guide her in what she can do to accomplish a physical connection with Prince Christian."

Who are these monsters? I rub my temples before standing. "I'm sorry to disappoint you both, but I don't think I can do that to Mary."

Her mother purses her lips and I fear she may hit me as

she stalks forward. She stands next to Mary. She grabs her daughter's chin and forces her eyes to meet mine. "Didn't you say she was a beauty?"

"Yes."

"Then what's the problem?"

"The fact that I believe she deserves better than this, ma'am."

Nicole brings her open hand across my face. "Do not presume to tell me *what* she deserves. Every day of her life has been devoted to preparing her to be the best choice. And nothing will stand in her way. If you do not help her, I will send you home and find somebody else to take your place. Maybe Dan? Or Trevor?"

Anger rises at the thought of my brother or friend putting their hands on Mary. "I apologize, ma'am. May I sleep on the idea and give you my answer in the morning?"

"That's acceptable, son. You think it over tonight and give us your answer tomorrow." Her father pushes to his feet. "Sleep well, kids. We will see you in the morning."

We walk out with our heads hanging low and our hearts heavy. Once the office doors close, I feel Mary's fingertips brush mine. I glance over and watch tears fall from her cheeks. "Thank you for standing up for me in there."

"I meant what I said, Mary. You deserve so much more than all this."

"You didn't call me *princess*. You said my real name."

When we reach her room, I brush her tears away. "Sleep well, princess. I will see you in the morning." She jerks me inside her room and shuts the door, before she drops to her knees and clasps her hands together. "Mary. Get up."

"Please don't let them replace you, Jeremy."

I grab her elbows and tug her to her feet. "Stop being dramatic. You will be fine. Don't ever get on your knees for any man. You are our future Queen. It is everyone else who should kneel to you."

She melts in my arms. "Tell me what I have to do to make you love me." I blink as she continues, her eyes resembling a puppy about to be punished. "You are the only one to ever stand up to me—and *for* me. Surely, after these last two years, you feel something for me too?"

"Mary, it's because I care for you that I have to leave. I could never sit here and train you to please another man, especially *him*."

"Please. Jeremy."

"Let's sleep on it, okay?"

Her icy eyes peek up at me and I know I'm in trouble. I need to run. But before I can stop her, she wraps her arms around my neck and presses her lips to mine. It's about as clumsy and awkward as any first kiss is for a teenager. A warmth spreads throughout my every nerve ending. I press her body closer and I hear her soft gasp as she feels me against her midsection. Her eyes investigate my face with a newfound curiosity, and I know I will never let another man touch her. I want this blue-eyed princess to only ever look at me like that. And no one else.

Mary ❧ Age 16

"Okay, you've proven your point. You can stop now."

"Aw, are you getting flustered?" I bat my lashes. A pillow flies across the room and hits me in the face. I laugh and throw it back at him. "Hey, watch the face, little boy. This is the moneymaker after all." I blow him a kiss as I try on another dress.

"I got your *little boy* right here, princess," he mutters from my bed.

"How about this one?" I twirl in a baby-blue evening gown that flows to my ankles but has a slit running up my thigh.

Jeremy's eyes sparkle. He walks over, scratching his stubble. "I like the first one better?"

"The black cocktail dress? But this is a Christmas party." I feign a pout, as he wraps his arms around my waist and tugs me to him, and shiver when he kisses the nape of my neck.

"Yes, but the black one is plain so you will receive less attention."

"I thought the whole point was to *get* attention. So the King will remember who I am when the time comes." Jeremy twirls me and I giggle. Then he bows and grabs my hand before dancing with me across the room. I clear my throat and stand straight, trying to act serious. "Those ballroom lessons are really paying off."

Jeremy grins as he dips me and places a kiss on my chest. "I believe they are well worth the time and money."

There is a knock on the door and Max pops his head in. "Sorry to break it up, your highness, but Mom is requesting your presence."

I release Jeremy's hand. My mom is always ruining

these precious moments. Before I stalk off, he tugs me to him and kisses me deeply. I pull back and smirk. "Are we starting another round of lessons?"

"That was for extra credit."

"Did I pass?"

"I can't seem to remember what your grade was." I lean in and kiss him again. "Hmm, yes, a B minus. Next time, try some tongue, then we can bump it up to an A."

I roll my eyes and follow Max out into the hallway.

"What took you so long," Mother snaps.

"I apologize, Mother."

"That dress looks perfect for the Christmas ball. Maria will do your hair and makeup for the event. Derek will meet you at the Palace and escort you inside. Understood?"

"Yes, Mother."

"Jeremy gave us a progress report this morning and it seems like you are still not trying hard enough."

I hold back my smirk, knowing damn well that was a lie to fool her. "I am sorry, Mother. I will try harder."

"Make sure that you do. We need you ready to go. And be certain Prince Christian acknowledges your presence at the ball." She adjusts my cleavage. "Even if you have to dance with the other Prince to accomplish that."

"I understand. Is there anything else?"

"Not at the moment. You may go." She waves me off.

As I head to my room, I hear her say to my dad, "She is much more compliant with Jeremy here. We should have thought of this years ago. It seems he puts her in her place."

I snicker. Jeremy, putting *me* in my place? Ha! What a

joke.

The sun sets beyond my window. The purple hues kiss the pond's shimmering surface, creating a surreal canvas. I rest my palm on the windowpane and the glass fogs. On the outside, my life appears as beautiful as the stunning landscape. But on the inside, it's like the clouded window. Dark and uncertain.

Jeremy comes up behind me and places a kiss on my shoulder. He whispers sweet nothings into my ear. And I moan and twist, giving him access to my neck. He takes advantage of the situation and has me trembling in his hands. "Stop worrying, princess."

"I wasn't worrying."

"After all these years, you think you can lie to *me?* You will do great at the dance. We have been practicing all week long. And you look breathtaking in that dress."

"I thought you liked the black one best?"

"I lied."

"After all this time, you think you can lie to me and get away with it, Jeremy?" I mock his words.

We laugh and lean our foreheads together. This is what I wanted in life. A man who loves me for who I am. A man who will stand up for me when no one else will. Is that too much to ask?

"Jeremy?"

"Yes, princess?"

"Tell me again."

His chuckle is husky. "No."

269

"Jeremy."

"I love you. There. You happy? Although I have not received anything in return."

"Tell me one more time." I rest my head on his chest and hear his heart beat faster.

"Nope."

"Come on."

He dips his mouth to my ear and tugs gently on my lobe, making me squeal. "Stop asking me to say it, if you aren't going to repeat it back to me."

"I have to keep you wanting more, otherwise you will leave me and never return."

"The only way I'm leaving your side is if they drag me out of here kicking and screaming."

"I would love to see that."

"You're so mean."

"When I am Queen and have successfully freed the rebels and poisoned my King, we can finally be together."

"And make sure it's in *that* order." He chuckles. "And when that does finally happen, I will storm the Palace, collect you in my arms, and love you like you deserve."

"You already love me like I deserve."

We both know we are discussing nothing more than fairy tales. We will not get that ending. We sway together, each afraid to let the other go.

"Jeremy?" I whisper softly into his chest.

"Yes, princess?"

"I love you," I push out the words, worried he may bolt.

"I love you too."

I let out a breath. This moment. I just need to hold on to this moment. With him. The man I love. The man I will never forget. My real-life prince. No storybook bullshit.

Sally  Age 39

I pound into the punching bag, imagining the guard's face. I grunt and shake my wrist, once the numbness subsides and the pain slips in.

"You still can't sleep?"

"I'm sleeping just fine. Thank you."

"I see that."

"Go back to bed, pretty boy." I continue my assault on my make-believe opponent until blood smears its white surface.

"Oh, so now you think I'm pretty?"

"You know what? I've got a wonderful idea. Why don't you stand right *here*? Like this." I bring my arm over, my fist attempting to meet his face, but Luke ducks. He swipes my legs out from underneath me, and I crash onto the floor. I should have seen that move coming. I rub the dark circles under my eyes. I'm losing my touch. First, I lost my husband to another man. Then, I lost Jeremy to Mary and her lunatic parents. And now, my mind is slipping into a constant state of instability.

Luke offers me a hand up but I clutch his wrist and tug him to the mat. The late hour slows his response time and he falls to the ground. I laugh at his shocked expression.

"I'm afraid you're getting sloppy in your old age."

"Hey, speak for yourself. I'm only thirty-nine."

"So am I, idiot."

"I thought women didn't like to talk about their age?"

"If they are trying to impress a man, they don't."

"Ouch. So you aren't trying to impress me?"

"Why would I do that?"

"Aw, come on. We have known each other for four years now. Surely you have some interest in me?" He smirks.

"Exactly. I have known you long enough to know I have no interest in you."

"Why not?"

"You are arrogant and…"

Luke rolls on top of me and pins my arms above my head. "And?"

I narrow my eyes. "An ass-kisser." I slam my forehead into his nose. He grabs his face and rolls off, laughing as he lands on his back and pushes to his feet. I stretch my sore muscles. Luke takes my bleeding hands in his and drags me to the medical bay. I lower myself onto the bench, and he pats my wounds with alcohol pads before applying the bandages.

"What anniversary is it?"

"None of your business."

"Come on. Tell me. Wedding? First date? Birthday?" I pull my hands away. He stands in front of me. "Talk to me, Sally. Please." My eyes shoot to his. I can hear the agony seeping through his words. I turn away from him, as I feel my own eyes start to burn. He gently grabs my chin. "Don't shut me out."

I open and close my mouth, but I can't speak past the lump in my throat. He lets me cry long and hard into his neck as he rubs my back until my body stops trembling. I'm not that girl. The one who's weak and falls for any idiot willing to listen. I push him away. "I already told you. It's none of your…"

Luke's pillow soft lips cover mine before my words can escape. He demands access to my mouth with his tongue. His desire leaves my lungs breathless and my knees weak.

Soon we are lying on the hospital bed, an entangled mess, while attempting to have our unspoken words heard.

Before it goes too far, Luke retreats. "I'm sorry. You are vulnerable right now and I took advantage of that. Forgive me." He rests his forehead on mine and his breathing begins to even out.

"It's my birthday *and* our wedding anniversary. When we got engaged, I told Willard that I wanted to get married on my birthday so I wouldn't have to spend another day of my life without him."

Luke places a kiss on my neck. "Happy birthday, Sally."

"Don't look at me like that."

"Like what?"

"Like you just committed murder."

"I feel like I did." He looks at the floor.

"Am I your first kiss since your wife passed?"

He nods and runs a hand through his hair. "That's pathetic, right?"

I squeeze his hand. "That is what true love is supposed to be like. Because until death do us part is a hard pill to swallow. You take all the time you need to mourn her. Then, when you are ready, you move on. Or you don't. It's up to you. There's nothing pathetic about it."

"I do want to move on, Sally."

"I know you do, Luke."

"Do you want to move on too?"

"My husband is still alive."

"You know what I mean."

"I look forward to the day when death parts us."

"He has given you permission to move on, Sally."

I pat his hand and jump off the bed. "When I said my vows, I meant every word."

"You have been separated for two years."

"Are you trying to convince me to move on?"

"Is it working?" He steps towards me.

I bite my lip as his warmth calls to my soul. When did I start having feelings for him? Why can't I stop imagining that kiss we shared? And why does my body crave more? I'm too old for this teenage drama. "Luke. I'm sorry."

"I've waited two years already. What's another two? Sleep well, Sally."

As he walks away, I grab his wrist and pull him to me. I kiss him with my own burning need. If Willard can move on, so can I. And who better and safer to move on with than my best friend? If what everyone says is true, that us rebels don't live long, then I might as well find a little happiness during my final years.

Jeremy  Age 18

I stand like a statue as Mary attempts to affix my tie for the third time. I try not to smirk as her mom glares at us.

"Mary. For goodness' sake, I am going to show you one more time." I'm choked as her mother tightens the tie around my neck. Out of the corner of my eye, I see Mary giggling behind the woman's back. Then she sticks her tongue out at me. She was messing this up on purpose. "There, like that. Now you try."

Mary pretends to study the knot again. I narrow my eyes at her and she complies. "Like that, Mother?"

Nicole beams as she inspects it. "Finally. Now you won't be the laughingstock of the Palace when Prince Christian needs your assistance. You may go and wash up for dinner. Your father should be home any minute."

After dinner, I lie on my bed in the basement.

"We could do it, you know," Mary coos.

"Not this again."

"I'm serious. We could sneak out in the middle of the night and just leave."

I sigh, hating to rain on her parade. "And go where, princess?"

"I will go to the compound with you."

"That is the first place they will look."

"I should be able to choose how I spend the rest of my life."

"We talked about this. If you are not chosen for the

276

competition, we will get married and run off together. Not before."

"You are a coward." She crosses her arms over her chest, daring me to contradict her.

"I am the only smart one. If you were thinking with anything other than your hormones, you would agree with me."

"Isn't it the guy who's always accused of thinking with his hormones? Not the other way around?"

"Not everyone is as intelligent as me." I grin.

"Whatever."

The next morning, there is a knock on the front door while we sit and eat breakfast.

"Odd… Who would be visiting at this hour… on the weekend? Boys, to the basement," the Governor mumbles as he pats his mouth with his napkin.

I follow Trevor to the basement but pause at the door as I hear a booming voice.

"Sorry to bother you, Governor, but we were tipped off that this boy was seen here with you. Do you recognize him?"

"Hmm, he does seem vaguely familiar, officer, but I'm hardly home nowadays—you know, with the election coming up."

"I understand, sir. Then you wouldn't mind if we searched the house. Here is our search warrant, signed by our commanding officer."

Who could have seen us? We never go outside. Never travel. I haven't seen my parents in years. I hold my breath and side-glance Trevor. He looks as worried as I feel. I nod towards the back door and we both tiptoe outside and into the surrounding woods. We walk for what feels like hours. Then we climb up a tree and camp until nightfall.

As the morning sun kisses the sky, we slowly lower ourselves from our makeshift hideout in the tree.

"Do you think they're gone yet?"

"I'm not sure. Either way, we need to leave. Otherwise, they might bring down the Governor and his family."

"Yeah, and that man would squeal under pressure for sure." Trevor spits on the ground.

"No doubt."

We make our way towards the house at an angle as we head to the main road. I squint in the early morning light as a figure approaches. No, not a figure. Mary. Mary is running towards us.

"Shit. Go ahead. I'll meet up with you."

"Are you sure, man?"

"Yeah, go." I wave him off and rush in the opposite direction. "Mary. What the hell are you doing? Get back inside the house before they catch you."

"I had to see you once more, Jeremy. They're after you. They know who you are. They tied you to your father."

"Shh. It will be okay. Go back inside the house," I repeat.

"No! We can leave and be together."

"Mary, you're talking crazy. *Go.*"

She pulls her hoodie over her golden locks and runs behind Trevor. I curse and quickly chase after them. For a girl, she can run like hell when she wants to. She meets up with Trevor first. "Mary?" He arches a brow in confusion.

"Get your ass back home before I throw you over my shoulders and drag you there," I blare.

"You don't scare me, Jeremy. Especially after living with my mother. No. I'm an adult now. And I choose to go to the compound with you." She locks arms with Trevor. "If you won't take me, I'm sure Trevor will."

I shoot a death glare at the boy in question. "No, he won't."

Mary sticks out her tongue and tugs him forward. "We need to hurry. We can't stay on the main road during daylight. They will be looking for us."

I grumble and follow with my hands shoved in my pockets. Thank goodness for the cooler weather or we'd look like idiots wearing hoodies, jeans, and a backpack. Wait. I blink. "Mary, what's in the bag?"

"I will tell you if you promise I can stay with you."

"No."

She pouts and looks forward again. When the sun reaches its peak and more cars appear on the road, we hide in a tall tree in the woods. Mary pulls out a piece of paper and marks it with a pencil as she bites her lip.

"What is that?"

Her icy eyes watch mine. "Let me stay."

"This is ludicrous. If they find you with us, you are as good as dead. And all this planning would have been for nothing."

"We won't get caught."

"Two grown-ass men and a princess traveling

together… and you think they won't catch on?"

"How about we make a deal? If we get caught, I'll run back home. But if not, you have to let me travel with you guys."

"That bag better have a freaking unicorn in it, princess, to be worth all this trouble."

"Give me your word. Both of you."

"Fine, you can stay, as long as we don't get caught." I rub my face as Trevor mimics my response. This is a bad idea. But Mary's grin is almost worth it. She shoves her hand inside the bag and tosses us granola bars and two bottles of water. "What?" I stutter. "You planned on running away all along?"

She shrugs as she chews her food. Then she passes me her piece of paper. It's filled with tick marks and circles. I arch a brow. "I made a map to the compound. One that only I can read." She winks. "So don't get any ideas. Plus, if we do get caught, they won't know what it is."

I shake my head as I watch her. This woman. My woman. "Smart move, princess. I'm impressed."

Mary's eyes moisten, and she nods as she looks away from us to stare out at the road. I think this is the first time I've rendered the little princess speechless. I close my lids, knowing we will be walking throughout the night.

After the third day of traveling by foot, our supplies run out. We are exhausted and beyond ready for showers. "Don't worry, boys. It's right past this ridge. We should be there by first light."

As we edge closer, we see headlights coming our way before we quickly duck into the bushes and hold our breath.

"Do you think they saw us?"

The car stops and two officers step out with their

flashlights moving side to side. I turn to Trevor. "They want me, not you. You guide Mary the rest of the way. Don't take her bullshit. Do you hear me?"

Trevor frowns but nods as he grabs Mary's arm.

"Mary, for once in your life, listen to me. Stay low — *no matter what.*" I slink away from the bushes to draw out the officers.

"I love you," she whispers. I turn, watching her silent tears fall, as she waits for me to step out of the shadows. I swallow and nod my encouragement.

"Who's there? Let's see your hands or we'll shoot."

I raise my open palms in the air. Their flashlights blind me as the officers slam me to the ground and handcuff my wrists.

"Well, looks like we got lucky tonight, boys. I knew you would turn up sooner or later, Jeremy Sumptor. Let's go have some fun. We are going to play a game of: where is the rebel compound? If we can't get what we need out of you, you're as good as dead." He shoves me into the car and speeds off.

I watch the bushes, knowing this will be the last time I see Mary. I lean back and take a deep breath. I did the right thing. Her life is worth more than mine. I just hope she doesn't do anything stupid...

I chuckle. Who am I kidding? If she didn't do anything stupid, she wouldn't be my woman, now would she?

Mary  Age 18

Once the enforcers are out of sight with Jeremy, I run until I can't breathe. I pound on the hidden back entrance to the compound. When someone opens the door, I shove past them and down the stairs. I'm frantic as my gaze searches all the wide-eyed, pointing people until I find who I'm looking for. "Sally!"

She pivots from her breakfast and leaps up. "Mary. You are drenched in sweat. Take a deep breath. Calm down. Here, come with me to my room and rest."

"Can't," I push out as my sides heave.

Sally lifts me into her arms like a rag doll right before I collapse to the floor. When she sets me on her bed, she asks Luke to get me some water. "Here, sweetheart, drink this."

"Sally. What the hell is the Governor's daughter doing here? I need to alert the Commander."

"Stop," I force the words between clenched teeth. "No."

"Deep, calming breaths. Luke, give her a minute to tell us what's going on."

The rebel crosses his arms over his chest, appearing doubtful.

I suck in air and will my heart to stop pounding. My lungs are on fire. But I push out all that I can. "Officers picked up Jeremy. They are going to kill him if you don't rescue him."

The color fades from Sally's face. I know she hasn't seen Jeremy in a while, but I also know her love for her son runs deep, just from the way he talks about her. Luke places a hand on Sally's shoulder and squeezes.

"Why the hell are you here, young lady." Willard

stomps in with a sheepish Trevor following close behind.

"Easy, Willard, she has been through a lot."

"A lot? Her father will have our heads when he finds out she ran away."

"Commander, they took Jeremy."

Willard blinks, then shakes his head. "It doesn't matter. *You* are our only concern."

I jump up with Sally. "What?" we say in unison.

"You heard me. Luke, call the Governor on a secure line and update him on our situation as discreetly as you can. The lines might be monitored."

"Right away, Commander." Luke gives me a sympathetic squeeze before exiting.

"But our *son*," Sally squeaks.

"He knew what he was up against when he volunteered for this mission. It's out of our hands."

"Stop. We can save him," Sally counters.

"Don't pretend you have a say in the workings of this organization, Sally. I am the leader. My word is law. Leave him, or so help me, you will be cast out next."

"I thought your family built this organization around the idea of democracy, not dictatorship." Sally spits venom.

Willard swings his open palm across her face, and I yelp as she crumbles to the floor. "I'm done with your holier-than-thou attitude. Remember your place." He turns his scowl to me. "You will explain to your father what happened and return home." He grabs the back of my neck and shoves me forward. "Let's go fix this."

I squeal as Luke applies ointment to my blister-ridden feet.

"I'm almost done."

"Jeremy sacrificed himself to save us and secure your location."

"He is a good soldier. I'm sure he will be back in no time."

I grab Luke's arm. "Please. Willard will listen to you. We need to save Jeremy."

"I will not go against my commander."

"Not even for the woman you love?" My eyes burn. "I love Jeremy and he loves me. We are both willing to risk it all for each other. Are you?"

Luke rubs his neck.

"She needs your help."

"Who?"

"Sally. Willard knocked her out cold. She is in her room on the floor."

He jumps to his feet and leaves at a jog. Good. Now that they are busy, it's my job to step up and speak to my people. "We need to protect our own. No matter the cost. Am I right? If I am to free you all, I need your help now. Jeremy needs us. Who will help me?" Cheers ring out as I stand on a table. "We are a democracy, and it is our right to *vote* on what we see fit. I say we elect a new leader. A more competent one."

There are cheers, and Sally's name is shouted out with fists pumping in the air.

"What the hell is going on here?" Willard booms.

The crowd quiets and closes around me protectively. "We want to vote for a new leader. A leader who has the empathy to rescue his own son," a man declares.

"Is that how you all feel? After my many years of dedication and service." Willard draws a gun from his holster. "Who wants to go against me now? We will not be rescuing Jeremy. I am the commander and you will follow my orders, or die as the rebels the King has deemed us to be." He cocks his firearm and aims for the onlooker who spoke out. "Starting with you, old man."

"Put the gun down, Willard." Sally strides over. "You are outnumbered." Everyone grabs makeshift weapons and stands by her side. "Mary is our future Queen. We will help her rescue Jeremy. With or without your permission."

The Commander turns his sights on Sally. "You have been a thorn in my side, woman. Do not go up against me. Or so help me, I will end your pitiful existence. Luke. Help me out here."

Luke brandishes a handgun and points it at my head. "Everyone needs to calm down and put their weapons away."

"Dad. Stop," Tammy cries out from behind Sally.

Sally tugs the girl to her chest as she sobs. "Don't do this, Luke. You know it isn't right. Mary is just trying to save the man she loves. Think of your wife. If she were standing here, what would she want you to do?"

His hand wavers. "She would want me to listen to my commanding officer in order to keep everyone safe. One man in exchange for the lives of many is not acceptable."

"What if it was your daughter out there? Wouldn't you go after her?" I question Luke.

285

Sally squeezes Tammy as Luke looks from me to the little girl. It happens so fast. Tammy quietly slips Sally a gun. And Sally raises it and shoots her husband in the head, then Luke in the foot.

The second-in-command screeches and drops his weapon. I collect it and aim for the middle of his forehead. "You may not be willing to give up everything for one man. But I am. Someone lock him up and take care of his wound." There's thunderous applause. I bask in their admiration as I stand tall. This is what my future will be like. Doing good in the world. Helping my people. "Now let's go rescue a rebel in need."

Our best soldiers gather around the conference table as we plan the attack. We all look up as the door opens and Luke stands there with Sally's support. She holds up a hand. "Luke has vital intel that will help us. Without it, we'll be walking in blind and potentially going on a suicide mission." Sally helps Luke to a chair, pain etching his face.

"This facility is the same one where they held my family hostage. There are four entrances to the building. Most of them are guarded on a timed schedule." Luke points them out on a map. Then he continues with a strategy to rescue Jeremy. I lean back. I'm glad Luke finally joined the winning team. My father speaks very highly of his military expertise, and with his help, Jeremy could be home before dinner. Once the meeting concludes, I jog to the garage as everyone gears up to leave.

Sally places a hand on my shoulder. "With all due respect, Mary, we have voted to keep you here at the compound. For your own safety."

My lips thin. My gaze touches each of the soldiers, and they nod in agreement. I squeeze my eyes shut. I wanted this *democracy*. It's time to let the system prove itself worthy of my sacrifice. "If the people wish that of me, then so be it."

Our extraction team loads up and moves out as quietly as they can. I send a prayer up for Jeremy's protection as Sally wraps an arm around my waist and wipes at her own eyes. I bite my cheek as they drag the Commander's body past us and towards our industrial furnaces. My father will not be happy that Willard is gone. But he will have to suck it up or I'll turn on him just as effortlessly as he'd turn on me. I lift my chin. I *am* marrying Jeremy when he returns. And *if* I am chosen for Prince Christian, I will accept my responsibilities and free my people. I wrap an arm around Sally.

Every single one of them.

Sally  Age 44

Luke snores with an arm draped across my chest. Images of Willard's shocked expression as I pulled the trigger replay in my mind like a bad movie. What was I thinking?

There're whispers outside our room. I rub a palm over my face. Jeremy must be awake. I slip out of the bed and toss my shoes on. The sound of grunts tugs my gaze to the training arena. "Can't sleep, honey?"

Jeremy swipes his forehead and my gaze zeros in on his brand. It feels like just yesterday when he was rushed into the medical bay with life-threatening injuries from the officers who arrested him. Now, here he is, twenty-one years old and getting ready to say goodbye to his wife, as she prepares to become part of Prince Christian's semi-arranged marriage.

"Have you heard from Dan?" he grumbles.

The sting takes my breath away. Once Dan saw that Jeremy was safe, my youngest hightailed it out of this hellhole. I look at my feet. "No. Have you?"

"You honestly think he would talk to me?"

"Why wouldn't he? You weren't the one who killed his father."

"Actually, I was at fault for that too." Jeremy smirks. "You know Dan will come around again. Give him some time to wrap his head around things."

"But what if they've caught him already? He won't survive it. He isn't strong enough." The last part slips out in a whisper. As much as I love my boy, his heart is too pure for this life.

"Dan is stronger than you think. Have more faith in him. Plus, our informants would have caught wind of his capture. He's probably just changed his name." Jeremy returns to his punching bag.

I bite my lip. Last we heard, Dan was heading to the city. But it's been almost two years since then. I rub my arms. I miss him. He's always been the clear-headed one in the family. Slow to anger.

Tammy waves papers in the air as she approaches. "We have a meeting in fifteen minutes. We just received the rest of the names of the girls selected for Prince Christian."

I step towards my room to give them their space to talk. Tammy has feelings for Jeremy and is trying to push her way into the space Mary currently occupies in my son's heart. I snort. Jeremy is a complicated man. His tastes are… *unpredictable*. I love Tammy, but she's anything but unpredictable. She loves numbers, maps, and timelines. Heck, even her book collection is mundane to say the least. In my opinion, she needs a soldier who speaks the same love language.

"Hey, I wondered where you went off to." I close my door and pivot to see Luke. He stands with a towel hugging his hips and his hair wet. My body instinctively warms as I check out his curves. When our eyes meet, I brush past him. He grabs my wrist, and we tumble onto the bed.

"No matter how hard you hide it, I *saw* you checking me out."

"I think your ego is inflating, soldier." My words are lost as I moan softly when he trails kisses over my neck in all the right places.

"When will you agree to marry me, Sally?"

"What is the point? You know rebels aren't allowed to get married. It's just a word here. It holds no legal standing."

"The *point* is we can announce and celebrate our love for each other, in the company of our friends and family."

"When did I ever say I loved you?"

Luke grins. "I think I've made you say it a few times under the covers."

"That doesn't count. I was coerced."

"Why are you so against this? You helped Mary and Jeremy plan and execute their wedding."

"That was different. They are young and hardheaded. They were going to do it with or without my blessing."

"You have to get a stronger hold on that boy," he teases.

I scoff, "Look who's talking. Your daughter is already trying to weasel her way into Jeremy's bed and Mary hasn't even left yet. Now stop messing around and get dressed. We have a meeting to attend."

Tammy reads the list out loud. These nine young ladies will be competing with Mary to win Prince Christian's heart. And the throne. "And the last entry is… Ann Marie Gable."

My heart sinks as the name reverberates through my body. No. I flip through the paperwork and my lip trembles. Anyone but her.

"Mom, is everything all right?" Jeremy whispers.

I force a smile. "These women do not stand a chance against Mary." I clear my throat. "When is the Palace dispensing the tutors? Mary needs to be back home before they arrive."

"Next week," Tammy all but sings as she taps the

papers together.

I nod. "Now is the time to put our plan into *action*. We only have one shot at this, so let's get it right. We have a lot of work to do before next week."

Once everyone exits, Governor Patrick turns to me and Luke. "I have information that can't leave this room. Not even Mary can hear of it."

Although the group doesn't have a set leader, it's been understood that Luke and I are heading up this mission. "What is it, Governor?"

"I have positioned a *safeguard* in the competition, in case Mary does not make it through."

"I don't understand."

"I pulled some strings, and Derek convinced Queen Elizabeth to add in the last contestant. She is a farmer, much like the Queen in her former life, so it wasn't difficult to secure her a spot. Under the table, of course."

"Was that really necessary? Why go through all that trouble?" Luke arches a brow.

"I looked through Ann's records and saw that Dan went to school with her. The two were classmates for three years. So, if Mary can't convince the Prince to choose her, I will shove Ann in her place. Then we can easily manipulate her into doing what we need with the leverage hanging over her head, whether that be her father or Dan. Either way, it's just in case. Our odds are high with Mary, but it doesn't hurt to have a backup."

I'm unable to speak. My best friend's daughter is now in grave danger. And so is my son. In one clean swoop. It's too much.

"Sir, with all due respect, no one has heard from Dan in some time now. Plus, you are talking about *elementary* school friends. She may not even remember him." Luke

291

frowns. "It's a huge risk."

"I'm aware of all this. I'll keep my spies on full alert. And when they find Dan and an opportunity to slip him into the Palace, they will." He stands and buttons his suit. "Make sure Mary is ready to go in the next few days." Then he leaves us alone.

"Do you want to talk about it?" Luke soothes.

"Talk about what?"

"How he is using Dan as a pawn for this girl."

"It makes sense to do what we can to reach our objective," I grind out.

"But he is your son. Surely you…"

"Dan has been missing for two *years*. I doubt the Governor will find him in time to do his part. And if that happens, I will assert my authority and make damn certain he doesn't get hurt. That dumb pencil pusher thinks he's in control, but I assure you he isn't. I easily put a bullet through my *husband*, and I won't even blink before I do the same to that man if it comes down to him or my children."

"Sal, you are playing with fire. Please make sure you don't get burned in the process."

The field is quiet as I take in the full moon. A cool breeze tousles my hair. My fingertip scrapes against the marble headstone. I came here to warn her, but I'm too late. I can't believe it. I've failed. "AnnaBelle. You told me you were strong enough to *win* the battle." I swipe at my eyes as memories strangle me. "I wish I would have visited you before this."

"She would have loved that, Sal."

292

I smirk at the granite as the voice sweeps up with the wind. "You were never a quiet walker, Jack."

"I never tried to *hide* my approach from you before. So why now?"

"Because I'm a murdering, cold-hearted rebel."

Jack chuckles as he consults with the night sky. "You were *always* a rebel in my eyes. But not in the way you are now."

I laugh and squint. "I believe we have been followed."

A black and white hen ambles up. She pecks at the tall grass by Jack's boot and chirps. "Pecker. You are worse than a child, little girl. Don't tell Ann I let you escape. Or she will never leave for the Palace."

The bouncing girl with pigtails flutters in my mind. "She still loves her chickens?"

"Yes. Now, if only she could use that same compassion on *humans*. She is always so focused on her chickens she forgets to take care of herself. But what am I saying? You know what I mean. At least with Dan. And I hear Jeremy is doing all right for himself too." He chuckles. "Remember that pact you and AnnaBelle had about marrying our children to one another so you two could finally be family? Those were simpler times."

That was ages ago. But I do remember. Even if those days died with Anna. I blink and stand as his words register. "Wait. Have you seen Dan?" Hope jump-starts my heart. Jack's lips thin and he doesn't meet my pleading gaze. "Just tell me that he's okay. We haven't spoken in years. Is he with Ann?"

"He's not with Ann." He rubs the back of his neck. "He came by here after Willard passed. He was mad at the world and in need of guidance. "

"Did he tell you what happened to his father?"

"I never asked. The less I know, the better."

"Where is he now?"

"Honestly, I don't know. I haven't seen him since he showed up on my doorstep."

I swipe at my eyes as my heart splinters. I miss my baby boy.

"Listen, Sal. He was looking for work. I sent him to a few farms to do some odds and ends. I even gave him a number to a contractor looking for a replacement after he retires. But that's it."

At least Dan is safe and making a name for himself. I'm proud of him. "Thank you." I pet Pecker and brush my hands on my tactical pants. "I should head out. I don't want to get you into any trouble with the law."

Jack collects me in a bear hug. "I'm sorry, Sal."

I squeeze him tight. "She was like a sister to me."

"I wish things could be different," he whispers. "That we could go back in time and be a family again."

"You're a good man. Make sure you take care of our little girl." I rest my forehead on his. "This'll be the last time I visit. I won't risk you or Ann getting hurt."

"If you ever need anything, Sal, I'll always be here for you. I'm just a call away."

"Goodbye, Jack."

Jeremy  Age 21

"Are you going to talk to me, Jeremy?"

"What's the point? You are just going to do whatever the hell you want anyway, princess."

"That's not fair. You knew this could happen. We agreed that…"

"We? We! No. There was no *we* in the decision *you* made."

"Please try to put yourself in my shoes."

"Stop." I can't do this with her right now. Red-hot anger burns behind my eyes. I slam open the door and breathe in the night air, attempting to cool myself off.

"I head out tomorrow. Please don't leave things the way they are right now. I *love* you."

"You love me? If you loved me, you would have talked to me before you killed *our* child," I snarl.

"I was only a few months along, Jeremy. Was it *really* a child?"

"Who are you?"

"I am your wife."

"No. *My wife* never would have murdered our defenseless child. She would have grown a damn backbone, stood up to her family, and told them that she would not be able to go through with it."

"We can have another one."

"No. There is no *we* anymore. What you've done is unforgivable."

Mary's hand smacks across my face. The pain can't match the anger in my heart. "How dare you talk to me like that. After all the things *you* have done, you think you can judge me?"

My face stings, as tears smear her perfectly made-up face. "What I've done is *protect* those who needed it."

"Stop with the hero bullshit. You are no better than I am. You kill innocent guards—men just doing their jobs— in order to rescue rebels. I aborted one life to save the lives of thousands."

"We will never see eye to eye on this matter, princess. How about we just agree to disagree. You go and do your *job* and I will do mine." I turn on my heel.

But she snatches my wrist. She presses her body to mine, and we embrace. "This is our last night together until the rebels are freed. Let's not waste it. I want to remember everything about you when I'm away. Then, when we see each other next, it will be like no time has passed at all." Her tears soak my shirt.

I'll never understand the choice she made. The agony in her voice pulls at my heart. But she's still my wife and I swore to love her through it all. And I intend to keep that promise. I lift Mary into my arms, as I had done on our wedding night, and take her to bed.

After I drop Mary off at the Governor's house, I enter the compound and hear shouting coming from my mother's room.

"Mom?" I stare between her and Luke as I close the door and frown. "What happened?" It's been a long time since I've seen her this mad.

"Did Mary tell you who performed the abortion?"

"I only did what she asked me to do."

I charge Luke. We roll on the ground until I have him

pinned down. *"You* killed my child."

"It was her *choice.* I never forced her to do anything. Jeremy. You know her better than anyone else."

"You should have talked to me. Father to father."

"She told me she talked to you about it. She said you agreed it was for the best."

My wife is a trained manipulator. Even using her tricks on her own people. I roll off him and lie there in a stunned silence.

"Luke, find another room to sleep in." Mom glares at him.

"Sally, please, you don't mean that."

My mom is a hard woman to crack. Yet, somehow, Luke has done it. I watch her face set firmly in place. Luke has screwed it all up with one action. "How dare you hide this from me. After everything I've been through, you should have talked to me! How can I ever trust you again?"

"It was for the success of our mission. That one mistake could have cost us the entire operation."

"Mistake?" I clench my fist but decide to punch the training dummy instead of the idiot in front of me. I shake my head and stomp out. I have always liked Luke. But this is hard to look past.

Suddenly, someone's standing in my path. I blink as he rubs the back of his neck sheepishly. "Did you miss me?"

I wrap him in a tight hug. "Dan. Where the hell have you been?"

"I couldn't stay around here any longer after Dad died. I overheard your conversation with Luke and Mom. Man, I'm sorry."

I shake my head as I lead him to the dining hall.

"What's done is done. I don't want to talk about it. I want to know what you've been up to. Sightseeing?"

"No. I've been writing novels and doing construction work under the table."

I cough on my water. "My brother, a writer? Never saw that coming. And working with your hands?"

"Hey, I work with my hands to build things, not to tear them down," he grumbles as he stabs his food.

"If you were so happy, why did you come back?" I pop a nut in my mouth and lean into my chair.

"I promised I would keep an eye on someone. The only way I can do that is from here." He watches me carefully.

I glance around the empty dining hall. "Who is it? Any way I can help?"

"No. The less you know, the better. For now. And I am trusting you to keep this between us."

"You know me."

"I do. That's why I'm warning you."

"*Warning* me? Man, you have grown since you left." I arch a brow. "Why do I get a feeling this has something to do with a girl? Maybe a damsel in distress?"

"Not just *a* girl, Jeremy." His eyes lock on to mine. "But *the* girl."

"Well now. *The* girl?" I rub my hands together. "Now we're talking."

"Could you get me a folder from Mom's office?"

"Defying Mother dearest already? Naughty, naughty, little brother."

"No. I just want to read the folder. I'll put it right back. I swear."

"How about we make a deal? I'll get you in the office and guard the door if you promise me one thing."

"What?"

"That you'll train with me, so you can hold your own out there." I toss my thumb behind me.

"Why?"

I shrug, as I replay the conversation I overheard between my mom, Luke, and the Governor after our meeting. The one about how they're planning to use Dan as bait for some chick. "Because I want to spend more time with my little brother."

"Fine. Help me get in and out, and you have a deal."

I grin as we shake hands. "This girl must be special."

"You have no idea."

I ruffle his hair and he shoves me away. It's good to have Dan home again. I've missed him. Even if he's wasting his talents on being a writer and builder. He'll be a good distraction.

Mary  Age 21

I glide my fingertips over my silk dress as the other contestants file in. I have this in the bag. These girls are inexperienced and half of them look like they belong in a circus. I paste on my signature fake smile and make small talk with my enemies, doing all I can to get any incriminating evidence. I make mental notes of juicy tidbits to report back to the compound. I scan the room. Where is the last girl? The one Derek snuck in. A small woman enters and lowers herself down next to me. After assessing her uncomfortable stance, I grin and introduce myself. Let the competition begin.

I do my best to make friends with Ann as we sit and eat. I catch her glancing at Prince Ryan more times than she should. I tap my fork against my red lips. Maybe I can use this to my advantage? "Ann, need I remind you that isn't the man you are looking for?"

"Mary, need I remind you that I know this."

I attempt to lighten the mood and stick out my tongue at her. But it backfires when I choke on my food and coffee squirts from her nose. As we clean up our mess, we see Prince Christian assessing us. "What's going on over here, ladies?"

"Prince Christian, I'm sorry. We were just giddy." I feign embarrassment, knowing how big of a control freak he is.

"We were laughing and got carried away." Ann smiles at him.

"And what about last night at dinner?" he blurts out.

"We like to laugh and have fun." Ann shrugs.

"Even if it's at an inappropriate time and you cause a disruption? Do you like everyone staring at you? Are you that desperate for attention?" He crosses his arms over his chest.

I feel like he's just punched me in the gut. How could he treat me like this? We have known each other for years. He should know I would never act out for attention. I watch as he walks away, shaking his head as he goes. I pinch myself under the table and force tears to fall. I need to separate myself from the other girls and remind him that I'm the most dedicated. Maybe he can be swayed by an emotional plea.

"Oh, no. Lady Mary, don't cry. We got carried away, but we did nothing wrong. Don't let Prince Christian get to you." Ann hands me a napkin.

I fake a sob and rush out of the room with all eyes on my performance. Perfect. Now to draw Christian to me. I glare at my maid and tell her she is to keep everyone but Christian out of my room. Then I turn to my writing desk and start a letter to my father, in code, for Derek to deliver.

I overhear the maid tell Ann I don't want company. I grin. That farm girl will be easily manipulated. I look forward to toying with her emotions. I lean back and watch birds flutter out my window. I will keep her as a friend for now. Until she no longer serves her purpose.

"Lady Mary, Prince Christian is asking for you."

I quickly pinch my cheeks and turn to see him standing in the doorway with a stern expression. "Lady Mary, Lady Ann informed me that I hurt your feelings. Are you emotionally wounded by my scolding?"

Maybe I misjudged her. Is she trying to sabotage me? Or is she really that naive as to what Christian wants?

"Prince Christian, I'm sorry for misbehaving earlier. You know I am more well-mannered than that." I lean closer to him and purr, "Especially after all that time we spent together at the Christmas ball. But I fear Lady Ann is starting trouble around the Palace already. I mean, it doesn't really surprise me. This is a competition after all. And she is just a farm girl."

"Do you think Lady Ann is trying to tarnish your image?"

I lean into his chest. "Do you blame her? You are the next King. And you will make history."

Christian steps back. "I am sure Lady Ann is just trying to get her bearings. Mother was a farmer before she came to the Palace, and she has made a wonderful Queen. I should be that lucky."

I swallow my shock. He actually *likes* Ann? Shit. I need to do some damage control before that little twit ruins everything. "I agree with you, Prince Christian. Lady Ann could make a wonderful partner. If only she didn't spend so much time watching Prince Ryan." I return to my desk with a hidden grin.

I'm rewarded with a sharp intake of breath. "Explain your statement."

I pivot and bat my lashes. "Didn't you hear about her arrival? She was found in the library, with Prince *Ryan*. There are even rumors saying they were mere inches from each other when they were caught in there alone."

"No, I haven't been privy to that information."

I grab his arm and sigh. "Some women just can't appreciate a *real* man. A strong and competent man. I mean, the girl surrounds herself with chickens all day long. Obviously something isn't right with her. But enough about Ann. You look pale, Christian. Have you eaten yet?"

The Prince blinks out of his thoughts and shakes his head. "I was on my way to lunch."

"Well, how about I meet you in the dining hall and we can eat together?"

"Yes, that sounds like a lovely idea."

He is fuming. I smirk. And that anger is directed at the exact person I intended. As I walk out after Christian, I jump when I hear her voice. "Hey, Lady Mary, do you want to go for a walk with me outside? It could help brighten your mood."

"No thank you, Lady Ann. Prince Christian wants to have lunch with me. Isn't that great?"

"That's wonderful, Mary. Good luck and have fun." She surprises me by wrapping her arms around my waist in an awkward embrace. What is wrong with her? This is a competition, not some damn *My Little Pony* episode.

After a successful meal with Christian, we retire to the sitting room with the other girls. Once we settle in, making light conversation about the Prince's recent excursions, we hear a loud splash. Everyone presses their faces to the large window. We gasp as we see Lady Ann attempting to pull Prince Ryan out of the pond.

"What's going on out there?" I feel the heat radiating off Christian.

"It seems, my Prince, that Lady Ann has *no* respect for you. Just look at the way she is touching Prince Ryan. She is an absolute disgrace. It appears she doesn't want to be part of the competition anymore."

Christian storms towards them. Yes, Ann will be no trouble at all.

My eyes scan the letter Sally sent. She's demanding I ignore my brother's insistence to get rid of King Mark. I crumble the paper in my clenched fist and glare at the messenger. "Did you tell her I was handling everything?"

"Yes." Derek tosses a cherry in his mouth. "But she feels your methods are too drastic."

"She just wants to run the show! Maybe I should remind her who's really in charge," I seethe.

"Don't let her get you down." Derek massages my shoulders. "The King is eating out of the palm of your hand. Prince Christian will follow suit, just give it time."

"Christian bought Ann an engagement ring. I saw it in his room. He is going to choose her."

Derek runs his fingertips over the curve of my neck. "Even if he chooses her, the King will never allow it. You will be his Queen—the King has ordered it. And we both know he gets what he wants." His hand runs along the length of my back to my rear.

"And when I am Queen, you will be the first to be hung." I shove him. "Keep your hands to yourself. Or better yet, grab the farm girl and make her squeal like a spring pig."

He snatches my wrist and shoves me against him. "Stop pretending that you don't like it. We have an understanding, remember?"

I grit my teeth and hold out my hand. Derek places a baggy in my palm before trailing his finger up my dress. I look down at the small plant. "This is the herb Max gave you. Are you sure this will do what needs to be done when the time comes?"

"Yes, it is guaranteed to make the King's heart fail. Now, it's time to reward me with what you promised me for my services."

I twist away from him. "After this works, *and* I'm engaged to Christian. That was the deal."

Derek snatches the herb, shoves it in his pocket, and begins walking away.

"Wait!" I can't let this opportunity slip past me. "How about a partial payment... for now?"

"I'm listening."

I clench my jaw before locking the door. Jeremy will have to understand. I can't take any chances. We only have one shot. I kneel in front of Derek before I undo his zipper.

Derek moans, "*Now* we're talking."

I hold out my hand and he drops the herb into my palm for a second time. Then he fists my hair and pulls my neck back. "Don't make a mess, sweetheart—that means *swallow*."

After the deed is done, Derek hums, "Christian is a lucky man." He runs is thumb over my swollen lips. "I look forward to my full payment. I'll convince the King to talk to Lady Ann tonight. So be ready."

Once Derek has Ann locked in the cell, I convince Christian to stay behind with the wounded guard.

"You fucked up!" I hiss at Derek.

"The King is furious that Christian ran off with Ann behind his back. So this course of action was necessary. Now, do what you have to do to expedite your part, or

Sally will have both our heads if our backup plan goes up in smoke. Because then I'll have no choice but to kill Ann." He shrugs. "Although, feeling her squirm beneath me might just make it all worth it."

Damage control time. Fingers crossed this actually works and I can manipulate the other Prince. I stomp out and make a beeline for Ryan's room.

"Lady Mary? What's going on?"

"Oh, Prince Ryan, it's horrible! Your father has Ann locked up and is going to kill her tonight." I fall onto his bed, grasping his hands. "We have to rescue her."

Ryan tries to stand but quickly grips his side. He's still tender after his recent surgery. "My recovery has me bedridden. But I need to save her." His puppy-dog eyes meet mine, and I know I have him in my back pocket. "Please, Lady Mary, what can we do to save her?"

I push out a fake tear. "I have an idea, but… no, we can't. It's too barbaric."

"Tell me."

"Even discussing it is punishable by death."

"I *demand* you tell me at once! We are running out of time!"

I bite my fingernails. "It's wrong… so very wrong. But it could save her, and that guard, from your father's wrath."

"If it can save Ann's life, tell me." Ah. Music to my ears. He's ready.

I drop to my knees by his bed and cry into my hands. I tell him about the herb and how to give it to the King. Once the words spill out, I sniffle, peering up at him between my lashes to assess his pale face. Did I misjudge the situation?

Just when I think I've failed and that he's going to back out, he offers me his palm. "Please ask my father to see me before he goes to bed tonight. I'll do what needs to be done."

I pretend to think about it and quickly feign shock. "No. Prince Ryan, this is a bad idea. We should forget it..."

He grabs my elbow and tugs. "We don't have time to argue. Give it to me."

Damn. He really does care for the decoy. I bite my lip, and my heart aches for the husband I left behind for this charade. I kiss Ryan's cheek. "Lady Ann is lucky to have such a devoted man by her side." When I pull back, I'm rewarded with a sense of bewildered interest. Maybe I can control him too?

I'll keep Ryan in my back pocket, just in case Christian messes everything up.

Sally  Age 46

I leaf through the reports, anger rising until it explodes. I slam the documents down on my desk. "How could this have happened?" I blare at Trevor. He helped train Max and knows him better than anyone else.

"We are losing control of our field operatives. Against our orders, Max kidnapped Lady Ann and didn't notice that she called the Palace, and they were able to hone in on her location."

I bang my fist on the conference table. "This ruins *everything* we have worked for! Why are they doing this?"

"It seems our once loyal trainees have gone rogue. And their parents are demanding we assist Mary and Max, or they are pulling their support and squealing." Luke scratches his chin. "Is there any way we can use Lady Ann to our advantage?" He scribbles on a piece of paper.

"Dan seems to think so," Jeremy scoffs.

I need to keep Ann safe at all costs. She has been through enough already. Especially after Max murdered Jack. I don't want to use drastic measures, but we don't have a choice. "We need to start planning our extraction of the siblings. The sooner the better. Get Dan to poke around the Palace and use his little girlfriend's insights to find us an entry point, rendezvous point, etc." I glance at Tammy.

She nods and jots down my demands. "We will sneak in and grab Mary and Max, maybe some evidence against the palace, and leave."

Everybody heads to the exit, and I fall into my chair.

"Mom?"

"What's wrong, Jeremy?"

"Are you sure we can pull this off with our limited resources?"

"We have to. Max and Mary know too much. We can't afford to let them spill all our secrets to save their own skins."

"Mary wouldn't do that."

"It's been two years since she left us. Things have changed. Plus, the Governor and his wife plan to sing like canaries in order to save their children. Our hands are tied. It's become survival of the fittest."

"Do you really think *they* care about their kids?"

"Either way, we are doing this. So be prepared, son." I slap him on the shoulder. "Tammy and I will run surveillance, you and Trevor will be a distraction, and Luke will head the extraction team."

"Luke? No. I need to head the extraction."

"You are too emotionally invested. Plus, Luke has medical experience that could save lives should it come to that." I watch as my eldest son stomps off. "Jeremy. You need to keep your cool, no matter what. Do not fail us." As I watch his departing back, I sigh.

Is he up for this mission? A lot is riding on his ability to remain calm and not bring down the entire Palace. I collect the mission papers. At least Ann will be safe. The boys thought I was dumb and hadn't noticed their pact to keep her alive and well.

I look up at the yellowing ceiling. "Don't worry, Jack, Max will pay for what he did to you. And your baby girl will remain protected." I glare down at the table. That little prick defied orders and killed Ann's father in cold blood. We were all in this mess because the boy couldn't follow instructions. If he wasn't Mary's brother, he would have been shot on the spot when I found out. But the weasel has been hiding behind his sister at the Palace or under the close eye of his parents.

Our reports on Ann are not great. We were hoping she would have married Prince Ryan by now. But she was consumed by her grief and grew bound and determined to uncover her father's killer. And that led her straight to us. The Black Rose. Presently, Ann is engaged to King Christian. And our Plan B has blown up in our faces. What a complicated mess we have weaved.

"Does everybody understand what needs to be done? Good. Now load up."

Our teams file into the school bus that we stole for this very purpose. It will fit right in at the university located just three miles from the Palace. Our soldiers will have to march to their destination in shifts, through the woods, but they are more than prepared for such a trek.

Before they leave, I grab Jeremy by the arm. "Son?"

"I know, Mom. I love you too." He winks and gives me a cocky smile. "See you soon."

They make their way to their designated entry point. Dan said it's the servants' entrance, which is situated off to the side and out of view. Most of our team have donned Palace guard uniforms so they can blend in. The others are wearing darker clothes to hide within the shadows. A majority of the King's men have been stationed near the jail, guarding Ann as she talks to Max; while Christian, Ryan, and the Palace guard commander are far away in the office, awaiting her return. They're in for a surprise.

Luke's team is the last one to head out. He pauses to tug me into an embrace. "If something happens in there, remember that I love you, Sally."

"Stop stalling and get your job done, Luke."

He smirks. "When I get back, we'll have to celebrate."

I shove him and my face pinkens, despite my attempt to remain unaffected. "Stop dreaming." I hear his chuckle as his team converges.

Tammy taps on her laptop and we stare at the screen as we watch our guys carry out their mission. "Here goes nothing."

Jeremy  Age 23

Sticking to the shadows, I sneak around a bend. My head shoots up as gunfire breaks the silence. The extraction team is supposed to be halfway out of the Palace by now. "Luke? What's going on?" I whisper into my earpiece.

"We have encountered some complications up here. Proceed with your objective, Jeremy."

"What complications?" When I don't hear a response, I draw my weapon. "Boys, we need to check on Luke's team. Let's go." We stay in the dark until we hear Max over the intercom. What is he doing? Is he luring Christian up to the office so Luke can escape with Mary? A woman's bloodcurdling scream rings out, and I freeze. Who was that?

"Luke is down. I repeat, Luke is down," Trevor sounds over the earpiece.

"Where is Mary? Is she with Max?"

"I have Mary and I'm making my way out. Keep them busy."

I train my weapon on their designated exit point. Then I see *him* walking *away* from his fellow comrades, letting them fight *his* battle. All the sins of his ancestors, just slipping away, unpunished. "I have the King in my sights."

"Hold, Jeremy. He's not our mission. You need to extract Max and Mary," my mom blares into my ear.

I lower my gun and bite my tongue, scanning my surroundings until my eyes land on Trevor. My gaze drifts to the limp body clutched in his arms. No!

Anger rises in my chest and all I can see is red as I aim my barrel at Christian. That bastard killed my wife. The shot is far but worth a try. I narrow my eyes and release a breath when I see him crumble to the ground. The bullet only grazes his leg, but now he can never walk away from his messes without the reminder of the war he began. Guards rush to my position and I curse.

Idiot... Idiot... Idiot... I sing as I haul butt in the opposite direction. I climb the stairs two or three at a time and reach the office to help Mary's brother escape. I glance around the King's desk and freeze. There's blood everywhere but no sign of Max. The walls rumble and groan as an explosion goes off. How did that happen? Who brought the dynamite?

"Mom, I need my orders. I can't find Max."

"Jeremy, things have gone pear-shaped. Get your butt out here before we're forced to leave you behind."

"What the hell was that, son? You weren't supposed to shoot the King," my mom spits as we all pile into the bus and attempt to escape the city limits.

"And Mary and Luke weren't supposed to die." I cradle Mary's body in my arms. Our unfulfilled dreams slip off my cheeks and onto her motionless form. "What do we do about Max?"

"Trevor stayed behind with his team to extract him. We will meet them at our rendezvous point."

I lean my forehead on Mary's. "Who shot her?"

"The Palace guard assigned to the jail."

"Who gave him those orders?" I hiss. My mom is silent, so I glare at the only survivor from Luke's team and press the question. "*Who*?"

He swallows. "Lady Ann, sir."

Thank You

Thank you for reading *Split Feather*. Without readers, I couldn't fund my writing adventures and life would be very dull! Could you please leave a quick **review** on Amazon and Goodreads? Reviews are so important, and I would greatly appreciate it. Just scan the QR code in the next section. And don't forget to follow me and see Ann again, in all her feathered glory, as she completes her adventure in Feathered Dreams Book 5– coming in 2023!

Also a big thank you to my hubby and kids for shoving me out of my comfort zone of introvertedness and forcing me to do my first convention (MegaCon Orlando 2022). After my fear melted away, I was able to talk to people and make connections! Plus share my love of writing with likeminded artists. You guys inspire me (and my stories) every single day. My love for you has no bounds.

A super-sized hug goes out to all my alpha, beta, and ARC peeps. You are amazing! Thank you for taking the time to help me make this story great! Especially my wonderful word witch editor, Kat Pagan! Melody, for never giving up on me and shoving me forward with financial contributions and late-night voice messages. Biena, for winning Karen's baby name contest with her entries: Carter and Olivia. Kayla, for your medical advice and shared love of spicy food. Courtney, for medical advice, beta reading, and a butt-ton of encouragement and love. Frankie, for your alpha read-through, stellar formatting, beta reading, and calling me with your incredible writing advice! This story wouldn't be where it is today without you. Alicia, for alpha and beta reading. All my Instagram stalkers: B.L. Twitchell, Dicky, Stephanie Whitfield, Stephie.writes, and many others with your funny videos, Etsy purchases, podcast listens, and great life advice. My adoptive mother, Cindy, who is one of my greatest supporters and Meme to my children. Becky, for being a sister, drinking buddy, Megacon booth babe, coffee dealer, podcast groupie, animal crossing junkie, adoptive aunt to my children, and second wifey to hubby. Heather, for beta reading, suggestions, being the best librarian, and for changing Cassy's name to Heather so you can be with your hubby, Kyle, in the Feathered Dream world.

Finally, all my pets! Where would I be without your massive amounts of hair and puke? I mean, who else could sit on my laptop and literally delete projects that took years to develop, in one single paw swipe? Oh, and for the many scratches I have that will last longer than your short nine lives. May the catnip and tuna never run out, my children. And to the many critters who have left us too soon, I can't wait to cross the rainbow bridge to see you. I'm looking at you Baby Girl, Moo-Moo, Silverbell, GuinGuin, Harley, Yogi, Queen Celestia, Pecker, Romeo, Red, Scarlett, Poxy, Fluffy Bum, Wiggy, and Aries.

Additional Titles by the Author

Feathered Dreams Series (a rags-to-riches, clean romance):

Join Ann and be swept into a world of swoon-worthy characters, glittering gowns, and unrelenting intrigue.

Ann is beginning to see how naïve she has been, though by no fault of her own. Farming side by side with her father, away from the drama of the outside world, is what she has always loved most. But now that she is at the Palace, she is forced to focus on other people and their daily struggles. In the midst of her personal growth, she starts to realize how cruel the world can be. Will she shy away and run back to the familiarity of her old life? Or can she share her unique sense of compassion and fierce loyalty to help those in need?

Feathered Dreams (Book 1)

Plucked (Book 2)

Molting (Book 3)

Split Feather (Book 4)

To Be Titled (Book 5) TBA 2023

Wolves of Cold Creek (18+, paranormal romance):

The Cold Creek packs are loyal—while bursting with mouthwatering, unclaimed shifters—all just waiting for their mates. Why not drop in and enjoy the picturesque views by day and scorching fires at night? Don't be shy. They don't bite... hard.

Scarlett's Tail (Scarlett and Sable)

Sky's Tail (Sky and Freddy)

Carly's Tail (Carly and Jackson) TBA

The General's Report TBA

Rebel's Revenge TBA

The Spell Caster TBA

Cooking Up Disaster (slow-burn romance):

Step into the Decadent Cup and grab something hot!

Blake has a tough exterior but a heart of gold. In the small town of Jasper, he owns the Decadent Cup café where he's selling handcrafted coffee, baking killer banana nut muffins, and staying the hell away from long-term relationships.

Amy's a struggling single mom with no time for love, because she had it with her deceased husband. When her best friend asks her for a favor, she jumps at the chance. But this change in events brews a challenging new blend of trouble, and she'll be cooking up a disaster with the town alpha.

Available now only on Kindle Vella.

About the Author

Brittany Putzer was born and raised in Central Florida, so the need for sunshine (and coffee) is imbedded in her DNA.

Growing up, she turned to books to escape, because it was easier to pretend to be a wizard, vampire, or damsel in distress.

Her books are a wonderful blend of dark and light, with colorful sprinkles of sarcasm, twists and turns, sweet kisses and, on occasion, dramatic cliff-hangers...

She hopes her books can help readers remember how strong they really are… if only they keep moving and fighting the good fight.

Scan to chat with Brittany on social media, **review** her books, get signed paperbacks, check out merchandise, and join her newsletter.